CADENCE OF CIAR

ZOE PARKER

CONTENTS

To my children, always.
HotBuns, you give me the strength I need to put one foot in front of the other.
To you, the reader. Thank you for joining me in this mad, mad world.

Cadence of Ciar

Zoe Parker

I wonder if Ciar
will let me walk
him with a leash?
—Keri

xoxo Zoe Parker

Deep within the winter forest among the snowdrift wide
You can find a magic place where all the fairies hide....
–Author Unknown

The First in a Multiple Mayhem series. Some call it Reverse Harem
but I like to be the weird kid.

CHAPTER 1
TOO ROUGH FOR PEPTO...

E ver have your life move in a terrifying direction, so fast that you get motion sickness? I have that feeling right now. The one twisting my stomach into complex little knots of absolute dread. I'm headed to a place that scares the crap out of me and my body knows it.

I'm not sure that even the pink stuff could help me now.

I'm standing at the edge of the forest, staring at the beat up wooden sign displaying the town name of Redwood in bright, red letters is adding nausea to the stomach cramps. Another thing reinforcing the desire to turn around and run as far away as I can. Flattening a hand against my stomach, I pray for it to calm down. I don't want to projectile vomit in front of everyone. That would suck and show them how afraid I am and that's not something I want to do.

This crappy pukey feeling appeared the minute Nagan told me I was moving back here to this place I want to forget but can't. No matter how hard I try, it sticks with me like a deep splinter buried inside of the most vulnerable place inside of me. This is the town where it all started. This is the mouth of hell I mistakenly thought I was never going to have to deal with again, but because I trust Mada - I trust Nagan, I'm here.

Redwood is the town I was born in. Where my mom went the rest of the way to crazy-land and tried to kill me. The woman who, although awful already, snapped and stabbed me twenty times with an enchanted dagger. I shove my hand in my pocket when I catch myself subconsciously rubbing one of the scars on my stomach through my shirt. It's a nervous tic I can't seem to shake.

"Keri, I know this is hard on you and I am sorry for that... but Mada has predicted that this is the next part of your journey and the will of the forest. All that horseshit that goes with it," Nagan says from where he stands beside me at the edge of the Dark Forgetful Forest. A forest that for me, has lived up to its cheesy name because I was forgotten about, until now.

I look over at Nagan - more like, up at him - my Centaur foster-father. His tail flicks in irritation, but for once it's not with me. He's no happier about me leaving than I am. Something he made abundantly clear while preparing me for this crappy journey.

I don't feel any bitterness about it, especially towards Mada, the Mother of the Forest. I've always known that one day I'd have to leave the safety of the hidden places and leave my adopted family behind.

That thought pulls my gaze over my shoulder. Squinting I look deeper into the shadows of the trees, feeling the Sluagh behind me. All them are just as sad as I am about me leaving. They're the ones who put band-aids on my scabbed knees. Who taught me how to run through the trees as nimbly as a squirrel and how to disappear into the shadows like a ghost. They also taught me how to fight like one of them and how to cuss even though, because of my mother's constant swearing, I don't very often. It's a protest against that life from before.

A remnant that I'm not ready to let go of.

They're a great family and no matter how much I wish it, none of them can come with me. The Sluagh are feared for a lot of reasons, the least of which is their inability to turn into a humanoid and blend in.

"You are not going alone, Ciar is going with you," Nagan reassures me and shocks me at the same time.

In surprise, I look beside of me to meet the green glowing eyes of the monster canine looking at me with a face covered in fur so black it disappears in the shadows. On four silent paws, Ciar creeps closer to my side. Even as a canine he's still a head taller than me and manages to smirk with all of those white teeth. I wasn't aware that dogs had lips.

Not that he's really a dog, in fact, Ciar is a Puca. To make it even more ominous he's the original one and up until now, I thought he hated my guts. On top of that - there's always more to the story with him - he's even older than Mada. She's so old that the dirt on her tree is petrified. So how does someone older than Mada's dirt plan on fitting into a Menagerie?

"I thought you hated me, Ciar?" I ask, voicing my true opinion on him.

Nagan raised me to be blunt and to speak my mind. But with Ciar, that's a lot easier to think than actually do. I'm a little afraid of him sometimes, something I'll admit without any shame. There's something about him that says the smart decision involves running in the opposite direction.

Stronger people than I get that feeling about him.

'Never that, Monster Girl,' he answers, in my mind.

The fact that his vocal chords in this form mean he can't speak from his mouth, he's always spoken to me in such a way.

But I can talk out loud, so I say, "Ciar, I can take care of myself. You don't—"

'Don't tell me what I need to do,' he interrupts turning away from me to look at the sign in front of us.

Well, there goes that argument. It's a guaranteed loss the minute he responds in a contrary way. I never win one against him, no matter what we're arguing about, which is often. He and I can't seem to see eye-to-eye on much of anything. For this and many other reasons, him coming with me makes absolutely no sense, and I have a right to know those reasons. Mada didn't order him to, no one orders him to do anything. Ciar may live in the forest but she isn't his boss. He does what he pleases. Something made him *want* to come with me, because that's the only reason he would.

He turns his big shaggy head - that, in my opinion looks more wolfish than the dog that Pucas are reputed to be and what I tease him about being - to study me with those eerie eyes. I shiver. I'm sure I'll find out soon enough.

Needing a distraction, I turn back to contemplate the sign and I am sucked down into a vortex of memories I wish I could purge myself of. I was nine years old when Ciar found me bleeding in the ditch, dumped there by my mother. Not that I remember it, but Nagan told me later on that I was minutes from death and they were barely able to save me.

My mother isn't someone I like to think about, not when I can help it. Every good memory I have of the woman is completely eclipsed by every foul act she perpetuated on me. Mainly the whole stabbing thing, she *left* me - her *only* child, to die like a piece of garbage on the side of the road. The only thing that saved me are the creatures standing around me. My friends from so long ago, my family now and they mean more to me than anything else in the world. They make up one of the most revered and feared groups of creatures in existence, the Wild Hunt.

Apparently, the Wild Hunt went after my mother a few days after I was found. Murdering a child, or attempting to, is one of those crimes in our world that you *can't* get away with. Not for long anyhow, and never without some kind of magical backup to protect you. Faerie has a list of cardinal sins that are a big no-no and the magic that gives us life and sustains us won't abide by it. Neither will the Sluagh. They saw through her fake persona while no one else but me did.

I don't really know much about my mother's past, truth be told. I know she was some type of Fae, because the Hunt going after her is proof of that - it's the specific type that I'm not sure of. She played at being human so well, even smelled like one, I was fooled right along with everyone else. I grew up with the false belief that my father was Fae and my mother was a human who was left to raise me alone.

I find out after her death that I'm not a Halfling at all.

Now, because she's dead, no one can give me answers about any of it. I know I'm full-blood because I never really looked human or even like a Halfling but I don't know what I am specifically. Even the Sluagh who saw through my mother's facade and chased her for weeks, don't know her actual Fae nature. All they know is that the magic exposed her as Fae. That's it. Nagan told me once whatever it was, wasn't the pretty elf-like kind. The Sluagh started the Wild Hunt before they were actually called. He said my pain called them. Which means I'm connected to them somehow through whatever Fae is hiding in my DNA closet.

With a sigh, I take one last, long look at my beautiful family and then step out of the wonderful safety of the forest onto the road. Taking my first reluctant steps towards a future I don't want but will face head on.

I'm many things but not a coward.

Nagan stomps the ground with a hoof and snorts. I can't

turn around to look again or I'll beg to stay. My pride won't let me beg, at least as long as I can keep from looking.

"I'll miss you all." With those last words I walk away and manage with an incredible amount of will, to not look back. That doesn't stop the tears from tracking unchecked down my face.

Screeches and roars echo behind me. While sobs burn in my throat.

MIRACULOUSLY, I MANAGE TO WALK ALL THE WAY THROUGH the town without turning around or acknowledging the people gawking at me. That's a solid win to me because I can feel them staring. Their unwanted gazes are like little bugs crawling all over my skin. I can't help but feel a little dirty from it.

Winding my way through the streets, with Ciar a silent shadow behind me, I find my destination at the end of a dead-end street. Stopping, I stare at the front doors of the Menagerie in trepidation. Above the door, in big golden letters is the year 2075. The year they started building these crappy places.

The training schools advertise themselves as a simple haven for magic users to learn and discover their places in the world. Nagan calls them 'chicken-coops.' He says the powerful and rich let the 'hens' - the students, get fat and compliant. When the time comes, they get plucked out like they're going to the soup pot. It makes a weird kind of sense and for the most part is true. When you're "plucked" out, you're becoming the property of someone, your Patron.

It's a convoluted mess but it's how they do it to try to have some semblance of order and cooperation between the species on our combined world. I have to agree that it's better than the previous crap. War.

When Faerie and the human world, Earth, collided hundreds of years ago, it merged into this massive one that they *cleverly* named, Faerth. That moment in history was aptly coined the 'Collision'. It lived up to its nickname, resulting in millions of deaths from the destruction and then war that followed. The end result of that event trapped all the races, from both worlds, together in Faerth. Which from what I've been told looks like two eggs leaning together in a skillet.

An unfortunate event for the humans who were here then, they didn't stand a chance against the waves of magically empowered races they were faced with. Especially not with the onslaught of natural disasters that struck following the influx of magic.

The magical reaction surprised both sides. It seeped from Faerie back into the human's dead realm and awakened the dormant magic in them and the other creatures of this planet. Changing them and the world around them into something that's a weird cross between the two. In the long run, it helped more Earth creatures survive but didn't stop the conquering of this new world by the Fae.

The Fae aren't known for being slow, the 'invasion' was a fast, brutal process. Initially, the humans fought back with large armies and their archaic weapons. The different countries united against a common foe and fought their little hearts out. There were quite a few messy battles but the humans lost every single time. Hundreds-of-thousands, died in those dark times. Behind closed doors the Fae call it the "Cleansing". They like to nickname things.

The humans should've paid more attention to the lore they'd compiled from Fae visitors to their dimension. Some of it was right and would've served them well against their invaders. It wouldn't have changed the eventual outcome but it would've delayed it and possibly saved a lot of lives. Fae conquer by obliterating the competition, there is no mercy as long as there's resistance. Luckily for survivors, the King of Lafayette - the current King of all Fae - decided to put an end to it. He offered them a life without slavery with the Fae put in place as the world rulers. The humans didn't have a choice at that point, they agreed. Those who didn't, disappeared from history and the land of the living.

Each continent was divided amongst the different Fae royalty or reigning powers with the King ruling over them all, well, most of them. Fae has some pecking orders that not even a Fae King can change. There are those that are termed 'Ancient' and have no recognized rulers, like Mada or Ciar. They're exempt from his rule and he does nothing to change that.

The result wouldn't be pretty.

The king is a bit of a mystery to me, honestly. I've only seen him on TV with his little pink Elven queen giving speeches about peace and whatnot. He's the one I can blame for this specific ridiculous place because he's the reason it exists. One of his ideas for cohabitation of the races, or as his motto carved into the archway states, 'Work together to mend the divide between all Faerth's creatures in order to live a good, harmonious life.' This Menagerie - yes, that's it's real name, is the place that they send all magic users under 30 for training. The point of it is for them to become productive members of society. It's a bunch of hoopla propaganda.

It's obviously a real place, since I'm standing here staring at it, but I know the truth of it. Chicken coop comparison aside, this is where they evaluate and train only the strongest. While the rest are sent to be some type of manual laborers. Like maids and construction workers to name two I know offhand.

A life of servitude for either direction. Your Patron becomes your "guardian" basically your boss with a lot more restrictions. For life. There's no quitting, no retiring. Once you have a Patron you're theirs, forever. Quite frankly, I don't want any part of this mess. I'm no longer a child of this world and its stupid rules. This world abandoned me in that ditch all those years ago.

My feelings concerning it apparently don't matter because Mada had a vision saying this was where I need to be. So protests aside, here I am.

Supposedly, my Awakening draws near.

Awakenings make me nervous. I've never seen one, but I've heard plenty about them. All creatures, since the Collision, are born with magic. Sometimes this magic is latent, sometimes it's not. A lot of it isn't strong magic, most can't light a candle let alone destroy the world. Like me for example. Awakening, however, changes things for everyone.

The basics as I understand are - supposedly - Faerie herself touches the person with some mystical woohoo that makes them grow magically stronger in order to accomplish their destined... task, I guess is a good word. The fancy title is 'Calling'. Some Callings are simple and their jobs become gardening or controlling and maintaining waterways. Some do the bigger jobs like dealing with the weather or powering certain technology. The list is endless and without those called do these things, the world wouldn't work the way it does.

I guess to some, a lot of it seems boring but they do get a more powerful punch than a run of the mill magic user. I appreciate everything they do. Clean water and food are the staples of life.

Now-a-days, Awakening and receiving their Calling is something folks go to great lengths for. Except most of them hope to be more than a useful Mage. That's why most of these places are sponsored by the rich and well connected.

The more useful and powerful Awakened ones are snapped up by those benefactors. The ones who don't? They're sent to do things under the patronage of the local leader, like roadwork, waste facilities - garbage removal, etc. You'd think those ones would be more sought after, they make the world move.

Lastly, you have those like the Sluagh. They were born for a specific task chosen by Faerie, they don't need to Awaken. And if you ask them, some feel cursed more than gifted.

The rest of the world prays to Awaken - and survive - you become a coveted powerhouse that's offered everything under the sun to reside in one of the wealthy houses. No manual labor, ever. Bloodlines don't matter when it comes to an Awakened. However, if you have no blood family strong enough to protect you, then a Patron can swoop in - against your will - and "protect" you. Stupid rules made for stupid reasons. In my case they're a bit concerning too. I don't want to belong to some Patron.

But if I Awaken, I won't have a choice. I'll be at the mercy of laws that I can't fight or change.

Mada said that I've already started to show signs of Awakening and she's never wrong. Personally, I'm content to stay in the forest the rest of my life and avoid all this mess. Unfortunately, the rules interfere with that because even though I'm part of her family, it's by love but not by birth or blood. If I do Awaken and she hides me it would bring unwanted attention to them and I can't have that.

And that's why I'm here.

As much as I want to argue it and say she's wrong, I know she's not. People come from all over the world to the Great Tree - Mada's tree - of the forest for their fortunes to be told. Those deemed worthy are given their fortunes, those no tend to disappear into the forest. Payment is required and they leave her the weirdest crap too. It's how I got the mPod in my backpack. It's considered an insult not to leave tribute and there are consequences. Mada is best at predicting Awakenings and sometimes even what their Calling will be, I remember her telling me that they're a lot harder to predict and they can be fickle.

I can't forget the most important part of the entire thing, at least concerning me. There's only a 50% chance of surviving your Awakening. The surge of magic entering your physical body can overwhelm and kill you. That's one of the other reasons Awakened people are so coveted because So many of them die. It's a complicated disaster, because there's more. There always is in situations like this. Anyone who Awakens also receives a Triad.

A Triad is three people, not counting yourself, who come together to bond with you to amplify and help control your power. They all have a specific function in your Triad and are all attuned to the Center - the Awakened.

There's the Pinnacle, who is the strongest of the Triad. They control the power of the group as a whole. The Anchor which holds the Center - the Awakened - to the group and keeps them grounded to use magic. Last you have the Hook, which draws power or magic in for the Awakened to use.

Magic aside, I've always looked at it like a prefabbed orgy because sex tends to be an uncontrollable side-effect of the bonding that a Triad goes through. It doesn't force them to be mates. It encourages them, because any other romantic bonds the members share with someone outside of the circle tends to be tame compared to the one they feel with their Awakened.

I'll be damned if I'll admit that it appeals to me, even a little tiny bit.

Sighing, I accept what's 'potentially' going to happen, I'll at least swim that far out of the denial river for the time being. Faerie chooses who gets what and Faerie isn't something I can stop. Gripping the nylon handle of the backpack slung over my shoulder, I suck it up and take the final steps to the front gate.

The guard, a Halfling - human and Elf mix specifically - looks at me with a frown of annoyance. His face pales when he looks past me to the ever silent Ciar. Ciar has that effect on people. Amused, I turn to look at him and my mouth falls open in shock. Ciar is no longer an animal and the dog joke dies on my tongue.

Holy meatballs!

Before me stands a stranger, an incredibly good-looking one. I know my mouth is hanging open but I can't seem to do anything about it except stare at him, hard. He's been hiding this the entIre time?

Spiky, messy black hair crowns a face that a devil would envy. Blood red tips graze his cheeks and forehead, lightened by the sunlight surrounding his face in a bloody halo. That particularly bright color is an indication of his power level and merely a peek. Ciar is so much stronger than I realized.

His eyes are pure green and bright, resembling glowing emeralds as they regard me with complete amusement. With no shame, I continue gawking. I genuinely can't help myself. My gaze keeps exploring the revelation that's him as a humanoid. Perfect red lips surround a mouthful of sharp teeth that are bared in a smile too big to be normal.

Still, that smile makes my heart beat faster.

My eyes trail down to broad shoulders and long, leanly muscled arms, and a perfectly formed, hairless chest that tapers to a slim waist hosting an eight pack of abs that flow effortlessly in a v down to - my eyebrow rises - well, that explains the fairies chasing him all the time.

It's hard not to admire it... uh, him. His legs are long and sinewy with the muscles clearly defined through his bronze skin. Even his feet are gorgeous. People should not be as pretty as the man I'm looking at now. The fact he's shown me now makes me a bit suspicious about the reasoning behind it. Ciar is the world's most ridiculously organized planner. He plans out everything, not kidding. Every action, every word. Nagan says that Ciar is the only creature he knows that can damn near equal Mada with the plotting.

Except that Ciar isn't a soothsayer.

From his 'Blank Space', a magic user's created spot that's hidden from others view, he produces a duffle bag. Without a care in the world, he kneels to dig through it, naked. Refusing to look away - no way will I look away from that - he stands and slide on a pair of worn jeans followed by a plain black t-shirt with the words 'I poop magic' on it, all sans underwear.

I laugh at the absurdity of it. I had no idea he had a sense of humor.

The icing on the cake is a pair of bright yellow flip flops. Oh gods.

As I laugh harder, he smiles at me again, showing a dimple in his left cheek. My stomach tightens as the suspicions of his plotting something goes into overtime. Which in turn makes me stop laughing. I swallow past an incredibly dry mouth.

"Who might you be?" the Halfling asks as he nervously clears his throat. The intrusion of the nasally voice brings me right out of the haze of the eye-feast of Ciar. In a roundabout way, the Halfling rescued me from saying or doing something stupid because I was well on the way to doing just that.

"Keri Nightshade," I answer. I know I'm on his list because Mada would've made sure.

"Oh, you're the late bloomer." That means they've discussed me here. No shock there - woman who's been missing for over a decade crawls out of the woods is news for the snoopy, bored people in town.

He eyes me up and down and says, "You don't look 25 years old. Do you have any identification?" he asks, in that same snide tone. I know what he's thinking. I'm dressed in home made leathers and boots. Not exactly the most fashionable look and it clearly marks me as someone from the forest.

Ignoring it, I swing the backpack around and search for the envelope Nagan gave me. Finding it, I open it and look at its contents. Paper money, a draft card and picture identification. Between Ciar and Nagan, I'm well educated on how the world works, including how to handle money. I hand the guard the identification card. He makes those little noises in the back of his throat that signify doubt, as he studies it and then scans it in a machine on the little desk in front of him.

"Smile," he says.

The camera flash momentarily blinds me. Ciar growls as the machine on the desk in front of the guard whirs and then spits out a card. The guard shakes it to dry it with a smirk on his blotchy face. When he hands it and my ID to me, that smirk drops.

I sigh when I look at it. The picture is horrible. One eye is looking weirdly to the left and the other is mostly shut. My nose is scrunched up above a mouth that looks like it sucked on a lemon. It's a horrible picture and proves that Halflings are as big of dicks as Elves.

The guard does the same task for Ciar, except nicer. Ciar states at the guard closely for a moment and I can smell his magic in the air. The brief glazing of the guard's eyes and the slight gaping of his mouth tells me that Ciar is putting a little magical whammy on him. It's gone in a blink and I catch it only because I know what to look for.

The man shakes his head and turns to me with the previous sour look once again on his face and says, "You can pick up your training schedule from the main office after you get settled into your room." He hands me a slip of paper with my room information on it. "I don't know how you convinced them to let you room with a pure-blood but keep the trouble to a minimum, or I'll report it to the campus office." He sneers as he makes that statement, looking a bit too happy about the prospect.

Ciar huffs in amusement. Which translates roughly to, the Halfling won't live long enough to report anything in that case.

Dismissing the guard from my mind, I walk towards the double doors of the building and yank them open to hurry inside. Thankfully, there isn't anyone about. I'm not afraid of the people here but I'm not excited about meeting them either. My presence here is under what I call, willing duress. Purely out of loyalty to Mada and my belief in her, nothing more.

So far, I'm hating every minute of it. I look at Ciar out of the corner of my eye, okay, maybe not every minute.

This is a mixed dorm house, so I'm not surprised when some of the rooms I pass have both sexes together, intimately. Fae aren't shy and apparently neither are some of these humans. It's obvious to my nose and ears and in some cases my eyes, they all like to... mingle.

Not that it bothers me. Sex is a completely natural, fun function and under certain conditions a powerful one. The only people who have hang ups about it usually, are humans. Except these ones seem to be lacking that problem. They're ahead of the curve and humping each other like happy Grub Bunnies. Those little boogers will hump till they're dead.

However, free spirits or not I hope that no one is doing the dirty deed in my room. That will annoy the crap out of me, especially since I'll have to deal with their left over smells and bodily fluids. The thought itself is fleeting. If I know Ciar even a little bit and I feel like I do, I bet we're supposed to have the room to ourselves. My presence here at 25 versus 13 which is the normal age of attendance is proof of that. If nothing else, the speed this went down ties a bow on the educated guess. Money greases the wheels of all machinations in this world and Mada has the wealth of the forest at her beck and call.

'You realize we'll need to blood-bond?' Ciar's voice in my head is not a new phenomenon but for some reason, it startles the crap out of me. Hand over my heart, I give him a dirty look and my cheeks instantly heat up.

Yep, same reaction as before.

Seeing him as a man was a shock and it kind of changes things. Definitely changes my reaction to him and I'm not sure I'll be able to look at him the same way again. Or stop looking at him if my inability to look away is any indication. Annoyed with myself I yank my gaze away and inwardly cringe when he chuckles in that knowing way that makes me want to smack him.

Given all of this... confusion, the blood-bond isn't my first pick. Him asking for it isn't unexpected either. In the back of my mind I accepted we'd form one, after all it makes the most sense and are relatively common amongst Fae. At least, before he up and changed things. For practicality sake, I know I'm going to give in and do it. It's a way for us to keep track of each other and since we're strangers to this place, that's necessary. I don't resent Ciar being here, in fact, I appreciate it more than I'll admit out loud.

"I'm aware that's an option," I say out loud. Talking to him in my head feels too intimate right now. I need a little space that isn't flush with the surprising and sudden attraction I'm feeling for him.

And the suspicions. Something is going on with all of this. Especially, how he fits into my life now that this has changed. With no other information I haven't even begun to figure it out yet. The silence stretches tight between us, this isn't anything new - he's not the most conversational person I've ever met. Plus, I always have trouble talking to Ciar. His presence is overwhelming at times and now that he's more than a wolfy-dog its overwhelming different parts altogether.

Relieved, I find our room on the third floor. Standing outside of the closed door staring at the brass numbers adorning it, I sigh. The significance of the room number hits me, 69, really? Can the mechanisms of whatever is happening be any more obvious?

Rolling my eyes, I open the door and pause to sniff the air. My nose is pretty good - not as good as Ciar's, but better than most. The musty, unused smell tells me that no one has been in this room for a long time. *Good.* I wait for Ciar to follow me in, then shut the door.

The lights come on automatically, which surprises me. I hope they don't do that when I'm trying to sleep. That'd be jarring. Nice peaceful dreams about some hot guy I saw on TV and then boom lights on I jerk up and fall off the bed.

'Magic lights. They won't turn on while you're asleep.'

I frown at him. For one, I don't know how I feel about him hearing my inner monologue about 'peaceful dreams of hot guys' and the asinine direction of the entire thought thread. For two, I didn't know that he can read minds, because that's exactly what he just did to me. That potentially means he's heard every single bad thing I've ever thought about him.

I fight to keep the smile off my face. A little part of me is glad he did.

Instead of saying anything about the mind reading, I ask, "Do you know the real reason she sent me here?" He stares at me for two seconds before simply raising an eyebrow. So yeah, he knows something. "Does it have to do with why you're here?"

Catching me off guard, he steps forward, closing the

distance between us. Automatically, my hands lash out to defend myself but he blocks the flight of my fist too easy. My instincts scream at me to freeze, so I do, while trying to stop the panicked tempo of my heart. I can be sarcastic all I want in my head - well, maybe not as much as I thought, but it's never good to show fear to Ciar, the Lord of the Wild Hunt, ever.

Not that fear is all I'm feeling.

"What she predicted is truth, Keri. *We* came here to find your Triad." As he speaks, the scent of him surrounds me. Spring, the smell of fresh turned earth, the dew on the grass at twilight. Distracting me momentarily from the words coming out of his mouth. "You are finally going to meet your destiny," he says, his eyes flaring to a bright green before he releases me.

The moment ends like the snap of a rubber band and deciding to play the coward, I go sit on the bed by the farthest wall. Why'd he have to go and bring up serious stuff? Having a Triad means power and that's not something I consider myself ever having. I like the simple life I led up until now and I'm not really in the looksee for something more.

I'm pretty honest with myself most of the time and it's hard to refute two powerful people telling me something is going to happen.

Instead of arguing I say, "I'm kind of dreading who my Triad will be. My luck it'll be the smelly guy that delivered groceries to us." He doesn't laugh so the joke falls flat as a pancake.

There won't be only one weird guy, I'll have to contend with three strangers. All bound to the soul strings of the Awakened so thoroughly that not even death is able to separate them. I'm more nervous about the Triad part of it than the potentially dying bit. Death is something that happens to everyone, this Awakening junk - isn't.

Another question pops into my head but before it can leave my mouth, he's answering it. "It was my choice to come with you. I won't return to the forest, Keri."

Well, at least he saved me the hassle of figuring out how to ask.

I guess in a roundabout way, Mada sending me here makes sense. If she truly believes I'm going to Awaken then this is a smart move and a required one. To keep me in the forest would break the Sacred Law. Ciar himself coming... that doesn't make sense to me. He's done nothing but tolerate me for years. Don't get me wrong, he's always around - wait. He's *always* around. Lurking at the fringes and watching and always full of snide comments and cold shoulders. Yet, he's a solid, constant presence in my life.

I tilt my head to the side to study him. In my experience with him, Ciar always has a motive. Always. It's one of the first lessons I learned about him. He can also be cold and unfeeling but *that* I never hold against him. I can't compare him to a human or a regular Fae.

Ciar is the Lord of the Hunt, Faerie justice incarnate. Some legends even say he's the first of the Sluagh. Looking at him standing there staring at me with green fire in his eyes, I find it completely believable.

Nagan and the others tutored me on what the world is like outside of the forest. How to act. How to fit in. We even had the Ley-net in order for me to search online and see the world from that perspective, too. In that respect, I'm not coming into this blind. He made sure to educate me about all the races and customs, including humans and their increasingly eccentric traditions.

Nagan also taught me to have an open mind and to never be afraid of being who and what I am. Because of him, I'll never be ashamed to be a creature of the forest, of the Sluagh. I smile and the tips of my teeth press into my bottom lip. I have my doubts about this Awakening hoopla, not that it'll happen - I'm pretty sure it will regardless of what I want - it's more about what the result of it will be. For all I know, I'll be the worst janitor in history.

Having so many things I want to ask forms a knot right in my stomach. Needing something to do other than stare at him awkwardly or even to voice my worries, I open my mouth. "What are you going to do while I'm doing all this classwork that I don't want?" I ask him, laying back on the bed.

It's surprisingly soft and as I sink into its lushness, I feel a twinge of longing for my bed in the trees. My ears strain for the rustle of wind blowing through the leaves. The high-pitched giggles of the Spriggets as they steal my shoes and lead me on a merry chase.

Mentally shaking myself, I look over at Ciar standing in the door as he says, "Joining you of course." His green eyes bore into me. "I'm your guard, remember?"

Guard, huh? Why do I feel like that isn't what he really means?

I stare at the cracked ceiling above me and I ask, "What do they think you are?" There's no way they know he's a Puca, they're so rare that they freak people out. Trust me, I've dealt with it every single time we came into town together.

"A Selkie." I snort at his answer.

It's feasible though. Selkies are typically dark haired, their skin color varies and they can have green eyes. But that's where his resemblance ends entirely. At least I know what he wahooed the guard into seeing instead of a Puca. His glamour is subtle but strong. I can only see through it because I know what's under it. Well, I know what's under it now. I had no idea that the - hot guy... yes, definitely a hot guy, resided under all of that fur.

"You lack fish de-toilet." I tease. Selkies are pretty, that's very true, but they tend to smell like rotten fish, bless them.

Ciar smells... not like fish.

Keri, shut up, because the last thing you need him to know is you think he's -

"Hot?" he says, finishing my thought out loud. The amusement in his voice is more than necessary.

I roll my eyes at him and correct it with, "A dick."

He chuckles, he doesn't believe me at all. We both know I'm a terrible liar but calling him a dick is nothing but the truth. This back-and-forth-goes-the-insult-banter is normal for us, it's a perpetual cycle. Except usually it involves a lot less levity. Typically, I'm pissed off by now and ranting about him in my head.

While I was growing up, he elected himself to be my weapon, survival and fighting-the-world trainer. Basically anything that involves killing or maiming someone. Grouchy poodle normally takes every opportunity to tell me how bad I am at everything.

'Keri, were you born with four feet? I have never seen someone trip on air.' He's said many times, 'Keri, do you expect everyone to coddle you? Stop being weak.' On and on like a bad habit. If I were less of a person, it might have affected me in a more negative way. Instead, I worked harder simply to annoy him. No, that's not completely true. I worked harder period. It took me awhile to realize that a tiny bit of it was in the hopes one day he would tell me good job. Just once.

He didn't, and I squished that hope early on for the most part.

He's still staring at me and I briefly wonder if he can hear my inner monologue. "Come on, we need to go get our schedules," he says, sounding like none of this is anything but normal.

I sigh and roll to my feet. If he heard me he's choosing not to comment. Which is fine with me. Still, his shirt should say 'Bossy Bastard' because that's exactly what he is. Grumbling, I follow him out the door, not really paying attention because my mind is already on what's ahead. Running nose first into his chest brings me right out of my thoughts. I step back, and he leans forward reaching around me to magically lock our room.

The hairs on the back of my neck stand up.

Ciar has always had an unusual effect on me, but this particular feeling is strange and new and I don't know what to do with it. This time I decide to do nothing. With a smirk on his still-new-to-me-face he turns, and I follow his yellow flip flopped feet through the hallway. I'm more careful this time to keep a little bit of distance between us. One face-smoosh to his chest is enough for me today.

"Why did you come here?" I ask him, again.

"Because you will go through your Awakening." He says it in a tone that makes me want to throw something at him. Chiding and laced with lots of "duh".

"Yeah, okay." I mutter and then switch tactics. "Why have you never changed into a human before?"

"It wasn't the time."

That's a very expectedly vague answer, not that I'm surprised by it. He always dances around answers and basically plays peekaboo in general with conversations. I think it's part of his nature. Giving up on having a genuine conversation about it, I look around me.

All the dorms are connected via tunnels to the main campus, for those that can't go out during a certain time of day. Honestly, they make getting around easier for everyone, in my opinion. There are several Fae that can't tolerate the sunlight, just like there are Fae who can't tolerate moonlight. I've never had an issue with either but several of the Sluagh can't go out into the direct sunlight.

Tuning more into our surroundings, I shake my head as I notice all the appreciative looks Ciar is getting. Their attention isn't that big of a surprise. I mean, look at him. Even I've caught myself admiring him a time or two as we walk, how can I not? Those jeans fit him perfectly!

The only question I have is, why do I want to smack every single one of his admirers?

It isn't jealousy. It's deeper and feels almost territorial. Oh no, the heck with this, I'm not falling into that trap. I push it all down and keep walking, some honeypots are poisonous and it isn't my place to feel anything remotely like that about Ciar. How many times in my life has he told me I'm not good enough to be a Sluagh? Even if I'm willing to admit a sudden attraction to him, I can't act on it. I'll never meet his standards.

Suddenly he stops and turns to me. Oh yeah, the mind reading thing must still be working.

"I made you strong," he says, then without another word he turns and continues walking.

He isn't wrong. His training did make me strong. His words, no matter how harsh, made me strive to be more so, but I'll be damned if I let him take all the credit. I made myself strong, too.

Physically, I can hold my own in a fight - thanks mostly to Ciar - with most creatures. I'm *not* powerful at all magic wise, but I have a little at my disposal. Enough to do simple things, move something or shut/open a door. Honestly, I don't want more. Magic means attention, strong magic means a lot of attention and Awakening means that everyone will be looking at me, gauging me. They'll also be looking closely at whoever my unfortunate Triad is and I don't want that. The looking or the Triad. I'm fine without any of that mess.

Right?

Staring at the dark hair of the man in front of me makes me think maybe not totally fine. If he were in my Triad I might not be so upset about having one. Not that I'm completely upset as it is. I *want* to be upset more than I actually am.

What the heck, Keri? Inner me yells at the other inner me.

What's so different now than two days ago when I was calling him every name in the book and laughing at his dislike of me? Why now? Have I ever been attracted to him before? I search deep within myself looking for the true answer, not the one I want to lie to myself with.

Yes, I did start feeling attracted to him but it's a very recent thing. Up until the last few minutes, it was the idea of him versus the physical him. I eye the butt in front of me. That's apparently not the case anymore. I'm definitely attracted to the physical him. It's not like I'm a virgin or ignorant about sex. I'm Fae, sex is big part of our lives. Per usual Fae standards, I've been having sex since I was sixteen. Not a lot, but enough to have a good bit of knowledge about it. In fact, I just had sex three -

Ciar stops again and turns to look down at me with a frown of irritation on his face.

- weeks ago, with a Fae that came to get his fortune told by Mada.

I give him my brightest, most innocent smile. I can tell by the look on his face he doesn't believe it. I'm not ashamed of my thoughts or actions concerning sex, I'm a healthy woman with needs. He's making me self-conscious snooping around in my noggin so freely. Especially when I think about anything related to him. Ciar himself taught me about shielding. I guess it's time to put that knowledge to use.

"Hello! You must be new here, I'm Sierra." The sultry - I'm not so insecure I can't admit the truth about it - voice states from behind Ciar. I peek around him and laugh. A human Mage. Ciar hates humans, no matter how pretty or magical they are.

This should be entertaining.

'There is way more Sluagh in you than people realize, Monster Girl,' he says, in a voice laced with amusement. My smile broadens, I like this comparison. It's the first time he's ever done it and if he handed me a million dollars it wouldn't feel as good.

I'll freely admit I love stirring up a bit of mischief too. Especially on humans. They're so easy to mess with. Look at this Sierra person, for example. She practically drips arrogance. Some magic wielders like her are under the false impression that having magic makes them better than everyone else. That's especially an issue with human Mages. Honestly, being able to toss a fireball should only make you arrogant if the thing you throw it at dies on the first hit.

I grew up around things that will simply eat it and then eat her. Ciar at the front of the line. Speaking of him, Pucas like mischief even more than I do. I see the sparkle in his green eyes that are staring at me right before he turns around to face her.

"Can I help you with something?" His tone isn't welcoming. Her beaming smile dims, his response to her is unexpected. Women like her are used to being adored by all.

"I haven't seen you around here before, so I wanted to welcome you to the Menagerie." She watts her smile back up and waits expectantly.

Ciar, bless him for entertainment value, looks at her like she has shit on her shoes and brushes past her. I shrug when her eyes fall on me and I follow him.

"Your brother is rude," she says to my back. I turn my head to look at her.

"My *brother*," Oh, this is just too much fun. "Likes to keep it close to the family. You know the closer the kin the tighter the skin?" I say as I barely keep from laughing at the look of disgust that crosses her face. I tuck my chin to hide my smile. Ahead of me Ciar snorts.

'Naughty Keri, talking about having sex with me,' he teases.

'I still think you're an asshole.' At my, tactful for me opinion, his laughter floats behind him.

'Liar,' he accuses.

Maybe a little, but mostly not really. He's totally an asshole.

CHAPTER 2

HE CAN WALK IN FRONT OF ME.. ALL. DAY LONG.

After grabbing some food at the cafeteria, we head back to the room. Well, I head back to the room and Ciar walks quietly behind me, staring, because the hair on the back of my neck keeps standing on end. I'm eating fries out of the bag of food I'm carrying, mostly his fries because food like this isn't common in the forest. Yummy, greasy, fattening goodness. I lick my fingers and smirk when I stick them back into his fry bag to find the bottom of it holding only crumbs. Whoops.

He has some raw burgers in there, he'll be fine without the rest of it. The burgers must weigh two pounds apiece. That's more than enough to fill up his stomach for a little while.

Unexpectedly, he steps ahead of me and opens the door, waving me forward like a gentleman. I nod my head in thanks and debate on eating one of his burgers, too. Mine is small in comparison. The flash of green in his eyes dissuades me. Fry theft is okay, burger theft not so much.

For a split second, the temptation strengthens. The bag is snatched out of my hands and I'm nudged towards my bed.

Flopping down on it, I laugh as the bag unceremoniously hits me in the chest. Digging my own burger and fries out of the bag, I dig in.

I wish I was part Moss Fairy or something similar because they have the metabolism of a marathon runner, so then I could eat all I want. Unfortunately, I'm something else and the calories go straight to my ass. I have to work out to keep in shape. It seems I have a penchant for chub, especially in certain areas.

I look down at my chest. Some places it's not such a bad thing.

"Why are you so against Awakening, Keri?" Ciar asks, and of course in my eloquence I choke on my mouthful of burger.

After clearing my throat, I chug some water out of the bottle that Ciar hands me and compose myself. "People like me clean toilets or take care of the animals and sometimes we even get to trim the shrubs. We don't have proper Awakenings," I answer, taking that last bite of my now cold burger. "And the whole Triad of stranger's thing throws me off."

It's nothing more than the truth. The entire point of this place is to gauge, groom and sell people to the Higher Fae or the rich humans. As janitors, maids, drivers, guards, occasionally tools and in rare cases, breeders. I'm not pure enough to be a breeder, so I figure that until I get bored or have had enough playing by the rules with this plan of Mada's, I'll get stuck as a maid or something similar.

"The people that encouraged your mother's actions are threatened by what you'll become when you Awaken." His words send me to my feet.

Why in the world is he talking about *her*? I hate talking about my mother. Yes, it's been years and she's dead and gone but it's a sore spot for me. Restlessly, I start wandering around the room and snooping through the dressers. I don't want to talk about her and what happened but Ciar isn't someone you tell that to and expect him to listen.

"Eventually you will accept this truth." As he speaks, I feel his presence move closer to me.

So, like a scared bird I flutter away from him and open the closet door just to look busy. Frowning, I lean forward and pick up the old dusty violin that's leaning against the back wall. It's a strange color of blue with faint lines etched into it. The strings on it are broken and curled at the base. Lightly, I run a finger down the neck of it. With a flare of heat the broken thing comes to life. The strings curl up and connect to the top and the lines lighten with red light.

In shock, I drop it and it twangs in complaint.

"What the hell is that?" I demand, pointing at the possessed violin.

"I do believe that's your Conduit," Ciar answers calmly, stepping around me to pick it up off the floor. He holds it out to me with a smirk on his face. Rolling my eyes, I take it by the neck and gently put it back on the closet floor and slam the door.

No, no and triple no.

"Keri, you can procrastinate about it all you want but it's going to happen. Stop being a child about it," he says, using that tone that makes me feel like the naughty child he's accusing me of being.

Turning to face him I cross my arms, mutinous.

"Procrastination works for as long as I want it to," I say in a very mulish tone. Go me, being a mature adult and all.

"This place will bring out what needs brought. Secure in the forest you will never spread your wings, monster girl," he explains, turning away to cross to his dresser.

He starts putting things in the dresser from his bag, like all of this is completely normal. It takes me a minute to notice that I'm staring at his butt. Disgusted with myself, I decide to follow suit. At least if I'm busy I'm not staring at him like a lust hazed teenage girl. His chuff of laughter makes my face heat. Gods bless it he's snooping again. Frustrated, I start the very detailed slow process of building up my shields again. It's something that can be done while doing other things because it's all mental magic. And it's a magic that I can do. Not so much some of the other stuff.

Which they'll notice right away when I start their stupid classes. I'm so going to get my ass kicked if they actually do things like I've heard they do. Maybe if I suck enough they'll throw me out and I can go home.

"Don't even think about it, Keri," Ciar warns without pausing in his task.

There goes that idea. Pouring more energy into building my shields, I start humming a song that Nagan taught me. It's a Centaur lullaby he used to sing to me as a kid. Ironically enough, it's about war and killing enemies but the melody is sweet and soft.

My voice isn't bard quality, but it doesn't sound like a mule getting strangled, so I'll take what I have gladly. Smiling at my own stupid thoughts, I keep humming and straightening things up.

Before I know it, I find myself with my sleeves rolled up, cleaning the bathroom. I'm only half surprised when I realize that Ciar is in there with me, pink rubber gloves on his hands as he scrubs the shower. When he realizes I'm staring at him, he smirks and flips me off.

The most amusing thing about the gloves... he looks freaking good in them.

CHAPTER 3

HERE THERE BE SNARKY DRAGONS...

I'm not sure what I expected from this place but the very first class is Familiars 101. A cliched name for a cliched class. This is dumb and I don't like it, I'm not 12. Looking around at the sea of staring faces I fight the urge to turn around and walk back out the door. I pick an empty seat towards the back. At least if they want to stare at me back here they have to turn around and look as stupid as I feel.

Ciar walks in the door a second after my butt hits the chair. Oh, my gods. He's actually going to take classes and play out this charade. The man is older than dirt why in the world would he play along with this? That's what I get for having any assumptions about him.

'Bodyguard duty, remember?' he says, his voice full of amusement.

Cutting a dirty look at him, I set to work again on my mental shielding. I started it yesterday but at some point, I got sleepy and took a nap instead of finishing it. That's something I need to remedy or else I won't have any thoughts to myself. Piece by piece I work on the three layers of shielding that will hopefully keep him out. Making sure to add a little alarm to each layer as I go. More than likely he'll get through, but it'll take him awhile. I feel his eyes on me and his displeasure, he doesn't like it. I smirk a little.

Anything I can do to annoy him is a plus in my book.

"Good morning. We have a few new members today. Here let me see..." The male voice comes from the front of the room and I look up dreading what's about to happen. I abhor attention from people and this teacher is about to make me a target. Who in the hell introduces new students anymore?

This antiquated place obviously.

"...right then. Keri Nightshade and Ciar Nightshade. Ha. Ciar did you know that there was a mythological figure with that name?" The teacher states, with a smile on his face.

I snort because I can't help it. Not only does Ciar know, he *is* that 'mythological figure'.

"Are you two brother and sister?" The man then questions.

I bite my lip to keep from laughing and shrug. Ciar completely ignores him and stares out the window. I get the assumption we're related, same last name and all. Which isn't his real last name either, I have no idea if Ciar even has one. The teacher clears his throat uncomfortably and moves on. He's smarter than he looks because pressing Ciar isn't the best option. Ciar shifts in his seat and I see something poking out of his back pocket.

"When did you get a cellphone?" I ask him curious despite myself.

'Weeks ago.'

Weeks ago? He knew that far ahead of time about this? I chew on my lip debating if I should be angry about it or not. The news that I had to leave - was made to leave - my home and my family was only days before it came to pass. My gut tells me this is just the beginning of a rough road. No one is being upfront with me. They tell me it's time to grow up yet none of them want to treat me like I have. It's frustrating. Then you add that he chose to come with me for some unknown reason he won't tell me about either. The guard bit is a load of hoopla.

Something is afoot here.

Wait - I look over at him and he meets my eyes. Lying to myself isn't something I normally do, I quickly reevaluate. Maybe I like the fact he's here, too much? I force my gaze to the surface of my desk.

Really, Keri? You're getting a crush on the creature who beat you bloody on the practice field? Who has never once had a nice thing to say to you or about you and pushed you until you collapsed?

Then a stronger voice in my subconscious takes over.

The man who bandaged and fed you when you were first brought to the forest, dying that's who. The one who sat beside your bed every single minute while your body raged with fever. The man that wrapped his furry body around you while you cried undeserved tears for the death of the mother who hated you.

Ciar, is the one who gave you your first sword and showed you how to swim. Ciar is the one who has *always* been there.

Okay brain, I get it! And also stupid subconscious, he didn't teach me how to swim so much as throw me in and say swim or drown. After swallowing half the lake and flailing around like a headless chicken, I figured it out all on my own. The memory of his distorted image through the water, pacing back and forth along the shoreline forces its way into my brain. Okay, *maybe* he wasn't going to let me drown.

"Miss Nightshade, are you ready to join the rest of us?" I jerk my head up, hearing my name and realize the teacher, Mr. Sputen - really? - is standing right in front of my desk looking down at me with that look of disapproval teachers have perfected.

"Do what?" I ask, suspecting that I need to know the question.

"Do you have a familiar?" he asks, clearly exasperated with me.

"No." I've never tried to call one. When I was a kid and failed horribly to try and light a candle, Nagan told me that I'd get a special one. Yeah, sure. A special imaginary one because that's the only Familiar I ever had.

"Well then, we will go to the arena today and do the summoning for those of you," he looks pointedly at me, "Who do not have familiars." He studies me a moment. "Typically, I am quite good at figuring out the heritages of my students. But you are a puzzle Miss Nightshade. Ciar is a Selkie, obviously. But you... you are not."

Neither is Ciar, moron.

"A half-breed," someone mumbles under their breath. It isn't a lie, so I say nothing. Mr. Sputen continues to stare at me expectantly.

"I have no idea." That's about all he's getting out of me. He stands there a moment longer staring and then turns towards the door dismissing me. Good, I'm not worth the aggravation.

"Come along class," he encourages, waving towards the people in the class as he walks out the door. The room echoes with the shuffling of feet and the scraping of chairs as the class files out the door behind him. Ciar and I are last. He brushes his arm against mine to get my attention, I look at him.

'Have you ever tried to summon a familiar?' He asks. Has his voice always sounded this deep and soothing?

Pulling myself out of my weird thoughts, I respond, *'When I first came to the forest, Nagan tried to teach me but I failed at it horribly.'*

Which is nothing less than the truth. I can shut a door

and maybe blow a piece of paper around but I can't light a candle. I have no idea how I'm going to summon a familiar. That takes more juice than I have. I don't see me being able to get out of it though, because this human teacher is still going to make me try - call it a hunch. I follow *slowly* behind the rest of them while feeling a little nauseous that I've got to participate in this fiasco.

Our destination is exactly what its name implies, including sandy floors and stone coliseum seats. There's even a dais for a royal to sit on high above us. I feel like I've walked onto a movie set. A really bad movie set.

"Those of you who have familiars, please go ahead and summon them. As for those of you that don't - who wants to go first?" Mr. Sputen doesn't waste time at least. A Sprite holds up her hand and it begins.

I glance over at Ciar when I feel his familiar magic in the air. Beside him stands a sleek black wolf about double the size of its natural relatives. With extra teeth and claws thrown in because Lancelot is a Sluagh, not a wolf.

"Lancelot!" I call his name and he runs to me. Kneeling, I allow him to cover my face in slobbery kisses. "Breath mint buddy," I tease. Giving me a toothy canine smile, he sits back on his haunches. Even in this position the big butthead is still taller than me.

Digging in my pocket for a piece of Berry Drop candy, I smile as I feed him a few pieces. It's my one candy weakness. Berry Drops are Fairy-made hard candies that are filled with strawberry gel. Nagan keeps boxes of them for me.

"Miss Nightshade, it's your turn." I reluctantly stop petting Lance and turn back to Mr. Sputen. "Do you know the incantation?" he asks. I nod. It's one of the first things Nagan taught me, except I only know the Sluagh version. "Well, stop staring at me like a sad cow and move to the circle." For some reason, this teacher has decided to dislike me. Even if he hadn't called me a sad cow, I can hear it in his voice and see it on his face as he looks at me.

This is going to make things fun.

I trudge over to the summoning circle drawn neatly on the sandy floor to protect users from wild magic. I have to give him credit, he takes precautions. Taking a deep breath, I center myself and whisper my chosen word of power, "Existence."

All words of power are whispered to magic users by Faerie at birth. It's the first word you speak when you learn to talk. The word that's special only to you. Nagan told me that mine is a special word, like the Sluagh's are special. I guess until now I didn't realize how different mine is from those other than the Sluagh.

One of the Sprites who went before me used a number, while some of the others used mundane words like sky or water. At least their magic worked, mine has decided to take its sweet time. Finally, the small pool of magic inside me begins to stir. I feel it twist and writhe before shooting out into the now silent room.

At first nothing happens, which doesn't surprise me at all. Then, after I start to become incredibly uncomfortable at all the stares I'm receiving, there's a small pop sound and a tiny yellow worm appears in the circle at my feet. Pulling myself out of my shocked stupor I kneel down to look at my Familiar. How very excited and he's so flipping cute! Kneeling, I scoop him up carefully with my hand and nuzzle him, whispering, "Fluffy," his name.

Stroking a finger down his lumpy spine, I watch him open a tiny little mouth exposing tiny little sharp teeth and bite the meaty part of my thumb. He's not doing it to be mean, he's doing it to cement the blood bond between us. My magic moves inside of me again, as if the spell is still active.

That doesn't make any sense.

"You got a slug for a familiar?" The voice intrudes upon my happy little worm petting moment.

Laughter breaks out around me. Only one person isn't laughing, Ciar. My eyes seek him out, he's staring at me with an odd look on his face. Is it pity because they're laughing at me? I hope not, their opinions don't matter—I'm perfectly content with Fluffy. My new little friend who is currently rubbing against my palm while making little growling noises.

He's adorable.

"Miss Nightshade, I'm afraid that we will have to have you try again. That worm is unacceptable as a Familiar." Mr. Sputen clears his throat nervously as he speaks.

Frowning, I look up at him. What? There's no way to break the bond with a Familiar except in death.

"No, you're not killing Fluffy." I tuck him protectively against my chest.

"Miss Nightshade, you need a familiar that can help increase your skill, not - that." He motions to someone behind me.

I feel the disturbance of movement and follow my instincts, curling over Fluffy protectively. Pain lances down my back. Claws. I know the feeling of those rather well. A deep growl silences the clamoring voices. I know that growl too. Ciar.

The arena shakes around us, raining dust down on our heads. A loud roar echoes in the air. I look up as another roar sounds and a hole appears as part of the ceiling is torn away, then another. Large clawed limbs reach through the growing hole and rip another chunk of ceiling away.

I look over at Ciar who is smiling and then back to the ceiling. What the fudge? A reptilian head pokes in the hole and black glowing eyes meet mine.

"Who dares attack my mistress?" His voice booms, as he slides through the mess he's made of the ceiling and lands with a heavy thud and a swirl of sand a few feet from me. Holy meatballs it's a Dragon! As I meet his dark swirling eyes, I realize something profound, he's mine too. I can feel him and as the magic connects him and I start to know him.

"She is your master, Dragon?" Mr. Sputen asks in disbelief.

"Zag," I whisper, as his name flits through my mind. In a bit of a haze, I close the distance between us. His big scaled nose nudges me when I approach and rumbles with satisfaction as I scratch the soft scales behind his ear hole.

"I have waited millennia for a proper master, girl, and finally I heard your call," he says, an eyeball the size of a dinner plate rolling to glare at the crowd of students. Straightening to his full height, he swings his head towards the people staring at us in shock. Turning back towards me by curling his neck he rests the tip of his snout lightly on my shoulder as he sniffs the wounds on my back. His forked tongue snakes out and flicks it. The texture of his tongue is rough like a cat's, but the touch gentle. The itch of them healing is forgotten as the blood bond snaps into place.

"Who caused your wounds?" he asks me softly. His breath hot against me.

I shrug. I didn't see who or what did it and I'm not going to blame the Familiar for acting on their masters order. Something pulls at me to look at Ciar again. He's holding a big chunk of bloody fur in his hands.

"Ah, I see. My lord has already handled the culprit." I don't miss the note of satisfaction in Zag's voice.

'You didn't kill it, right?' I ask Ciar, instead of assuming. I hate to think something happened that wasn't the Familiar's fault.

Ciar shakes his head and tosses the chunk to the sandy floor. Grimacing he wipes his hand down his jean clad leg. That makes me feel a bit better. The poor thing - whatever it is - I look over at Mr. Sputen knowing that my eyes are swirling with color. They always do when I'm angry. He takes a step back putting more distance between us. Even further when Zag turns to look at the human Mage.

"Keri called and therefore I answered. And now that I have ingested her blood, we are now permanently bound. Do *you* contest my choice human?" Zag is to the point and being intimidating on purpose. I like him already.

Mr. Sputen shakes his head, his face pale.

I can feel Zag's irritation with the man through our bond, which is growing even stronger as the minutes pass. I can feel it pulsing between us like it's alive. In response to my wonder, Zag's shadow thickens and swirls around us. Considering he's a Shadow Dragon—the rarest kind in existence—this isn't a surprise. That doesn't make it any less cool, though. The surprise in all of this is his appearance at all. Only the strongest magic users can have creatures like him for a Familiar.

'I am not surprised, Monster Girl,' Ciar sounds very smug.

'Well Ciar, that makes one of us.' I don't have any good comebacks. I'm fully aware what this event means.

With a whoosh and small explosion of shadows, Zag shrinks and alights his house cat sized self on my shoulder. Well, that's a handy trick.

"Zag, are you sure you're my familiar?" I ask, managing to stop gawking.

"Without a single shred of doubt." Amusement laces his words.

"Well, that's crazy. I don't -"

"It seems that you have two familiars, Miss Nightshade." Mr. Sputen interrupts. There's a bite to his words this time. He isn't happy about it, at all - which doesn't make sense. Why is he pissy about me having a Familiar or two, when he should be pleased or somewhat that I have one at all?

"Although, I have no idea what good a worm will do you," he finishes.

I give him a smile full of satisfaction as I say with nothing short of triumph, "Fluffy is a Corpse Worm, Mr. Sputen." The look of absolute shock on his face gives me enough gumption to keep from laughing out loud. I choose instead to laugh on the inside. No reason to start too much trouble on my first day. I have plenty of days ahead of me to do that.

Fluffy is just as special as Zag. A Corpse Worm feeds on the body and souls of the damned. Fully grown, he'll be as big as Zag, minus the sparkly wings and feet. Fluffy will be all teeth and appetite.

"How is this possible?" Mr. Sputen mutters, waving for the class to continue with their summoning.

I spend the rest of the class time getting to know my new companions. The bells chime, indicating it's time for the next course. Zag nestles himself into my hair. Typically, familiars are dismissed to a user's Blank Space, but I'm not about to do that - to either of them. I've no idea what it's like in there, but I imagine it's not a happy place. My imagination has it painted as this big dark hole full of floating junk.

I tuck Fluffy between my breasts and absently play with Zag's tail that's wrapped around my neck, as I try to stay awake through my potions class. The water I chugged in between it and magical history class is hitting home. I raise my hand, unsure of what else to do and politely ask to be allowed to go to the restroom. Calmly, I stroll out the door and then when the room is out of sight, I pick up my step. I really got to go.

I wander through the halls for a good two-minutes before I finally find the women's bathroom, all to Zag's amusement. Hurrying in I take care of business and happily relieved I stop at the cracked porcelain sinks to wash my hands.

Inevitably, I end up looking at myself in the mirror. I hate seeing my face and my mismatched eyes. As a kid it just reminded me how much I didn't fit in anywhere, not even in the forest. I'm too humanoid looking to be a Sluagh but too alien looking to be a human. Mockingly my green eye swirls while, at first, the yellow one does nothing. Then like a match being lit it flares to life and joins its partner. Two vastly different colors moving in an identical pattern.

They go well with my stupid pointy ears.

Forcing myself to hum a happy tune, I dry my hands and turn to leave. That's when I spot the blue violin from my closet leaning casually against the inside of the bathroom door. The door I came in. Crap, the cursed thing followed me. Snatching it up I duck out of the bathroom door with it tucked under my arm, I stop long enough to stuff it in the janitor's closet and before I can change my mind, slam the door and practically run away. I don't want the mess that having this thing entails. Maybe someone else will find it and it'll follow them around everywhere.

Ciar gives me a knowing look when I slip back into the classroom. He knows I feel guilty and I have no idea how but he always does. I guess, Ciar just has a nose for my guilt. Gods know he caught me out enough as a kid. To avoid looking at him and feeling even more guilty, I stare at the clock. Chewing on my thumbnail, I watch the second-hand tick around it like a hawk. A nip of sharp teeth at my wrist stops the bad habit before I worry it down to the quick. Zag is already being useful and demonstrating how bossy he's going to be in the future.

I wonder if I can win an argument against a Dragon? I'll have to try it in the near future.

Finally, the teachers dismiss us for lunch. I'm so hungry and eager to get out of the class, I'm first out the door. The rumbling of my stomach hastens the trip. The good thing about magic is the Fae working in the cafeteria know exactly what you want or need to eat and because of this your food appears right on your table.

I laugh when ours pops into existence. A platter full of meat - lots of it - which I love, the rarer the better. This place provides the best and it's practically still mooing. Ciar gives me a wolfish smile before grabbing a large hunk of it and taking a toothy bite out of it.

Amused, I give Fluffy tiny pieces as Zag hops onto the table to feed himself. Smiling at the Dragon tossing a piece of meat into the air and swallowing it whole is entertaining. And a bit cringe worthy, my imagination keeps supplying flying cows. Still, I chew my own piece of steak with gusto.

"Do you have all of the same classes as me, Ciar?" I ask, around a mouthful of food.

He nods but his eyes are on something over my shoulder. I glance behind me, not the least surprised that everyone is staring at us and whispering. It reminds me of what I realized with blinding clarity earlier in the hallway.

"There aren't very many like us here, are there?" I ask. He contemplates me a moment while he chews. He then holds a piece of meat to my lips. Absently, I take it between my teeth and chew.

"At the moment, no." I frown at his answer.

What does that mean? Pushing the issue with Ciar is pointless and I'm not sure I feel like having an argument right now. If he wants to tell me, he will, and the food is too good to spoil with bickering.

"Have you found any company yet?" I ask, because Pucas have one heck of a libido and I'm being snoopy, too. His green eyes take on an eerie glow as his teeth flash in that too big smile again. It makes me instantly suspicious, which makes me double check my shielding, only to find out that it is holding firm.

"Oh, yes." At his answer, a shiver wracks me.

Those two words sound so dirty and my body responds to it that way. I have no idea why.

Nervously trying to continue the conversation I ask, "Who? One of those humans?" He shakes his head and takes another big bite of meat.

Frowning, I continue chewing to keep my mouth occupied enough to not say anything else stupid. For some reason the thought of him being close to anyone else... bothers me. Something I have no right whatsoever to feel and something that never bothered me before.

Fudge.

Just how attached am I to him, really? I look at his green eyes and otherworldly face and those long sharp teeth of his. My heart rate jumps. Gods, this is flipping ridiculous. Why am I suddenly so self-conscious about having an attraction to someone? Is it because of who it is? Anyone would feel attraction towards him and I'm a healthy woman and he's a healthy man. It's not like he's the first man I've been attracted to.

Ciar's eyes narrow. Is that sneaky bastard in my head again? I feel around for him in there and there's nothing. Hm.

"You're at the cusp of Awakening." Zag's whisper against my ear makes me jump.

"Zag, I don't think my Awakening is going to be that big of a deal," I whisper back fiercely.

Denial isn't working and procrastination is out the window, because the fact of it is that I received two familiars. I've honestly never heard of anyone getting two before and any idiot could determine that no matter what I want, I'm going to Awaken. His loud chuckle echoes as he raises his eyes to be level with mine.

"I have lived for thousands upon thousands of years, waiting in the darkness for my chosen to call. You Keri, are that chosen. Only *you* were strong enough to call me forth and it is only *you* that I will serve for the rest of my life. Yes, your Awakening will be a big deal." Done with his speech, he tickles my cheek with his tongue and calmly goes back to his lunch like what he said isn't a life bomb.

A giggle of disbelief escapes me, I can't help it. This is ludicrous - me having power of any kind? I can't transform water and most toddlers can transform water. I'm the unwanted, almost murdered, child of a loony dead woman.

Then Mada sent me here. This entire situation is just one big messy fiasco. Somehow getting a Dragon and Corpse Worm for familiars - a flipping magical violin following me around. The icing on the cake is Ciar coming with me - voluntarily - and looking so damn hot. There I said it. *Hot.*

Fudge.

Nervously, I shove the last piece of my steak in my mouth and look for a napkin. There's blood all over my hand and I can feel it dripping down my wrist. A large, clawed hand grabs mine and I sit there helplessly watching while watching Ciar take that long dexterous tongue of his to slowly lick my hand clean. Even in between my fingers. So sensuously is it done, that certain parts of me are aching to feel it on them.

I'm in so much trouble. Breaking the spell of his eyes, I yank my hand out of his grasp and practically run from the cafeteria. His chuckle follows me out.

CHAPTER 4
PAY SACRIFICE TO THE PORCELAIN GOD...

W hy is it that when you run away from something in a public place, you always end up in the bathroom? Because that's exactly where I'm headed. I guess I can tell myself it's because I need to wash my hands. When the reality is that its because Ciar can't come in the bathroom and he's the one I'm hiding from. Smacking the door to open, I pause at the sound of "mean" laughter - you know, the kind that reeks of menace - and is always accompanied by someone crying.

Peeking around the half-wall at the entrance, I see three women standing over a fourth one who's curled up on the floor. Now, I'm not big on sticking my nose in other's business but I know bullying when I see it. I won't tolerate it only pussies bully people. Stepping around the wall, I clear my throat.

"Hey, some hot guy was asking for you in the cafeteria. He's new - black hair green eyes?" I lie, suspecting that hormones and egos will pull their attention from the gal on the floor.

Ciar can forgive me later.

The level of lead-gal's intelligence is demonstrated when she makes a snotty face at me and flounces out of the bathroom with her two side-kicks in her wake. Wow, I can't believe they fell for that. I expected a smart remark or something. I guess I underestimated Ciar's attractiveness level.

"Thank you," the woman on the floor says as she climbs to her feet. A quick glance at her confirms she's in one piece, just a little wet.

"No problem," I answer, heading for the sink. Since I'm in here, I might as well actually wash my hands. I look up and meet her eyes in the mirror. She's human, and very pale. She smiles nervously and wrings her hands in front of her.

After studying her, I say, "I'm not going to lecture you on learning self-defense and all that garbage, but I can see - very clearly, that you have more than enough magic inside of you to defend yourself. So why didn't you?"

"I'm a pacifist," she answers, after staring at me for a solid minute. A pacifist in our world? How has she survived this long?

She flips her long brown hair over her shoulder and regards me a bit less nervously. I smile, using my lips only. My teeth are sharp and tend to make people nervous when I show them. Well, humans anyhow and magic or not, she's human.

"You're clearly one of them, I can see the point to your ears. So why did you help me?" she asks, quietly.

"You're asking that because the girls doing it are Fae?" I dry my hands as I talk, holding her blue eyes with my own mismatched ones. She nods. "Just because I'm different than you doesn't mean I like bullies of any species."

This gets me a tentative smile, which I'm pleased about. I don't want her to be afraid of me because I'm Fae. As I turn to toss the paper towel in the trash, a flash of purple catches my gaze in the mirror. Frowning, I turn back to it and I spot the splash of color in my plain brown hair.

The tip of one of the slightly curled ends is purple. A light lavender type purple. What the fudge?

"Guessing that's a surprise?" she comments coming up beside of me.

"A bit. What's your name?" I ask, tucking the hair over my shoulder and out of sight while trying to put what it means in the back of my head.

"Lucinda," she answers, giving me another shy smile. "Yours?"

Smiling back, I turn to leave and say as I look over my shoulder at her, "My name is Keri. Stay safe okay?" She nods, and I walk out of the bathroom. Thankful, as I duck and weave through the throng of people in the hallway, that we don't have to carry books around.

The only reason I'm avoiding most of the attempted shoulder checks - a result of the bathroom incident I'm sure, is because of the training Ciar made sure I received. Reflexes honed from avoiding, or trying to avoid, his attacks. Otherwise the floor and I would be intimately acquainted.

It's rather childish when you think about it. Most of the people trying to knock me about are adults in their twenties. Very immature adults and without lumping them into stereotypes, spoiled rich adults. Apparently, I'm going to get the high school experience at twenty-five.

The more logical, less bitchy part of me chastises the 'I don't wanna' part, *Oh, stop whining about it and just keep going, the day is almost over*. Sighing, I keep mucking along. Music class is on my schedule next, which makes me think of the violin I stuffed in the janitor's closet. Guilt worms its way in. With a little bit of effort, I shove it aside. I can deal with that mess later. This is the one class I'm genuinely looking forward to and I don't want anything to color it. I can't sing to save my life, but I love all types of music.

Powerful spells can be wrapped up into the notes of music. Not that the ability to do such spell-work is a skill of mine. There's no harm in attempting to learn about it, so I chose the class. I expect that the best in it will obviously be the Sirens. Music is their thing after all but that doesn't mean I can't have fun.

Thankfully, once we're settled in, I'm not called to do anything. Ciar is chosen instead and he can sing like a god. He used to sing to me as a child when the nightmares kept me up at night. That's the song he picks, it is and always will be one of my favorites. A poignant, soulful song about a river who loves a woman but doesn't have a body to be with her. The magic he is weaving with his voice calls to me, taking me to that place of comfort and safety that he created for me.

My eyes burn, and hastily I blink the tears away. He paid more attention than I realize and for some strange reason, that fact makes me want to give into the tears. The sound of applause saves me from that overly emotional response.

The teacher, Ms. Cobbleson, says, "That was absolutely beautiful. I will most definitely have you sing again in the future, Ciar." Given the way she's looking at him, that isn't the only thing she wants him to do. I snort at my own thoughts while she continues, "Now, as you all know - except for our two new members - I will be putting you in pairs. I want you to write the music for a creative dance."

Crap. Who will I be paired with? I look at Ciar who is looking at Ms. Cobbleson intently. The feel of his magic in the air raises goosebumps on my skin. I see that decision is already made.

As soon as the slightly glazed look leaves her face she says, "Miss Nightshade, do you mind being paired with your," she squints at Ciar closely trying to see a resemblance. "Relative?" I cough to cover a laugh.

"That's fine," I answer quietly while my tension eases. Ciar and I have never danced. He was an animal most of my life, but I've danced many times before. Including with partners. I've learned some of the new dance styles, as well. I'm Fae after all, dancing is encouraged but it's usually a prelude to something more intimate.

The disappointment written on the faces of the others in the class is a because they weren't partnered with Ciar. Somethings that's funny and eye rolling at the same time. I get it too, he's pretty. The smile fades off my face as the nerves associated with the reality of the situation hits me. I've got to dance with Ciar. I'm going to be body to body with someone I, may or may not, have a wicked crush on.

Well, this'll be fun.

The smile he gives me is wolfish and purely Lord of the Hunt. The feeling rising in me floods into my eyes. I smile back at him with all my teeth. I almost forgot in the newness of this place and in the sadness of leaving home, that I'm Fae. I'm family to the Sluagh, the big bad monsters of this world. I'm a child of the Dark Forgetful Forest and I fear nothing.

Dance challenge accepted, Ciar. I wink at him.

The rest of the day passes rather as expected. By the time I drag myself back to our room, I'm absolutely fed up with people. I'm sick of them staring at me and disgusted by them gawking at Ciar. In our last class, one Djinn girl had the audacity to sit right on his lap, uninvited. She ended up on the floor but it's a point of principle. I also didn't make a new friend when I laughed at her. Or the next woman to have a trip to the floor for draping herself across his shoulders. She ended up getting the crap scared out of her too.

All of this from Ciar himself, I had nothing to do with it.

Do any of the Fae in this place understand their own

natures at all? They seem to have the lots-of-sex part down pat, but the intricacies involved with other things seem to be lost on them. If a Fae - especially one like Ciar - is interested in someone, there's no subtlety about it. He'll doggedly pursue his chosen partner until he catches them. Then he'll either *do* them or eat them, maybe both. But if there's any romantic intent he'll do little things that a creature of his nature does. He'll feed them and then he'll care for them like... lick their hands clean. My eyes jerk to his. He's sitting on his bed across the room from me - shirtless - staring. Those eyes of his are lit up like green torches.

As a full body shiver runs down my spine, I ask, "Ciar, are you courting me?"

With animalistic grace, he slides to his feet and crosses the room. Prowling towards me like he owns the world - wearing those well-fitting jeans, riding low on his hips. I can't help but appreciate what I'm seeing, a lot. Leaning down, he places a hand on each side of my hips. Bringing his face so close to mine that I can feel his breath on my lips. Feel the heat pouring off his body. I can't control my body's reaction to his proximity. Straight lust flashes through me like a forest fire.

"Are you ready for that bond, Monster Girl?" His nostrils flare, scenting my reaction to him.

The heat rises to my cheeks but I keep my eyes on his. I will not cower or be ashamed of how this makes me feel. "Bite away," I offer. My voice wavers slightly, exposing my false bravado.

Smiling, he rubs his cheek against mine and dips his head to my shoulder. The sealing of his hot mouth against my skin is pure bliss. Enhanced, because he's choosing to let this be purely pleasurable. I'm Fae, pain and pleasure are intertwined in our world, so his teeth sliding into my skin is one-hundred percent sexual. The first draw of blood he takes from me, orgasmic. A moan escapes me before I can catch it. His teeth dig deeper into my body, his weight pushing against me until I'm lying back on the bed with him draped over me. His body fits snug between my open legs. My hand digs into his soft hair and pushes his mouth closer to me.

Instinctually, I rub my face on his shoulder, tasting his skin with the tip of my tongue. Hesitating only a second, I bite into it and the essence of Ciar floods my mouth. His blood tastes like moon lit nights and waterfalls, the crisp clean air of the forest. He tastes like home.

His flesh rips as he tears it from my mouth. Instantly, my body feels the loss of him. Taking several deep breaths in an attempt to calm the confusing emotions rolling through me, I push myself up on my elbows to study him. He's standing several feet from me in the unnaturally dark room. Those green eyes glowing eerily are the only parts of him I can see.

"Ciar?" He growls, when I speak his name.

Goosebumps rise on my skin because of the way he's looking at me. That consuming lust rolling off him is like an aphrodisiac calling me to it without protest. I feel his intent before he moves and relax in preparation, I have no desire to stop him.

In a flutter of leather wings mini-Zag is between us, roaring at Ciar. Ciar, who looks more monster than man and - holy meatballs, is he beautiful. Those inhuman eyes are blazing with hunger, hunger for me. Hunger I feel for him.

"Regain your control, dark lord!" Zag yells at him, standing his ground against Ciar, who is pacing side to side looking for a way to get around Zag and to me. I want him to get to me, to become part of me. Something loosens inside of me and shakes free. Pain lances through my head, laying me flat on the bed from the strength of it. My back bows as my body convulses from another wave of pain.

"She has claimed you. Hold her!" Zag orders, sounding muffled and distant, like he's at the end of a tunnel.

With effort, I force my eyes open to see Ciar's face above mine. I feel the steel of his arms wrapped around me holding me tightly to him. A clawed hand lashes out at him. Calmly, he takes the assault as jagged cuts open up on his face and then just as quickly heal, leaving slashes of blood in their place. Fighting the magic force holding me, I reach up to touch the bloody lines on his face and his eyes meet mine. That's when I see the claws and realize that the hand that damaged him belongs to me but something isn't right, none of this is right.

Another wave of pain rolls through me. Panting I let out a moan mixed with pain and pleasure. I need something to make this awful burning fade. To take the wrenching pain away. To sate the need. "Please, Ciar... I need..."

'Shh, my Monster Girl. I'll take the pain away.' His voice in my head is a soothing balm on the jabbing shards of magic inside of my body. As his mouth descends and merges with mine the pain recedes. Leaving the coolness of relief and tempered arousal in its wake. On his seeking tongue I taste the tang of my blood. I taste the power of Ciar, the Lord of the Hunt and feel him in every beat of my heart.

With one last deep kiss, he pulls away from me.

"Sleep." His magic weaves around me, a lullaby to my senses.

My eyes are heavy and I fight to keep them open. My gut is telling me that something will be different when I wake up, something important.

"They will hear that summons, my lord. She has claimed..." loud heartbeats in my ear drown out the words. "... earlier than expected."

The smell of Ciar surrounds me as I burrow in deeper, needing to be close to him. "Do you have any idea of the others? You are the..." Soft lips brush my forehead and cheek. Feather light touches on the edge of my mouth. "These foolish mortals in this place should be treating her with proper..." A burning hot mouth takes mine and the taste of forest floods me. I open to it as if it's the most natural thing in the world to do. More, I *need* more. Before I can beg for it, demand it, the warmth pulls away from me.

"They will not be the only ones to sense her, others will come and try to claim her." Not that Zag's words are making a lot of sense but that last part I understand perfectly. No one will claim me unless I allow it.

So, I let them know that in no uncertain terms, "I will... feed them to... Ciar."

Two masculine chuckles follow me into oblivion.

CHAPTER 5

GUILTY GOO-GOO EYES...

I wake up in my own bed with the blanket pulled up to my chin. Someone tucked me in like a child. Shaking my head, I sit up. Rubbing my forehead doesn't ease the pounding inside of my skull. This is the worst hangover I've ever had in my life. Debating on flopping back down in the bed and passing out for a few more hours is interrupted by my screaming bladder. Before I do anything else, I'll take care of this need and brush my teeth. My mouth tastes like something died in it. Ugh.

Climbing slowly to my feet, I stumble into the small bathroom. After taking care of nature's necessities, I brush my teeth - twice, and wash my face. Feeling a little better, I check the time only to discover that it's almost noon.

"Crap. Crap. Crap," I grumble, as I run around trying to get dressed for the rest of my classes. I don't want to disappoint Nagan by getting thrown out this soon or failing because failing is worse.

"You have been excused from classes today, mistress. My lord took care of it earlier." Zag's voice startles me so hard I fall over with only one leg in my jeans. Giving up a little on life, I lay there as bits and pieces from the night before come back to me with blinding clarity.

"Where's Ciar?" I stutter out.

Zag pads over to me to look down into my face and with quite a bit of amusement, says, "He's getting you food." May the gods bless Ciar for that.

Closing my eyes, I try to remember everything that happened, because it's important to remember and I know this. "Zag?"

"Yes, mistress?" Is that guilt I see in my familiar's eyes? Why yes, yes, it is.

"Who was I going to feed to Ciar?" I can feel Ciar drawing closer, feel his heat, his heartbeat. With that comes the memories of the taste of his mouth and the feeling of his body against mine.

Well, shit.

"Whoever you want." Ciar's voice - at least - doesn't startle me. At this point, I don't even care that I'm lying on the floor in my underwear with my jeans only on one leg. Not after what transpired the night before. "What are you doing, Monster Girl?"

All his attention is on me and it's much more intent than his nonchalant question implies. Rolling over, I gain my feet and pull the jeans off, tossing them onto my bed. Crossing to the small dresser we share, I dig a pair of yoga pants out. This is definitely a comfy pants day. I slide them on quickly, still feeling him watching me.

"I smell coffee," I say instead of the myriad of questions burning in my brain. Turning I smile at him.

Amazingly, he smiles back, and it's a smile that transforms his entire face. For a gaping-mouth minute, I stand there and drink it in. There are no doubts whatsoever about that smile being genuine because his *emotions* are bleeding into mine. Amusement... arousal.

What the heck?

Dumbed down from the flush of being near him after... last night, I take the offered coffee. The luscious smell informs me that it has the right amount of sugar and cream in it. Ciar knows me so well and the first sip lets me know exactly how well.

Gods, it's perfect.

"So, what exactly happened with my biting you?" I ask, finally getting some caffeine fueled bravery. The tick of the ceiling fan is the only sound in the room. "Well?" I prompt, turning and pinning Zag to the floor with my gaze. He shuffles a little. He'll answer me.

"You claimed him," he finally answers. Wait, I did what?

"Claimed? How is that different than a normal bond?"

"Well," his beseeching gaze turns to Ciar. "A little help here, my lord?"

Ciar hands me a brown bag that smells heavenly, almost as good as the coffee. Taking it, I hop onto the bed and dig through it with glee. My mouth is watering from the smell of the sandwiches inside of it. I begin stuffing big bites of one in my face while I wait for an answer to my question.

Fluffy growls from under the bed. I climb off the bed to look under it and laugh when I see how big he has grown in just twenty-four hours. He's already as big as Zag's mini form. I feed him the bacon off my sandwich.

"That piglet has already eaten today," Zag comments from beside of me.

"I'm still waiting." I'm not the most patient person, especially with something like this.

"You made out with me," Ciar says, sitting on my bed a mere foot from me.

"Nu uh, you made out with me first." The maturity of that statement is incredible. Go, me.

"So, you're not denying you made out with me?" He teases, completely deflecting my questions.

Seeing that he isn't going to answer anything, I shove the rest of the sandwich in my mouth to keep from talking. Nothing I can say at this point will get me out of this mess. I like the making out part... looking at him through my lashes I realize that I kind of want to make out again. His gaze jerks to me and his eyes burn as they search my face.

Flipping bond, he knows exactly what I'm feeling.

Climbing hastily to my feet I go to the bathroom to wash my hands, needing something to do besides stare at him like a lovesick idiot. Love? Yes, love. Frowning, I dry my hands and flick a glance at him. Ciar?

The answer smacks me in the face. I won't lie to myself.

"What has you thinking so hard, Monster Girl?"

"My period is late. I'm wondering if maybe my last little romp resulted in a mini - womph -" The ground is suddenly farther away because I'm dangling by an arm from a large clawed hand, while wolfy-dog man sniffs my stomach. "I'm joking you idiot, put me down." With a huff he drops me to land lightly on my feet.

"That was not amusing," I laugh at the annoyed tone of his voice, it's hilarious. "Children are to be protected and cherished. A child of yours will be doubly so." That's all noble and sweet and stuff. Now I feel like a jerk.

I don't know what to say to that because it speaks of intimacy that I'm still reconciling, and because I have no idea what to say to that. I go and tuck myself away in the window alcove to read a book, or at least pretend to. I'll never admit to him how many times I look at him throughout the day.

I'm pretty sure he catches most of them. After all, he's looking at me every time I look up at him, so what does that say?

CHAPTER 6
THE VENGEFUL VIOLIN...

A cringeworthy screech drags me from the pleasurable dream. Covering my ears, I sit up in the darkness and look for the offensive source of it. However, when I discover it's source I sigh and lay back down. The flipping violin is on the dresser next to my bed, glowing a pale eerie blue in the darkness. The strings are moving to a phantom bow causing the awful sounds that resemble a Boggart getting strangled.

Determined to not acknowledge the persistent thing, I roll over and shove the pillow over my head hoping the fluff will block it out. The violin only gets louder. Gods that's an awful noise.

"Okay! Fine!" I throw the pillow aside and get up, gracefully tripping over Fluffy who's laying on the floor next to my bed. Fighting to regain my balance I careen right into a warm, solid, very male chest.

Well, hello there, Ciar.

"What are you doing, Keri?" His warm hands grasp my shoulders. His touch is nice and it's hard not to lean further into it. A fact that has nothing to do with the bond or whatever mojo is going on, it's quite simply because I like him.

The slow sensual smile that splits his lips makes me regret admitting it, even if to myself, immediately. Flipping bond. Stepping away from him, I grab the violin and fire shoots up my arm. In vain I try to drop it, swinging my arm in the attempt to sling it away. Still it remains firmly in my grasp. The pain fades and Ciar's chuckle breaks the silence.

"What?" I demand.

"It tried to befriend you and you cast it away. Now it's taking the choice from you. It's your Conduit, accept it." As he speaks, his hand slides down my arm to wrap around my hand and the burning sensation instantly stops.

"I have no idea what to do with the flipping thing, Ciar. I can't play a violin."

"I bet you can play this one. Try," he encourages.

A bow magically appears in my other hand and I let Ciar guide the violin to rest under my chin and against my shoulder. Rolling my eyes, I lightly run the bow across the strings and am rewarded with one of the most beautiful melodies I've ever heard.

That enthralling sound is all due to the magic of the violin but, for a moment as I stroke the strings, I allow myself to enjoy the music coming from my contact with it. Reluctantly, I carefully set the violin on the dresser and rest the bow across the top of it. The ethereal glow around it dims and it's almost like it goes to sleep.

"Did that really just happen?" Ciar huffs at my question.

"Of course it did, just like you got a Dragon and a Corpse Worm as Familiars... among other things." As he talks he moves closer to me pressing his body lightly against my side.

Part of me is tempted to give into the offer he's subtly giving me. Yet another, more cautious part of me says to wait. Wait until I'm not still magic drunk. Wait to make the choice to commit that's not influenced by whatever magic wahoo is going on. Although, I suspect that there isn't as much wahoo as I keep telling myself there is.

Stepping away from him is a bit difficult but I manage it. Grabbing a bottle of water out of the stack that Ciar bought earlier in the day, I sit back on my bed and stare at him. He's lounging on his own bed with those eyes of his bright in the darkness and intent upon me.

"Your hair is turning purple," he comments after several minutes of silence. That's a fact I'm aware of and trying hard not to think on. "It's a sign of your impending Awakening. The violin another. The Familiars yet another. All of these facts in your face and you're still doubting?"

"It's not completely purple, just the tips of it," I defend the one thing that I can. I know full well that the purple is half-way up my head and he's right about the rest of it. The hair is new it wasn't purple even at the tips a few days ago. Then we had that bite each other things the other night and everything started changing, dramatically. I'm not like him I can't roll with all the punches, I have to have my little bit of breathing room.

A lot of new shit all at once. Like Ciar wanting me.

"Not quite, Monster Girl. I've wanted you for a long time," he says while smirking. My mouth opens and closes several times but nothing comes out. Do what now?

He continues, "Do you think that I'm the type of creature to allow magic to control my choices, Keri?" I shake my head because my tongue has deserted me. "I've known since the first time I laid eyes on you how things would turn out."

I remember that day well. It was the first time I came to the forest, I had set a snare - something my nanny taught me - to catch a rabbit for dinner. Money was tight and my belly was empty. Instead, this pitch-black wolfy-dog lay at the edge of the forest lying in a pool of blood. Those green eyes looked at me and at that moment I knew he wouldn't hurt me, but he was hurting and I couldn't abide by that. I ripped up my shirt and made him bandages and fed him the rabbit I caught.

I was all of five when that happened.

"Wait, you knew when I was five that you wanted me?" I say it with a serious look on my face.

His smirk disappears, and he sits up with an alarmed look on his face. "That's ridiculous! You were a child. I simply knew one day I would," he sputters.

Unable to hold it in any longer, I laugh. Ciar is a lot of things but a pedophile isn't one of them. He gives me a disgusted look and leans back against the wall.

"Your humor is not appreciated," he grouches. Which makes me laugh harder. The pillow hitting me in the face shuts me right up. Ciar throws hard.

"Ow!" I exclaim throwing the pillow back at him. He laughs at my attempt to hit him with it and catches it instead. Before long it's a straight up pillow fight, with both of us dodging and laughing and hitting each other hard enough to send feathers flying everywhere.

Tired from the game, I end up sitting on the floor laughing, out of breath and surrounded by white feathers. Inches from me, Ciar is also laughing and surrounded by them. I'm not sure who moves first, but somehow his lips are on mine and it's sweet and languid and goes on for minutes before we break away from each other breathing hard. I stare into those eyes I know so well and smile.

That kiss was my choice, not magical wahoo.

Sitting back on the floor, away from temptation I say, "Why were you so sure of my Awakening, Ciar?"

Crossing his legs in front of him, he rests his elbows on his knees and steeples his hands at his chin. "Because of me," he answers simply. Raising my eyebrows, I wait for the rest of the answer. "Only an Awakened is strong enough to survive truly mating with me, Keri."

Oh, well, that's good to know. I frown, "Wait, what do you mean by 'truly mating?'"

He leans forward, that smirk returning, "You know exactly what I mean, Monster Girl." I do, but true mating means forever. Like, forever-forever. It means something more too. The only way I can mate with anyone is if they're part of my Triad. "Exactly," he adds, reading my thoughts again.

The shields are up so that means the bonding is allowing him to get around them and there's nothing I can do about that. Because this bond is different than what I was told to expect from a bond. If I concentrate hard enough I can feel his heart beating.

Ka-thud. Ka-thud.

The sound of it makes me want to crawl on his lap and put my head against his chest. Instead, I say, "I don't understand, Ciar, I really don't. You haven't exactly been nice to me over the years. There was no indication that you liked me at all. Yet, you're telling me you're my mate AND a member of my Triad?"

Scooting towards me he closes the distance between us, touching our knees together. "Do you know how hard it is to see something you want, every single minute of every single day and not be able to touch it?" He leans towards me. "To taste it?" Even closer. "To rightfully claim it as yours?" He smiles then, so gently that for some reason it makes my eyes burn.

"I had to wait until you were ready to even contemplate saying or doing anything and that time is finally upon us. You will Awaken and when you do, I'll finally be able to claim my place at your side and taste what has been denied me for so long." His lips lightly brush mine and then he pulls away.

"Why did it have to be purple though?" I blurt out.

"You love the color purple, so hush."

"Why a violin?" I ask quietly.

"Have you never wondered why you loved music so much? You're drawn to it, are constantly humming it when you do things, even eating your food. Music is in your blood. Now, do you see?" I hate when he makes sense, because then I can't argue with it.

So instead of saying anything, I nod. It's a bit overwhelming. Surprisingly, not so much the Ciar part of the equation as the Awakening.

"There's a chance I'll die, Ciar," I whisper. I don't want to die. There are so many things in life I've yet to see or do.

Instantly, his eyes alight in anger and he spits out between his gritted teeth, "You shall not!"

Unsure of what else to say because death is not something Ciar can stop, I pat his cheek and climb to my feet. I'm sleepy and my brain hurts from all of this.

"Keri, you will survive because you're too damn stubborn to die," he whispers in the dark.

Climbing into my bed I pull the covers up to my chin and snuggle down into the bed. He sounded so sure of it and if life has taught me anything, it's that if Ciar says something will happen, then it will. Ciar is never wrong and this time I really want him to be right.

CHAPTER 7

ALL HAIL THE GREAT DOG BREATH...

The next two days were rather uneventful. I was expecting something to happen because the of the magical wahoo and bupkis. I now understand why they tell you to be careful what you wish for because the headache starts in music class.

Ciar keeps giving me sideways glances wearing that somehow attractive frown of his. For the first hour I roll my eyes at his concern. Now my head feels like it's going to explode and the room keeps doing this weird weeble wobble. I'm actually starting to worry a bit. Fae of any species, don't get sick like humans do. That narrows the field on what's wrong with me. It also forces me to dig my head out of the sand of denial. Normally, I hate when Ciar is right and this particular moment is no exception.

Cradling my head, I lean it on the cool top of the desk. Briefly the pain lessens but it comes back with a vengeance and I can no longer hide it. Cold sweat breaks out all over my body, instantly soaking into my shirt, and a moan of pain escapes me before I can catch it.

My stomach is clearly debating on showing my lunch to everyone.

Another wave of pain rolls through me and I seriously doubt my ability to remain sitting up much longer. Warm strong arms scoop me up and instantly the pain lessens. Ciar. I can feel us moving but I have no idea where he's taking us. I hope it's some place that has pain killers. Pain lances through me again and I cry out. Maybe just knock me unconscious, that will work too.

"I got you, Monster Girl," he whispers against my hair.

He lays me on something soft, but it doesn't feel like my bed and then cool hands gently rest against my forehead.

"She is in the throes of Awakening. How long has she had symptoms?" A woman asks above me.

Ciar took me to the healer, I can smell the clean scent of her magic. It's a little bit of a surprise and show's a facet of him I've never seen before.

"Take her pain away," is Ciar's curt response.

"That is not something I can do. It is a painful process and no amount of magic can lessen that pain. From the looks of things, there's a good chance she will not sur - "

"Then you're useless," he interrupts, picking me up again.

I force my swollen eyes open and try to smile at him but instead of smiling back, he kisses my mouth. With the light touch of his lips, the pain fades again. It returns in a rush when he pulls away.

"I'm sorry, Keri. I can only take it away for seconds and the healers in this place are fucking worthless. Mada has forbidden me to bring you back to the forest until she gives permission, which means I won't be able to find it even if I disobey her. I cannot take you home." He kisses me again and I force the smile to happen.

Trying to talk out loud causes more pain, so I try to

communicate with my thoughts. He may be able to telepathically communicate but I'm not a telepath.

It'll be fine. I can sleep it off, dog breath.

A surprised chuckle bursts out of him. My eyes drift shut again, it hurts. It hurts so bad. Multiple doors slam and I hear yelling and then a thud as something fleshy hits the ground. I'm pretty sure someone got in Ciar's way and he took exception to it. The cold blessed feeling of water embracing me makes me moan, I sigh as the sharpness of the pain dims. It isn't gone but I'll take what I can get.

"Ciar... did you... Awaken?" I manage to get out.

His warm body moves against mine and I realize he's holding me in the water. I fight to open my eyes, but they won't budge.

"I was born as I am. I didn't need to." That's something to puzzle on later and it speaks volumes about the power of the man holding me.

"I leave for ten minutes and you allow something to happen. Explain yourself." I feel the tickle of Zag's tongue as he investigates me himself. "Oh, oh my - it's happening. Fluffy, get your fat ass in here!" Zag calls.

A laugh comes out as a cough and then a moan as a fresh wave of pain rocks me. Ciar's arms tighten and I feel the weight of Zag on my chest. A splash and then a bulbous body wraps itself around my legs. It's rather cute really, my boys all trying to cuddle me and make me feel better.

Sing to me, dog breath. You have the voice of a damn Siren.

I feel his laugh more than hear it and then the melodious voice of Ciar fills the room. Other than music class, it's been many years since he's sang to comfort me - not since I was a child in fact - and it is no less potent now than it was then. He still has the power to lull me, to tug my spirit free from the pain of this reality. Letting it all go, I ride the cadence of Ciar into the darkness of unconsciousness.

CHAPTER 8

FAERIE AIN'T FOOLING...

I have no idea where I am but there's bright colors everywhere. Purples, pinks and vivid reds painting a kaleidoscope of color vomit in my mind. What kind of crazy place did death drag me to? II always thought death would be rather dull and gloomy. Curtains made of spiderwebs and crap. I poke a cloud of color that floats nearby and it ripples from my touch. This is so far removed from my imagination that floating around in it might normally be fun. Unfortunately, there's a crappy reason I'm here.

Daughter...

That's the reason.

Your time has come to embrace the power you were born to wield.

"I have to be honest and tell you straight up I don't want it but seems like a bad idea to refuse Faerie." Laughter echoes around me. Well, at least I made her laugh.

Your gift will bring you pain...

Something she sounds a little pleased by. That's what I get for cracking jokes at a deity.

"I really am going to Awaken?" I ask, a bit dumbfounded.

Or die, the choice is yours. Accept this gift and you shall live. It is unique among my children.

Unique isn't good in Faerie. Look at Satyrs. "What's this gift?" I can't believe I'm running my mouth and questioning the creator of all. What's wrong with me?

You are to become my chosen Fate Caller.

Fate Caller? Where have I heard that before? I search my mind trying to find the memory but come up empty handed.

With your musical soul you can call the fate of any creature instantly upon it... but beware the cost. For every fate you call early, a brand shall appear upon your skin that can only be removed by the 'Giving.'

This doesn't sound good at all.

Your Lord of the Hunt shall stand true as your Pinnacle.

"Ma'am," clearing my throat I try again, "Ma'am, I'm not sure you have the right person for this."

You think I would make a mistake such as this, child?

I know menace when I hear it and there is a lot of it in that sentence. Well, then, Fate Caller I shall be and I finally have the intelligence to shut my mouth.

"Of course not." As if I'd say anything else after that.

You have always been a clever child. When you open your eyes, remember my words. Do not call fate lightly and use the Conduit, it was made for you. Now, daughter, Awaken!

With the last word, there is a loud boom and a tunnel appears sucking me into it, pain spears me and I scream as I'm sucked down into darkness.

WHEN THE ACHE IN MY HEAD HITS ME AND THE LIGHT filtering through my eyelids makes it worse, I know I'm alive and that fact thrills me. I attempt to roll over and roll right off the bed. Thankfully the floor isn't that far of a trip. Fluffy mostly catches me, so I simply lay there with my face resting against his soft leathery skin.

"Ciar, Faerie has a sense of humor," I say, my face smooshed against the worm.

"Mistress, you might want to move your face, he hasn't had a bath this week," Zag informs me with more than a touch of laughter in his tone.

Rolling over, onto the floor, I open my eyes and look up into his swirly ones above me. "Zag, where is Ciar?"

"I believe he is... out," Zag is not a good liar.

"All right, then. How long have I been asleep or whatever?" If Ciar doesn't want me to know where he is, then who am I to push it?

"Three days and you smell like every one of them," his delicate nostrils flare but the humor remains in his eyes. He isn't wrong, I smell awful.

Rolling slowly to my feet I stagger into the bathroom, peeling off clothes as I go. Turning the water on as hot as I can take it, I climb in and lean against the wall, letting the water pound down on me. It burns but feels good at the same time. I stand under it until it starts to make me sleepy, then I hurry and wash off. My hair is last and when I see it I sigh, defeated. It's mostly purple, all the way up to the edge of my vision. Now I had new concerns, being awakened means others can start eyeing me for their clans or families.

Now the evaluations will begin.

Gods, why did you send me here, Mada? Did I make you angry? Resting my head against the wall, I decide to stand there until I'm wrinkled like an old raisin. It always feels like someone else is controlling my life, when do I get to make my own choices?

"Are you in here feeling sorry for yourself?" The quiet question pulls me right out of my self-pitying moment. I was so lost in it I didn't feel him coming.

"Shup," I say, in a voice thick with the tears that snuck out.

"We need some groceries for Fluffy, they refuse to feed him here. When you are finished blubbering in the shower, we'll go get them." Although, he's making fun of me his voice is still quiet, soothing. It's the same voice he used with me when I was young. The coaxing one when I still cried over my mother. Gods bless it.

Slapping the tap to turn it off, I reluctantly climb out of my shower of self-pity, grabbing my towel as I go. Sucking it up I look in the mirror when I'm finished drying off my body, only to stare at the changes. Because there are changes. My hair is indeed solid purple and curlier.

My eyes are different, too. They're still mismatched but now they have that eerie back glow like Ciar's. This might mean I can finally do real magic! Curious and excited, I focus on a few drops of water to try and change it to ice. It's a simple spell, but after a solid minute - nothing happens, absolutely nothing. The water doesn't even move.

Annoyed that my magical ability isn't any different, I dry off my hair and walk - naked - into the dorm room, making a beeline to the dresser. I feel his eyes on me but attempt to ignore the weight of them. This isn't the first time he saw me naked, so I have no idea why I'm so aware of it now. The hair on the back of my neck stands up, which causes me to hurry a little more than I want to.

Apparently, hyper aware.

"Did you use your word?" Ciar is leaning up against the doorframe closest to me with that all knowing smirk on his face. Turning my face away, I mimic him sarcastically. No, I didn't use my word because I was too excited and forgot but he doesn't need to know that.

Staring at the violin on the dresser in front of me I bite my lip and pick it up. The zap of magic when I touch it arcs up my arm. Whoa, that has a kick to it. I roll my eyes at the ever-present smirk on Ciar's face and turn back to the half-empty bottle of water on the dresser.

"Existence," whispers out of me and I feel the magic move this time. The bottle starts to shake and with a faint pop explodes liquid all over the place. "Holy meatballs, it did something," my voice squeaks with my excitement.

"Yes, it exploded. What were you trying to make it do?" Zag asks alighting on my shoulder.

Refusing to let him ruin my sense of accomplishment, I snark, "I was trying to make it turn into a useful Dragon Familiar."

"Why do you need a useful Dragon Familiar?"

I twist my head to look at him with my eyebrows almost at my hairline and see the second he gets what I said. If Dragons can blush, then he's doing it. In retaliation, he nips my ear. Laughing, I rub under his chin, something that turns him into a puddle of goo every time it's done. He's more like a cat than he realizes at this size.

Casting a glance towards my bed, I sigh. Fluffy is under there and I can feel his discontent because the poor thing wants to come with us. He's in his larval stage and hasn't grown any legs yet. I can't carry a hundred-pound wiggly worm to the grocery store, either.

Or can I?

The idea hits me like a lightning bolt and happy with it I run from the room. Several minutes later, Ciar is still muttering under his breath as he pushes the clunky wheel chair we 'borrowed' from the school that's now holding a happy Corpse Worm wrapped in a trench coat. I even put a baseball hat on him to add to his adorably creepy look.

"I can't believe you insisted we bring him," Zag chastises.

"Oh, I can. Keri has a soft streak a mile wide," Ciar's

amusement is contagious. *And it's not a mile wide.* "Yes, it is," he teases, snooping in my brain again.

Flipping bond.

"Fine, so I like being nice and there's nothing wrong with it. The world needs more nice people in it. Imagine how awesome that would be." I realize I sound defensive but even the Sluagh are capable of kindness. And they eat people.

"They're kind to *you*, Keri. Never mistake it as part of their character." Sticking with my maturely mood, I stick my tongue out at Ciar for his unwanted comment.

I can think what I want to, delusional or not. They were always kind to me, and that's how I formed my opinion of them. Nothing will ever change that. They were kind to me when no one else was.

"He does seem rather happy to be going with us. That noise he's making sounds remarkably like laughter," Zag muses, eyeing Fluffy.

The worm is happy, I can feel it radiating from him. Who knew that it could be this easy to make his big blubby butt happy? Although, when he finally grows legs our method of travel will be less fun. I'll no longer get to watch Ciar push a worm wearing clothes in a wheelchair carefully over holes in the sidewalk.

The fact that he's here looking the way he looks, smiling as he pushes that wheelchair, is mind-blowing. It's nice to see his sense of humor. I like it and gods bless it I like him. How did I get to this point? A week ago, I'd have sworn on every god in existence I hated him and that he hated me. Now we're walking to the grocery store with a worm-on-wheels semi-incognito.

How weird is it that I think Ciar's the most beautiful creature I've ever laid eyes on?

Ciar stops walking, the smile on his face changing into something more male. His eyes swirl, satisfaction bright in them and then he turns back to the wheelchair and starts pushing it along again. For ten solid seconds I stand there staring at his retreating back unsure of what to say or do. I don't want some pull of Faerie to determine who my mate - mates are, but I also can't deny that I think Ciar would be my first choice in any situation.

The world fades away as I stare at his back, catching the flash of his green eyes as he glances over his shoulder. I didn't miss the smirk on his face, either.

Ugh, he can still hear me.

"Mistress, there's drool coming out of your open mouth." Zag nips my ear to bring me back to reality. Shaking my head to clear it, I start walking again.

Really Keri? You just went all gaga over someone you've known your entire life. Wiping my chin, I flick the tip of Zag's tail. There's no drool there. His chuckle wafts through my hair.

"Has anyone ever explained why Familiars exist?" he asks, settling himself like a mantle around my shoulders, his chin resting near my ear.

"Not really. I know the logistics of it, but it's not something I expected to have to deal with." True facts.

He clears his throat and in a serious voice begins with, "When Faerie created her first creatures of magic, it was a lot like whittling a piece of wood. Pieces of them fell away as they were shaped into life and those pieces became other things." That's something I didn't know. "Some of those pieces were absorbed by other creatures of magic being born and sometimes they were absorbed back into the body of Faerie." He pauses for dramatic effect. "Some came into life on their own, however, their life was tied into the life form from which they fell. Hence, the first Familiars were born."

Frowning, I look at his flashing eyes, "Then how are you my Familiar since you were born first?"

"Every soul came into existence at the same time,

mistress. Some were just held longer in the arms of Faerie than others." It makes a weird kind of sense.

"How exactly did Faerie create us all?"

"She dreamed us into being. Except the humans, those are the children of other gods." It's not often that the lore matches the truth of it and I'm sure it's not as cut and dry, but this particular thing always fascinated me.

"What about the whole bond and Awakening thing?" The heat of his breath hits my cheek as he laughs at my question.

"Remember those pieces that were absorbed by others? That is how Triads came to be. The first soul is so powerful that they cannot be contained in one body, so pieces are given to others to help balance that," he explains.

I snort in disbelief.

"Okay, I can't deny that I Awakened." I flip a purple curl towards him. "Although to be fair, it's all been relatively anti-climactic. I made a water bottle explode so I don't see this 'all powerful' crap. For one of my Triad to be someone like Ciar - it doesn't make sense, Zag. None of this does."

"You're a Fate Caller." Rolling my eyes, I flick his tail again. "Flip at me all you wish, it won't change the fact that you're the one creature in existence that can bring fate to another, with your will alone. Don't cheapen your Calling because you can't shoot fireballs out of your eyes."

I open my mouth to defend myself and snap it shut. I can't, he's right. Whether or not I like it, he's right. Fudge. Fudge. Double fudge.

"Why do you so rarely curse?" Zag asks, his eyes up level with mine. Apparently, I mumbled it versus saying it in my head.

"My mother used to yell and swear at me all the time," and that's as far as I'm explaining. She did it while clobbering me with something usually, but he doesn't need to know that. Zag being awesome doesn't push it and settles down on my shoulder again. At this point, we've caught up to Ciar and the noisy gurgles of Fluffy. Catching sight of something on the front of the coat I jog to catch up and stand in front of them to force them to stop.

"Why is he covered in bloody feathers?"

"He was hungry," Ciar explains, straight faced. "So I gave him a pigeon."

"Well, okay then," I dust the feathers off Fluffy and fight to keep from laughing at the ones stuck to his 'face', or at least the general area of his face. It's where his eight eyes are. Ciar apparently has a soft spot for Fluffy. I learn something new every day about him and I can't help but wonder what I'll learn next.

The grocery store is another learning experience. I remember them from childhood, but it's been years since I was in one. This one is a rather large one for such a small town, probably because of the Menagerie and all the creatures it accommodates. There's even a section with 'live' food. Which happens to be the first aisle that Ciar walks down. Unsurprised by his choice, I turn on my heel and go down the household aisle, trusting in him to get the meat Fluffy will need. Unlike my three companions, I might eat it but I'm not keen on killing for the sake of killing. I have and will again but it's not something I enjoy doing.

Ciar is another story and that's something about him that doesn't bother me. He is what he is, and he doesn't pretend to be anything other than that. Fae aren't human and should never be compared to them. The fact that I have more morality than most is probably more bad versus good and sets me apart from Fae even more. They're creatures of their natures, something that doesn't make them evil or good.

When it comes to things they love, Fae are perfectly capable of being compassionate and even gentle. Perhaps I'm not too far apart from them after all? And incredibly fortunate of the other Fae in my life.

"You're thinking very hard on something, mistress," Zag muses from his perch on my shoulder.

"You gotta stop calling me 'mistress,' Zag. Keri is my name, silly lizard." He huffs at me as the tip of his tail pokes me in the cheek, a prod to get me to speak my thoughts and answer his question. "I was thinking about Fae nature, and how even the more monstrous of them can be gentle and loving."

"It is a rare thing, but true - in your case, at least. You have some of the more volatile that care for you, including myself." He brings his reptilian head around to meet my eyes. "Just as I treat you with kindness, as does the dark lord and his ilk. But Keri," he uses my name with a little discomfort, I'm proud of him for the effort. "You're an exception. Don't expect it to be shown to or by others and you'll never be disappointed."

He's right, I was raised with gentle hands. I've seen the results of a Hunt and of people incurring the wrath of Mada.

"Keri, you need one of these." A cart is pushed in front of me and then Ciar is gone again. It's not empty, either. Something is wiggling around in a brown paper bag.

'Don't forget to get your 'girl' stuff,' Ciar reminds me.

Oh! Grabbing the cart, I hurry and grab things for our room like toilet paper that doesn't feel like sand and head straight towards the health care aisles. Humming to myself, I start grabbing all the things I think I'll need and a few things I simply want. Shampoos and bath stuff goes in first. I pick through the organic Fairy products, tickled about the broad selection. The human manufactured stuff can't touch the quality of it.

"I had no idea you were quite so feminine." Instead of responding to Zag's unappreciated observation, I flick his tail again. "What are those things?" he asks eyeing the blue box I toss into the cart. This time I tug his tail, he doesn't need to know about that kind of hygiene.

Mine doesn't happen that often anyhow, but I like to be prepared.

"What do you want to eat? I mean, you're normally as big as a truck. I imagine that a few chunks of meat aren't satisfying." I start pushing the cart again.

"I go off in search of my own food in the mornings." That explains his absences. I'm curious what he's eating but not enough to ask and then regret asking.

"And at night?"

"The moon calls, so I fly sometimes."

The idea forms in my head and immediately leaves my mouth, "Can I come sometime?" I miss the moon and the night and the idea of flying sounds spectacular.

"Of course!" He sounds excited at the prospect.

Smiling, I start enjoying the shopping trip. Dancing around behind the cart, I push off with one foot and send us coasting down the vegetable aisles. A feeling of unease tickles my spine as the cart is jarringly stopped by a tall, ageless looking Fae.

Great, it's an Elf. Aristocracy, if the fancy clothes are any indication.

His face is lean and almost delicate, perhaps even a little feminine, his eyes are a pretty blue - I can't deny that -but they're cold, no life in them. His hair is long and a light blue that almost looks like a soft, touchable cloud.

"Can I help you?" I ask tucking my hair around Zag to keep him quiet because I can feel his irritation and his desire to say something. My time with the Sluagh taught me many things, but my time with my mother taught me when to keep my tone civil. Now is that kind of moment.

"Who do you belong to?" he asks, stopping me from

trying to go around him with his finger to the end of the cart. Looking closer, I see it, the magic he's using. This Fae is packed full of it.

"Myself." *Arrogant tool bag.*

"Are you one of the," he pauses, making a face like there's a bad taste in his mouth, "Students at that zoo?"

Ciar's sudden presence and the darkness of his emotions wash over me. Uh-oh. A warm hand runs across my shoulder and down my arm, hesitating long enough on my wrist to run a finger across the pulse before continuing across my hand, ending its journey by resting beside mine.

Double uh-oh. Ciar just did the Fae version of peeing on a tree. Any other circumstance and I'd say something sarcastic, but not this time. Aristocrats are dangerous and powerful. Ciar can hold his own against them. Me? Not so much.

'You do not fear this Elven trash.' His voice carries a command I haven't heard since we've been here.

"Your guard is looking for you, Elf." Ciar's words carry an unspoken threat and a quiet menace that runs a chill down my spine.

The Elf turns to look at Ciar and I watch his pupils expand and then shrink when the realization hits him that danger is standing right in front of him. With a curious look thrown at me, he turns without a word and stalks off. Ciar drags his hand slowly over mine and then steps away, his posture nonchalant like he didn't just have a minor face-off with an Elf.

In fact, it was nonchalant the entire time, but I know his danger level and now so does that Elf. Speaking of that Elf. "Why was he curious about me? I've run into them many times before and nothing?"

"You don't know your own appeal at all, do you?" he asks, tucking a curl of purple hair behind my ear.

Oh, I look different now, don't I? I don't really think

about it because I don't feel any different. There's no fantastic powers and fireworks. There's more inside of me than before, I can feel the magic hanging around in there but it doesn't feel like it's anything spectacular.

"I'm talking about your appeal as a woman, Keri. Not the magical aspects of you." His voice holds his exasperation. Frowning, I meet his gaze.

Do what now?

"Were you sneaking and drinking wine or something over there?" I lean forward and sniff near his mouth. Catching me off guard he plants his lips on mine in the briefest of kisses before dancing out of the way of my swat.

"You need to learn to use your magic to protect yourself. One day we won't be there to save you and you'll need to save yourself in a way that doesn't involve you punching them in the face. Now, let's finish our shopping, I have some things I need to do this evening." And off he goes. Shaking my head, I turn my cart into my skateboard and off we go, right into the banana display.

Fudge.

CHAPTER 9

THE BOMBED BATH...

Having a few moments alone is so surprising that at first, I don't know what to do with myself. So I stand there in my pajamas eyeing the empty room. My gaze pans around to the bathroom door and the decision is made quickly. Grabbing my big ratty fluffy pink robe - I love pink, no shame - I run gleefully into the bathroom to do the one thing I rarely get to do.

Take a hot bubble bath.

Turning the taps to steam-your-skin-off, I toss in my Fairy made bath bomb and practically rip my clothes off. The bomb bubbles the water with pink glitter and the smell of cherry blossoms fills the room. Humming to myself, I check the temperature with my fingertips and quite happy, I slide into the hot water.

Bliss fills me from head to toe.

Grabbing a towel from the shelves next to the tub, I roll it up behind my head and lay back to enjoy this quiet, relaxing moment in life. A deep sigh leaves me as all the stress and the junk associated with it, does as well. At least for this stolen moment in time.

The hot water soaks into my skin and the warmth soaks into my bones. Another sigh and I relax deeper into the water, as my body becomes pliant and limp. There are so few times in life where one can truly relax, I'm thankful I have this one.

Now, I can think.

I'm used to being surrounded by noisy creatures, but I'm also used to being able to get away from them. Lately that hasn't been an option. If Zag isn't there, Ciar is and if neither of them are there, Fluffy is wobbling around somewhere. I know that it's part of being in a family and all, but things are changing drastically with Ciar.

There will be more. Two more big problems in fact.

Since I'm Awakened now – which I don't really see the big hoopla about it – then Ciar is the Pinnacle, he can't be anything but. Plus, I *feel* it. That means that one will be my Anchor and one will be my Hook. Both of them will probably be hot and more than likely have attitude problems. I mean look at Ciar? He's the epitome of broody bad boy. Even with all the stupid angst and worry, I can't help but be curious about them. Strangers that won't be strangers for long.

Holy meatballs, how will I deal with three men? I've done some kinky stuff, but these ones I have to keep around. No sneaking out in the morning anymore. I have no idea how to be in a relationship because I've never actually had one. One-night stands or week-end stands is the total sum of my romantic life. This is all unexplored territory for me.

A buzzing sound breaks the bubble of quiet around me. I know that sound, it's a phone. Why is there a phone in here with me? Sitting up, the water sluices down my chest and I try to keep it from dripping onto the robe sitting next to the tub. I dig around in the pocket for the phone, that I'm betting Ciar had the foresight to put in my robe pocket. Because somehow, he always knows stuff. Ineffectually swiping on the screen to answer the call, I use a towel to dry my hands enough to finally slide the green button.

"Are you in the bathtub?" Ciar's voice comes through clearly before I say hello.

Laughing, I say, "Yes, as you apparently expected me to be."

"I saw the bath bombs in your bags. Are you enjoying yourself?" There's an undertone in this voice that gives me goosebumps.

"I was."

"When you're finished with your bath, meet me in the park," he pauses and then continues, "Please." The line disconnects and for a solid two seconds I stare at the phone.

Did Ciar just say please?

Leaning back into the tub I continue to look at the face of the phone. I might as well make use of it. Let's look up information on Triads and such. More than the bits and pieces I know because in my idiocy, I didn't think it was important to learn. I had in my head I'd never Awaken.

The Ley-net provides the answers.

Everything is about the Center, which is me. When a person Awakens, it sends out a magical call to their Triad. Since Ciar is already here, where are the other two? Who are the other two?

I flip through the next Ley-page, reading quickly through the stuff I already know. I'm looking for a specific thing and there it is - the call. When someone Awakens it sends out a magical call to the destined members of their Triad, but there's a catch. If they're reluctant to bond, it leaves the bond open and susceptible for someone else of equal power that is compatible with the Awakened to hi-jack it.

However, they have to be accepted by the Awakened for it to cement. They can't force it. No one can force it. This relaxes a worry in me that was causing me all types of issues.

'See, it's all about choices, Monster Girl.' I startle at Ciar's voice in my head and almost drop the phone in the now tepid water. "I realized that you'd stand me up at the park." He's not wrong.

I was so lost in reading that I didn't feel him return, but I feel him now. Standing a few feet from me in the doorway of the bathroom unabashedly staring at me with that knowing smirk on his face. Shooting to my feet, I toss the phone on the robe and grab the towel to hastily dry off, wrapping my robe around my chilled body. The phone goes back in the pocket and I brush past Ciar to grab a drink and crawl onto my bed.

I think it's time he and I have that talk we've been avoiding.

"The Ley-net gives some explanation and then I know what I've been taught. Now old-man, what's the rest of it?" The pillow goes onto my lap, mostly for comfort. Maybe a little for me to hide behind.

Strolling across the room he slides onto the bed beside me, close enough to reach out and touch me with hardly any effort but not actually touching me. I don't mind it, I like him this close. Plus, he can't hide his emotions as well from me at this distance.

The bond is getting stronger now that I'm no longer denying it, which was stupid of me to begin with. I do need to figure out how to understand it and use it. I wish I could say I'm one of those people who can read emotions on someone's face like a book but, I'm not. Especially with someone like Ciar who can snoop inside of my head like he's watching a TV program. That gives him an unfair advantage, so I have to work with what I can.

Ciar leans against the wall and crosses his arms over his chest, giving me a slow half-smile that's full of the audacity of the man and says, "You know the logistics of an Awakening."

His smile broadens. "The moment your teeth sank into my skin, instead of a simple bond you claimed me."

"And that claiming Awakened me?"

"Yes. Your Awakening sent out an irresistible call to your Triad and since you claimed your Pinnacle first, the call was potent." I suck at reading faces but there's no mistaking the abject satisfaction on his face.

"Why are you so happy about it? You don't strike me as the sharing type."

He leans forward, intensity saturating the air around him. Uh-oh.

"Because I have waited almost two decades for you to be ready for this, Keri. A Triad is a sacred privilege that most creatures don't get to experience, so I count myself blessed by Faerie for allowing me to be one of the fortunate ones. And," the smile blooms into something that's all teeth and promise and instantly makes me flush with heat. "This bond between us is not a surprise to me. I've had decades to accept the implications as well as everything that comes packaged with it."

Leaning away from him, I rest my back against the rough wood of the wall and mull over what he's said so far.

"Now, what are you really worried about, Keri?" His voice is soft, coaxing. How can I resist that? The bond between us in a tangible thing. I can see it crossing the short space between us, a dark and tight thread connecting us together.

"I don't want to lose myself because some wahoo magic says so. You have been hard on me my entire life and never once did I think you liked me as a person. Now, I'm supposed to just accept that I'll be sharing a life-bond and more with someone who didn't like me a week ago?" It spills out of me like verbal vomit and I don't even try to stop it. It needs saying.

His green eyes are luminescent in the fading light of the

room as they study me, swirling with emotions I can't read yet but can feel the seriousness of.

Finally, after staring at me an uncomfortably long while, he says, "You have to be strong for what's coming and to be strong, one of us had to be the bad guy and push you. Mada didn't want to do it because she considers you her daughter. In her eyes, you're her fragile little butterfly."

He's not wrong, Mada is horrible about babying me. He continues, "Nagan won't hurt a hair on your head, let alone push you to be who you are today. Which left only me to do what needed done. I pushed you until I knew you'd survive anything this place could throw at you. Until I knew that you could handle anything this fucking world throws at you," he moves close to me, the energy rolling off his body brushing against my skin. "I pushed you so that you can survive being bound to me."

"How," I lick my lips as my voice quivers, "Scary are you really, Ciar?" In a blink, his face morphs into the monster I know him to be, but I'm not afraid - not anymore.

Achingly gentle, his warm soft lips touch the very tip of my nose while simultaneously running a finger over the point of my right ear. His touch sends a shiver through me. He's flipping dangerous alright, to my libido. His face melts back into the one I've grown rather used to seeing.

Hiding a smile, I look away from his eyes before I'm trapped by them. He might have accepted everything, but I'm not sure how I feel about being someone's property. Fae males are all about ownership.

"Never in a million years will I consider you my property, monster girl. If anything, I belong to you." With those quietly spoken words, he slides to his feet and walks out of the room.

Well, that's a twist on things. He's upset with me, I can feel that but I'm not sure why.

"You accused him of wanting to own you, after he's done

nothing but sacrifice for you. That is insulting for such a creature as he." Zag crawls across the wall like the shadow he is. More than likely he heard our entire conversation and I guess since he's my Familiar that's something I'm going to have to get used to.

He's also probably right about Ciar.

Hurrying to my feet, I dig in the dresser for clothes and shove my feet in my shoes without untying them. Grabbing that steel thread that ties us together I leave the room at a jog and head right for him.

It's the weekend, so the Menagerie is mostly deserted. I'm not sure where everyone goes but I do know they can't go home, it's one of the many dumb rules here. There's an entire book on them that I haven't read very much of yet. I probably should.

Behind the school is a small wooded area and that's where I find him. Sitting on a bench with his elbows resting on his knees, head down in thought. It looks almost like a pose of defeat, like the weight of the world is heavy on his shoulders. Given everything, maybe it is. On quiet feet I approach him. I know he senses me, but he doesn't move.

"You know, when I was little and afraid of something, you were the one person I always ran to. Even when I worried you'd grouch at me for it." Sliding onto the bench beside him, I rest my leg against his. "You were the one I always ran to, regardless of the reason. It was always you." The words leave me feeling lighter, the truth of them removing a weight I didn't know I carried.

"I followed you everywhere, I realize how creepy that sounds, but I did. When I was older, I didn't understand why the Fairies giggled when you walked by or why they whispered about you behind their back. You were this big bad wolf, you know? I didn't understand why they weren't afraid."

Slowly, carefully, I slip my hand into his larger one. There is no hesitation as he grips mine tightly.

"To be honest, I was a little jealous once I realized why they tittered. I always assumed that you had a Fae form, but I didn't think about it too often. Thinking about it led to other questions and feelings I didn't want to explore because even though I ran to you when I was afraid... I was afraid of you too." His hand tightens on mine to the precipice of painful then relaxes.

"When you reached adulthood, I wasn't sure I could control my impulses concerning you, so I stayed transformed around you. Your smell, your closeness pricked at my Fae nature like a rusty nail. It was not because of magic or your Awakening - it was... is because of you. Your quiet strength, your humor. The little noise you make when you eat certain foods or the kindness you show to everything, even the things that don't deserve it." He turns his head to entrap my gaze with his own, "Magic has nothing to do with my wanting you. *You're* the reason I want you and you can't get any more real than that." His voice is hoarse towards the end and the emotion in his words is raw and unfettered.

There is no room to doubt the truth of what he's saying.

And in my lamely graceful way, I say the only word I can think of, "Okay."

CHAPTER 10
HUNGRY LIKE A ... WOLF...

We sit there for a long while, enjoying each other's company while watching the sun set and the night come alive around us. As a treat, the Fairies getting ready for their busy night at their various jobs, dance around with their glowing glitter leaving flickering trails behind them. Most types of Fairies are under four foot tall, delicate, beautiful and gentle natured. They have a variety of hair colors ranging from pastels like mine to bright oranges like the sunset we just witnessed.

They're also some of the horniest Fae in existence. Ciar had an entire troop of unwed Fairies who pursued him fervently in the forest. Smiling, I wink at one who gets close enough to blow a kiss to Ciar.

Anyone magical can see the tie that binds us. If I look hard enough I can see it. Dark red lines run from my aura to his, whereas his much darker aura wraps and entangles it in rootlike appendages. There is no breaking a bond like that.

Not that I want to.

"The other two will come, soon I imagine." It's the first time he's spoken since giving his rather impassioned speech.

Pulling his hand onto my lap, I absently play with his calloused fingers.

"How does a Fae who can heal themselves get callouses?" Letting him in is all I can handle right now, thinking of two others? Complete strangers? I'd rather be in denial about that a little while longer.

"I chose to let them remain. They remind me of how hard I worked to learn to fight." That's a very honorable reason. Gods, I'm a tool-bag. I open my mouth to apologize and a quick meeting of his lips to mine shuts me up.

Part of me is disappointed it's over so quickly. Maybe because he senses my disappointment he gives me another quick kiss. The giggling of the Fairies pulls me out of la-la land. And his warm lips away from mine.

"No more apologies, Monster Girl." The tone of his voice stops me from insistently doing it anyhow.

Smiling, I stand up and run towards the remaining Fairies who scatter in all directions, their laughter floating behind them. I do love their playful nature. Ciar can have one too. When I was very young he used to chase me through the forest making me laugh and scream in joy.

"Come find me," I whisper, knowing he can hear it and then I run.

In that moment I feel free, running through the trees dodging the grabbing hands of a man I sorely misjudged. A man who will never leave me, no matter what happens. Maybe all of this isn't so terrible?

Hitting the ground hard enough to knock the wind out of me makes me question that conclusion. Spitting out the moss that I inadvertently ate when I slid into the tree base reminds me that I didn't completely misjudge him. Rolling onto my back, I look up into his wolf smile and laugh when my foot connects with his chin. Rolling backwards to my feet I run again. He has no one to blame but himself since he taught me the move.

As my hand pulls away from a tree, I feel something cold and alien to this hot evening. I flitter a glance at it - it's a leaf with frost on it. Ciar's closeness pulls me away from the curiosity and I discard it and let it fall from my thoughts like it fell from my hands, and keep running.

I have a big bad wolf to outrun.

CHAPTER 11

NOT A BROTHER FROM ANOTHER MOTHER...

T he weekend is over way too soon. I swat at the blaring
alarm clock and end up catching a little Zag face in the
process. He squawks loudly for something so small and falls
off the edge of the bed.

"Sorry, Zag," I mutter, rolling over to bury my face in my
pillow. Which is suddenly jerked away, the movement drag-
ging me halfway off the bed. Hanging mostly upside down I
look up into Ciar's amused face.

"Why are you yanking me out of bed?" I allow myself to
slide the rest of the way off the bed onto the floor. Maybe if I
can blend into the carpet he'll leave me alone and let me
sleep.

"If you don't get your ass moving, we're going to be late
for these ridiculous classes we temporarily have to attend.
There's only one that I'm looking forward to and we have to
practice for it today." As he speaks, his voice fades away and
then something soft hits me in the face.

Oh, pants.

Calling him at least twenty names not his own, I climb

blearily to my feet and head towards the bathroom. I'm already mostly done with my morning business when I realize the water in the sink is running and Ciar is standing there with a toothbrush in his open mouth staring at me.

"What? I had to pee." Finishing up my business, I slip by him and wash my hands.

"I'm pretty sure your eyes were closed the entire time." He's probably right, otherwise I'd have noticed him in there with me. Shrugging, I put on the pants he tossed at my head and grab my own toothbrush. My mouth tastes like Fluffy pooped in it.

Rolling my eyes at his laughing face, I brush my teeth and go in search of a shirt that is clean. I forgot to do laundry over the weekend, my clothing choices are limited. I could use the laundry service, but I don't want strangers touching my clothes. Something about it feels icky.

Washing clothes isn't hard to do, the machines do most of the work. I don't have that much to do anyhow.

"Why are we doing this since I already Awakened? Aren't we supposed to report it to the Headmaster and be 'chosen' by some fancy such-and-such to serve their house or whatever. Not that it's what I want to do." It sounds logical in my head but he's looking at me puzzled. Maybe it didn't come out as clearly as I wanted it to? I'm a slow waker.

"No one but us knows. I cleared the memory from the Healer and the other witnesses. We need to continue like normal until we can establish our own power base. I will not be a servant, and neither shall you." There's that bossy Ciar again.

The insistent knocking on the door wipes the last vestiges of sleep from my brain. Who in the world is that? Ciar glances at me before casually strolling towards the door. He yanks it open and blocks the uninvited guest from seeing me.

Which is good, because my pants aren't buttoned and I'm pretty sure my shirt is on backwards.

"Message for student, Keri Nightshade," a small voice chirps. A messenger Seraphim for me?

Crossing to the door, I lean around Ciar and say, "I'm Keri Nightshade, what is the message?"

The Seraphim is all of eight inches tall with the face and body of a baby. Golden wings dust the area behind him with flakes of gold. Big blue eyes, haloed by curly blonde hair, look at me with the wisdom of a hundred-year-old man. After the once over he gives me, I realize it's the wisdom of a perverted hundred-year-old man.

"The Headmaster is requesting your presence at first chime in his office concerning your unreported Awakening." With a rather saucy wink he pops out of existence.

I give Ciar a look. "I thought you spelled them?"

"Obviously I missed one." He doesn't' sound happy about it either.

"Do I have to go with whomever they say?" This is concerning.

"Of course not. You need the protection of old power, which you shall have."

Do what?

"It's simply going to take me a little while to ensure it." Okay, no explanation is forthcoming yet.

"Why didn't I get some super dooper fireballs or lightning bolts?" I ask, purely for education purposes, and maybe to distract him a bit into giving me more answers.

"You got something better."

"How is calling fate to someone better than fireballs?"

His sudden stillness makes me look at him as he asks, "Keri, you silly girl. Don't you see how fucking special this is?" I shrug. "You can control someone's fate. Your precious fireballs don't compare to something like that."

97

"There's a cost - apparently a brand will show up on my body that only my Triad can fix or whatnot. Fireballs are free and I like fire." The look of, 'You're an idiot, Keri' stays firmly on his face.

"There's always a cost to great magic. Gods Keri - if death by bear is someone's fate, you can literally call it to them right then and by some magical way a bear will end them. Don't you understand that?"

Oh. "Like... it's a literal thing, right then and there?" He nods.

Well, that's cool. I look over at the violin resting quietly on top of the dresser. I locked it in the closet last night and I know no one else touched it. The thing has a mind of its own and a bad sense of humor. I notice the new stickers on it from a band I liked as a kid. Sneaky thing, using something like that to make me notice it. Doesn't matter that it works.

"You're going to need to accept it in your life at some point, Keri. You need the conduit as much as it needs you." There he goes with his logic again.

I can see why I might need it to work whatever mumbo jumbo Faerie gave me, but why would it need me?

"I imagine it has a form of sentience like all objects of power do, and this one isn't a commonly used one," Ciar patiently explains. He always patiently explains and I always express my opinions on it with sarcasm.

A single note drifts out of it. Haunting and magical it expresses one emotion more clearly than any other. Loneliness. I hate it when Ciar is right.

"Fine, but I'll need a way to carry..." A flash of blue and in place of the violin sits a small glowing blue bracelet. "That's handy." Grabbing it off the dresser I slide it onto my wrist, it's warm and I swear it feels like it sighs in relief. My reluctance didn't hurt it, did it? In apology, I rub a finger across its super smooth surface, looking at the detail of it.

The metal rope is blue, exactly like the violin and it feels soft like gold. The only adornment is the circle with the etching of a violin on it. Simple, tasteful and something I'd probably pick out to wear for myself. Magic at work for sure.

"Keri, you're always a nice person, always too nice for a Fae." He crosses the space between us and with a soft touch of his fingertip lifts my chin to raise my gaze to his. "Why are you running so hard from this?"

Looking into his piercing eyes I clear my throat and swallow the tears that rise to the surface. It's a valid question and I'm not sure I have any answers for it. He's right though, I am - was running. "A Triad means more than sex. It's a bond that transcends everything. My mother told me it wouldn't happen to me because I don't deserve that kind of love."

The rage that flashes in his eyes is so profound that for a moment his shape wavers. My heart rate jumps nervously and I tense. Ciar never loses his temper. As he blinks, the rage fades and in its place is a soft look that I can't fully interpret.

"Keri, your mother was -" I can see him searching his mind for words to describe her and failing. " - is dead, and nothing she said to you is worth remembering. You're a very special, unique woman who still leaves milk out for the Ballybogs."

My cheeks heat. "They like milk."

Ballybogs are tiny little Fairy-kin that look like little brown balls of mud with legs. They're incredibly shy but sweet and loyal. The forest is full of them and ultimately, I befriended a bunch. They're lifespans are incredibly short, a couple of years, but their time moves different than ours.

Myrtle was the first one I found, caught in a Fairy trap. I released her, and she stayed with me the rest of her life. Only leaving for a few weeks to return with a husband and a child on the way. Ballybog babies are smaller than the tip of my pinky finger. She had twelve children who then had their own children and so forth and so on. The children left and her husband died but Myrtle stayed.

The day she died I felt like I lost a sibling.

"Sad thoughts show that soft heart. Accept what you know is coming and move forward and grow stronger from it. Nothing will make it go away." With that said he turns away from me and goes to finish dressing.

Yes. I sneak peeks at his shirtless condition, a state that I was feeling too sorry for myself to initially notice. Taking his lead, I finish dressing and get ready only to find him waiting by the door with earbuds in his ears, singing. The melody of his voice is eerily beautiful and leaves no question to what he's listening to. The song he wrote for our project. He hums it often when he's doing other things and I'm pretty sure he doesn't realize he's doing it. Because of those peeks I've been able to start piecing it together.

"Let's go see what this idiot wants. After you," he motions for me to proceed him out the door.

"You're going with me to his office?"

"Of course I am."

Smiling I feel Zag's weight sink onto my shoulders. Sneaky booger has been silent since I knocked him off the bed. In affection and appreciation, I stroke his back between his wings.

Ciar isn't wrong. I'm a big old softy and it's gotten me into so much trouble over the years. I can't stand to see something in pain or killed needlessly. Never could leave an injured animal or Fae behind, that's why I collected quite a zoo growing up. I always let them go when they were ready. Nagan even took me on a road trip to another state to return a Kelpie to their family waters. That one I didn't find so much as free. Some Fae think they're superior to other types of Fae. Especially the Unseelie type like the Sluagh or me... even Ciar.

We're all Unseelie. In human lore, the Unseelie were the darker Fae, while in our reality the Unseelie are the ones that are not as pretty. Ciar is pretty, in fact he's ungodly pretty, but he's dark and menacing and animalistic. Which makes him Unseelie in their eyes. Not that they live long enough to make too many judgements. Ciar isn't like I am. And right now, he's not wearing a kind look on his face. Ciar and the Headmaster aren't going to get along.

Not one bit.

Impulsively, I snatch his phone out of his pocket. I pick through the songs on his playlist and find one that's upbeat and one that will pull at his Fae nature. Finding it, I gently stick one headphone in his ear and the other in my own. As the song starts and the bass kicks in, I begin to skip. Then I start to sing, and it takes me several seconds to realize I no longer sound like a strangled cat. Oh, no, I sound like -

'A Fae?' he cuts in.

Elbowing him, I sing louder and dance beside him while we make our way up the hallway. For the first half of the song he's stone-faced and watches me with an occasional eye roll. Full of mischief I up the ante. Grabbing his hand, I spin myself, coming to rest against his body and with a laugh spin away. He's a Puca, he can't help but chase me. This is how we made our way to the Headmaster's office, two dancing singing fools without a care given to those early risers left staring in our wake.

Skin flushed with pleasure, I stop at the secretary's desk and try to put on my best serious face. I'm not the best at it and the look on hers reaffirms that. Her hair bun looks a little tight and maybe if she smiled more she'd be pretty. Well, if she lost that sour look on her face too. Her face is round and full, her blue eyes beady behind the glasses that look too small for her head. She even gives Ciar a look of distaste. Oh yeah, she's a sour one all right. Her desk is cluttered with pictures of her and cats, several of them.

'A sour puss,' Ciar adds in my head. I cough to cover up a laugh.

"We're here to see the Headmaster," Ciar says to her, his voice like honey. Knowing him and his tones that one is especially dangerous.

"The Headmaster requested the presence of Miss Nightshade, not the Nightshade siblings." Although she didn't look at him the first time, I catch her subtly check him out, then turns to me with such a scathing look I felt slightly singed from it.

"Shall we see ourselves in then?" Grabbing my hand, he pulls me along behind him, taking the choice from the woman to let us both in or not. Not that there was ever a choice.

Without knocking, he opens the door labeled 'Headmaster' and then heads straight for the large cherry desk dominating the room. Well, this guy likes fancy things. The curtains are made of velvet, the cushions on the seats of the chairs, a matching fabric. The plush red carpet alone is thick enough to sleep on. There's even a fishbowl on his behemoth desk that's holding what looks like a Water Nymph in it.

Do what now?

Staring at it, my head tilts to the side and my purple hair falls forward, blocking my view of the rest of the room. The Nymph mimics my movements.

'It's an illusion,' Ciar informs me, cutting off the burgeoning plans of rescue.

Smiling benignly, I turn my attention to the two men in the room. What do I call this toad? Headmaster, master? Your grace?

"You asked to see me, sir?" I finally get out, deciding on the term that I think covers most of them without sounding too insulting. When the frown deepens on his face and those big bushy red eyebrows of his draw even closer together, I mentally sigh. Sir isn't the right word. Wide-eyed I stare at him, weighing him in a similar way to the look he's giving me.

He likes to eat, evidenced by the size of his paunch hanging over his too tight tailored pants. Which I think might, in fact, be made of silk. Aristocrats wear silk but not usually silk pants, although one never knows. They wore them hundreds of years ago and it quite possibly might be back in style again.

Fads tend to be something I avoid. I'd rather do my own thing and be happy with it than rely on other people to decide if my butt looks big in those pants. Mister Headmaster doesn't have that same problem, his butt does look big in those pants.

And those chops he has going on, bright red against the sickly paleness of his shiny white bald head. At least the few hairs on top are combed and pomaded down. As my eyes work their way down his head, I see that he's staring at me with a look of disgust and his jowls are droopy with his displeasure.

He looks a bit like a put-out bulldog.

"Young lady, I was informed that you have Awakened and not followed the proper procedure to report it. Given the color of your hair, this seems to be the case indeed. What have you to say for yourself?" As he talks, I'm reminded of the many times I was chastised as a child for speaking with a full mouth. Except he sounds like he has a mouth full of marbles or pebbles. The only reason I understand what he's saying is because he speaks slowly.

The disgust in his eyes increases, as if this human Mage has any right to look at me that way. Or demand answers from me. I'm only here because Mada insisted, otherwise I'd still be in my home.

"She Awakened, yes – but keep in mind human, we are here as a courtesy only. Your Pact laws have no impact on creatures of the Dark Forgetful Forest." Ciar speaks quietly, but the Headmaster reacts as if he is physically slapped. Yeah, his reaction I completely understand, Ciar threw out the DFF card. Although I'm not sure what Pact he's speaking of.

'They cannot control or hold a member of the Dark Forgetful Forest for breaking their laws.' Ciar fills in the blanks.

'I'm not a blood relative, Ciar.'

My eyes drop down to the nameplate on the desk, Headmaster Patton – clears his throat nervously. "I was only aware of the sponsorship, I was not aware that one of you were clan there. Which one of you is it?"

I bet my eye-teeth he doesn't know that Ciar is the Lord of the Hunt.

"It doesn't matter. Miss Nightshade has indeed Awakened, but she has not received her full Triad. Until that event transpires, we will remain in this town unhindered by your Regulators." Regulators are the military that enforces the customs of Awakening. They're a nasty lot from what I've heard, and I'd rather not have to deal with them.

"Now, is there anything else we can help you with today, Headmaster?" As the last syllable falls into the silence of the room, I fight the urge to cheer.

That was one heck of a speech.

Headmaster Patton's face is so red it's nearing purple. Ciar might want to tone it down or the poor man's head is going to pop like a full balloon.

"Ahem," he coughs nervously, "Has any of her Triad been discovered? An Awakened typically only does so once one member of the Triad has been claimed."

Automatically, my gaze goes to Ciar who's eyes happen to be on me. Slowly, his lips spread into that smile that's all teeth and intent. The red of Patton's face hits purple, him having a different reaction than I do.

"Indeed, I'm her Pinnacle. Any more questions?"

For a split second, I feel sorry for him as he looks back and forth between us blinking like a sleepy owl. It's hard not to laugh out loud.

"Pardon?" he blurts out.

"I'm. Her. Pinnacle." Ciar leans forward, his fingertips spread out on the desk in front of Patton, his face mere inches from the much shorter man's.

Ciar's out of patience.

"But you're her——" Ciar keeps smiling and shakes his head.

"No one ever said we were siblings," he answers, then turns and walks towards the door. This meeting is apparently over. With some pep in my step, I practically run out ahead of him to keep from losing it and laughing like a hyena.

"I can tolerate many things, but I will not have some pompous Mage giving us any kind of order. Mada be damned," Ciar mutters under his breath, as his long legs eat up the distance to our room. I'm jogging to keep up. I'm not super short, probably a hair's breadth from five-foot-nine and I'm still pushing it to keep up with him. There's more to the story I'm sure. Pompous or not, there's no way that Patton got to Ciar that quickly over something that simple. I ask him.

"He was trying to spell you," he grits out between his teeth.

Well, fudge. Why would the Headmaster try to spell me?

"Someone is very interested in you and your Awakening, but since I can't actually read minds I don't have the answer I want."

Do what?

"What do you mean you can't read minds? You've been reading mine forever."

Ciar stops so suddenly I run right into his back and I immediately find myself in his grasp facing him.

"You are an exception to everything." Releasing me, he turns and continues walking, leaving me staring after him like the idiot I'm starting to think I am.

CHAPTER 12

CAREFUL WHAT YOU WISH FOR...

"What's up with the hair-do?" The rudely snapped question basically yelled in my face pulls me out of the thoughts of the mysteries that my future holds for me. My eyes focus, and I find myself staring at the human Mage Sierra that we ran into in the hallway our first day here.

"What's up with your breath?" I ask instead.

Yes, I'm a nice person but I'm also a firm believer in boundaries and right now, she's breaking mine. And her breath is rather foul. Sierra likes fish. Sputtering and red faced she pulls back away from me and stares at me like she wants me to catch on fire. Considering the sudden attention of Ciar, she might have actually tried to set me on fire.

Fantastic, I can sing now and play a violin, but I can't protect myself from a magical attack. Not that I ever could before, but still, this should be part of the perk package

'I'll teach you, it's something you'll have the magic to do now.' Ciar offers.

Finally, something useful!

'Really?'

'*Yes, really. You can do all kinds of crap and all I can do is sing pretty now.*'

He chuckles. '*You'll see.*'

Sierra gives me one last dirty look and flounces to her seat. A quick flash of heat fills my eyes and I know they're swirling. The change of them brings her Aura into focus. She hasn't Awakened, but she's close. How I know this I have no idea but there's this... lack of something there. A thread spirals out from her, lightly tying her to whomever is on the other end of it. It's pulsing like a heartbeat so that person is moving closer to this room with every passing second.

When he walks into the classroom, I choke to cover up the laugh. The Fairy is all of eighteen years old - and that's being generous - with spiky brown hair, his tall form is so skinny he looks like a good wind will blow him away. Not what Sierra expects, I'm sure.

He's strong though, not as strong as some others in this room, but still, surprisingly so. Well, well, she just found her Pinnacle. Sierra's head jerks up and their eyes meet. The thread between them snaps taut and instead of her smiling with happiness or whatever they're supposed to feel over an Awakening, she starts to cry instead.

Seriously?

"Why are you crying, he's your Pinnacle. Which means you'll Awaken and get some cushy job with the Aristos," I whisper to her.

"He's a Fairy," she sobs out.

Turning back to the boy, I kind of shake my head. Why does that matter? He's wingless and for the most part looks human. The only difference is his slit pupils and pointed ears. Why be ashamed of that? He's stronger than her.

"So? He's strong, which means you'll have a solid Triad. Isn't that better than a human boy with weak magic?"

'*She's racist,*' Ciar interjects. I cut him a dirty look and turn back to Sierra, but it doesn't shut him up like I hoped. *'Nothing you say will convince her otherwise. Why bother with it?'*

Because the Fairy deserves for someone to speak up for him.

"I get it, I really do - you're getting paired with a Fae and it means he isn't your dream guy, but it's something you're not given a choice about and Faerie doesn't make mistakes." Silently, I add that she also doesn't like you questioning her choices, either.

Gods, I really am a hypocrite.

"But... but look at him," she continues, in a whiney, snot choked voice.

Sighing, I look at them and it isn't her I feel sorry for, it's him because he's going to be stuck with her the rest of his life. For the first time I pay attention to the look on his face, he looks completely shocked and no happier than she does. It doesn't stop him from drawing up his courage and stopping at her desk.

"I'm Bean." The chit has the audacity to wail loudly when he says his name.

Doesn't she know that all Fairies name their children for a fruit or vegetable until they come into their power fully?

Then he surprises all of us by saying, "I'm not any happier about this than you are. I was hoping it was her," he says, pointing at me.

Ciar growls and Bean takes a step back. Ha.

"Why wouldn't you be happy with me? Look at me, I'm gorgeous and my family is wealthy and—"

He interrupts, "You're pretentious and close minded and only worried about yourself," he finishes. Two spots of color burn high on his cheeks. Bean has a spine, hooray.

"Sierra, is there an issue here?" the teacher asks, coming to stand beside Bean.

"Bean is her Pinnacle," I supply the answer, a little satisfied that she can't deny it.

"Well, this is...uh... fabulous. It means you'll Awaken, Sierra!"

Fabulous isn't the word the very human teacher wants to use. I take in the frazzled look about her and the sideways looks she's giving poor Bean. I don't know this one's name. I search around for a name plate but find none.

'Mrs. Radish.'

You're kidding me? Radish? Faerie save them from their parents picking names.

"I don't want to Awaken now," Sierra wails again.

"Well, Sierra, there isn't a choice involved. I imagine it'll happen soon since you met your Pinnacle first." Although Mrs. Rubbish, inner giggle, is saying all the nice words and right things to try and calm the situation - her body language is saying something drastically different. Radish is angry about it, which is odd. Why is a teacher angry about Sierra's potential Awakening?

'Look more closely,' Ciar encourages.

Flash of heat and her Aura snaps into view, she's a mid-level Mage, nothing spectacular. Now I can see the blacks swirling in and out of her Aura like a school of fish. Definitely angry. That's when I see, or don't see, something - there are no threads leading away from her, connecting her to someone else. Rubbish didn't Awaken. Which explains the greens and puke yellows now spinning about in her Aura.

Jealousy.

That's not very teacher-y of her, but then again, now I see why she's a teacher. Fae are all about the untrue adage that those who can't do, teach. Out of curiosity I'm going to check the rest of them today, too. I didn't realize that Auras told this type of truth. If not for Ciar and my connection, I still wouldn't.

I choose to disregard the blue thread that branches out of me. I know what it means, and I'll deal with it when whomever is on the other end makes themselves known. It's not like it's pulsing like Sierra's - which means whomever is on the end of it isn't here yet. If what Ciar says is true, and I'll admit - if only to myself, that I'm pretty sure it's true - then they're coming regardless.

'How much time do I have?'

'Enough, although you act more like it's a prison sentence than the gift it is.' His answer is fast and decisive, he's probably eavesdropping again. *'I can't read every single thought, just the ones you're projecting loudly or not protecting.'*

That's mighty honest of him to share with me, but I don't really see the point in closing all the gaps now. It will take a lot of effort to lock him out completely and he'll still feel my emotions through the bond, just like I can feel his now. Amusement is the strongest one that I can feel coming from him. Well, isn't it peachy that I can amuse his majesty?

Turning my attention back to the drama winding down in front of me, I watch Bean's face as he stares at Sierra. His emotions are written on it plain as day. He's not happy about his Center, but I can see the fascination and disgust warring on his face and I can also see the moment the disgust wins.

Which is the most interesting part of this entire encounter.

I mostly believed that the connection between a Triad and their Center is more force than anything else, until now. Yes, there is some 'encouragement' from the magic but if Bean can overcome it, then someone like Ciar can decimate it.

I'm an idiot.

'The moment I realized what you are to me, Monster Girl - you weren't Awakened, there was no magical pull.' His attention intent upon me draws my gaze to his. *'Magic has nothing to do with it.'*

Since this began, I assumed that he meant the Pinnacle thing, but what he's saying now has nothing to do with being a Pinnacle and everything to do with being -

' - *a man.*' He finishes the thought for me. I make a face at him and turn away. Heat crawls up my face and into other places, which make me smile.

Carefully, almost slyly, I spend the next several moments building up my shields, giving myself the freedom to think about how he wants me for *me* not because of some magical wahoo. The sense of relief is different and new, and I let it settle inside of me.

Looking at him through my lashes, I study his face with my self-imposed blinders off. The green of his eyes is luminescent, and I've always thought the color was intriguing. Now with it on a Fae face it's incredible.

No, not a Fae face, *his* face.

'What's in that head of yours? Something important for you to block me out so hard.' His eyes narrow but that ever-present smirk hovers around his mouth.

Smiling benignly, I turn back to the soap opera, a little disappointed that it's mostly over and that Sierra is now looking at Bean in a purely calculating way. Poor Bean, he's in for a ride with this one, not the good kind either, but I'm sure that'll happen too. She doesn't strike me as the demure type.

Radish points out the door for Bean to leave and harrumphs at the rest of us to settle down. Resting my elbow on the desk, I lean my face on the meaty part of my hand and take the time to look at the people around me. Readily, I admit that I didn't really care enough to pay attention before and I don't necessarily care about them now, but I should at least know who and what they are.

Most of them are humans, not too surprising. Humans breed easier and more quickly than Fae. However, there are Fae around us. Mostly Elves and Fairies and even a few wearing the purple and gold of Aristocracy or some other High Fae bloodline. Some are even looking back at me with the same measuring gaze.

Those ones look on with indulgence and disinterest are pure Fae. We don't age like humans, but there's something in the eyes that shows it. It reminds me of how some wines get darker with age. Some of these Fae are incredibly old. Why are ones that old in this place?

Looking over at Ciar I ask him, *'Did you know you would be part of a Triad one day?'*

Without hesitation, *'I suspected but I didn't know for sure. I already knew that I would not have a Triad since there would be no Awakening for me.'*

'I wonder how many of these will be part of a Triad or become an Awakened?'

'Possibly none of them. Some shouldn't be here anymore than myself.'

Chucking I say, *'They're as old as you, eh?'*

'No, but too old for this place.' That's interesting to know. What he says next even more so. *'They keep coming here in hopes that they'll Awaken or become part of a Triad. Being a High Fae doesn't make you automatically safe. There are several families, Fae and human alike, who will cast aside or sacrifice what they consider mundane children and make new ones.'*

Wow, that's harsh and something I kind of understand, except mine is an opposite situation. My mother tried to kill me to keep me from Awakening, something I don't understand at all. This power, that's growing - the Aura peeking thing is proof - doesn't seem so great to me. And my gut tells me it will get worse before it gets better.

'But you'll not be alone when it does.' The sincerity in his words make me want to hug him and smack him at the same time.

He said *when*, not if.

Opening the pack of gum in my pocket to distract myself, I go to pop a piece in my mouth only to be shoved backwards when a force hits my hand hard enough to almost break it. Only one person can catch me off guard so completely.

"Ciar?" I question the man who's standing over me holding my hand in an iron grasp. The burning green of his eyes are focused so intently on the piece of gum clasped between my fingers that, for a moment, I worry my hand is going to catch on fire.

With a deep growl that I feel as clearly as I hear, he snatches the gum and shoves it in his mouth. Blood dribbles out of his mouth, trailing down his chin to disappear down his neck.

"Ciar?" I demand this time.

Casting his eyes around the room, he spits on the ground and I watch as the lump of bloody gum melts through the floor.

"Faebane, which would kill you," he whispers, pulling me to my feet. The earthy smell of his magic is strong in the air and I feel it break over my skin. Why is he glamouring us? Because that's exactly what he's doing. He says nothing as he practically drags me out of the room, heading outside instead of to our dorm. Digging my heels in, I fight his pull until he stops in the courtyard outside.

"What are you doing, Ciar?"

"Someone had access to your things in order to place such a potent poison in the gum."

"I bought it at the school store."

"Are you absolutely sure?" He looks me over and his hands cup my face. His breathing is rather ragged, and his color is bad.

"Why did you ingest it, Ciar? Faebane kills Fae, you idiot." I push his hands away and start checking him.

"I'll be fine, I'm a different kind of Fae." He smirks but

it's a little shakier than normal. "It still has a little kick, but it won't kill me."

"What kind of kick?"

"It's the equivalent of you being drunk."

Frowning at him, I refuse to go anywhere until his breathing calms and the color returns to his face. Taking a deep breath, he exhales and rests his forehead against my own. It's a reminder to me how close this creature and I really am, because when I was a child this is something I did when he returned all bloody from his hunts. Not all Fae are so easy to kill, not even by the Lord of the Hunt.

"Come on, I need to brush my teeth twenty times to rid myself of the foul taste of this shit." Smiling at me in reassurance, you know like he wasn't the one that ate Fae killing poison or anything, he tugs on my hand and reluctantly I follow.

It really does make his breath horrid.

CHAPTER 13
OPEN MOUTH INSERT STEAK...

S ince Zag found out about the whole poison thing, he's
been a regular mother hen. Apologizing a hundred times
for something that wasn't his fault. The silly lizard. He thinks
that somehow, he was sleeping mind you, he should've been
able to smell the poison before Ciar.

"Zaggggg, enough! Nothing you could've done." I chastise, flicking his tail to get him to move off my chest. Grumbling, he moves but only a few inches to lay beside of me on
the bed.

I look at the clock and groan, it's three am and because
he's checking on me every ten seconds, I haven't gotten any
sleep. Of course, there's a good chance I wasn't going to sleep
well anyhow.

Who's trying to kill me now?

"Monster Girl?" I raise my head up to look at Ciar
standing a few feet from me.

"What?"

"Follow me," he says, ducking out the door.

Flinging the covers and a complaining Dragon off me, I

run after him uncaring of my bare feet and pajamas. My important parts are covered so it doesn't matter. Ciar moves like a demon, flitting in and out of shadows like he has no substance. The few times I get close enough to reach out and grab him, he slips through my fingers like water.

Laughter is left in his trail. Smiling, I pick up my pace. We've played this game before and occasionally I actually almost win. Except this time I'm not chasing a wolfy-dog, I'm chasing a half-naked man who wants me in the ways of a man and who I... who I want too.

Well, shit.

Rounding the corner, dirt flinging in the air, I skid to a stop, he's standing still in front of me, his eyes lighting up the darkness in a faint moonbeam. Extending his arm, he beckons me with a pale hand and almost like he's pulling me with strings, I go to him. But it is not against my will, I go because I want to.

The air is a warm caress but the feel of his skin when I put my hand in his is an inferno that spreads up my arm, across my shoulders and all the way to my toes. He pulls me against him until we are firmly touching – with me fitting against him like I was made to go there.

"You know we've never danced together? How else shall we practice for our class project?" Placing my hand on his shoulder and his other hand on my waist, he brings our clasped hands into position and then I feel the magic seeping out of him as he begins to hum.

And since I've heard the song so often, I begin to hum with him.

Small Moss Fairies appear out of the tall grass and flow around us in a swirl of blues and reds, their lights bright and their giggles loud. The magic of this dance calls them too. Smiling, I look up into his eyes and stop fighting. And just dance.

Effortlessly, he leads me in a dance that only Fae can do. Our humming takes on a life of its own, the notes appear on the fog wrapping around us in its magical embrace. This is true Fae dancing and the beauty of it leaves me breathless. Laughing with pure joy, I follow his steps that are so fast it feels like we're flying. Faster and faster we go, his eyes holding me prisoner, his smile making me feel more aware of his closeness.

When his arms tighten, pulling me closer to him, I allow it. Ciar is a beautiful man who smells like home and feels like the strongest thing in the world and right now, he's looking at me like he wants to eat me up.

I love it.

Resting his forehead against mine for a brief second, he lets his lips touch mine and then he's twirling me away, laughing. Spinning, I try to catch my breath and manage to fall right into the thick grass. The magical lights around us fade and the Fairies, sensing that the dance is over, go back to their hidey holes. All that's left is Ciar standing above me, his hand out waiting for me to take it.

After holding his gaze for what feels like an eternity, I slide my hand into his and smile as he pulls me to my feet. The tension between us is thick, giving more heat to the warm air around us. It's a good kind of tension, it's just one that I'm not quite ready to explore yet.

Once I do, I know it's forever.

"Well, it's fair to say I think we'll get a passing grade." The tension eases at his jest.

"Gods, I hope so. Either way, I have a feeling that at the end of it we won't be the only ones sweating." The mojo we were putting off was at its base nature sexual. To me it's so much more.

He smiles and links my arm through his as we head back to our room. Ciar talks about nonsensical things like laundry -

which I forgot about again - and asked if would I like to have a TV and then if I want to go to lunch.

The man is always about feeding me.

CHAPTER 14

A BROWNIE TO THE RESCUE...

M ost normal people have magic to do their laundry or Brownies to do it for them. The Menagerie doesn't have either for folks like me, so we're stuck going to the laundromat. Which is not a friendly welcoming place. It's in the shadier side of the town.

I have a fat Corpse Worm, happily munching on a rodent of some kind, once again dressed up in the trench coat and in a wheelchair. A Dragon who is being super protective and watching everyone like a hawk, and then there's Ciar, who surprised me by coming at all. He's even carrying the laundry basket full of clothes.

Strangely, including his clothes.

I know that when he does choose to wear underwear, he's a boxers kind of man. I'm not sure if I could've remained straight faced if he wore those little girly underwear. Then again, picturing him in them is at war with the humor. He doesn't have many clothes. I watch him shove them into one washing machine while I take up two. I had no idea I owned so many clothes. It will be nice to not have to smell them before I put them on.

Tossing in the laundry tablets, I'm politely shoved aside by a small woman in a green dress. Oh, a Brownie.

"Who taught you to wash clothes, little bit?" I blink at her, unsure what to say.

"No one, really," I finally answer.

I read the instructions on the machines, truth be told, but for some reason I didn't want to admit it out loud. Silly pride.

"Well, go on with you. I'll take care of this mess and babysit the Worm. Lord, take the girl for supper, she looks about starved to death." This is said without her turning away from the task of sorting out my laundry.

Why in the world did a Brownie just adopt me? Because that's absolutely what happened. Brownies only serve their chosen master and it's considered bad taste to argue with them about it. Well, fudge. I don't need to collect anymore strays. Ciar tugs me out the door towards a diner across the street.

"She decided to collect you this time," Ciar says his voice full of amusement.

"I thought that they only served those who own property."

"But you do." His voice is quiet, careful.

It stops me in my tracks. There's only one place he can mean. My mother's house. Gritting my teeth, I start walking again, that house can rot for all I care. I walk right by him into the diner. The door jingles as it opens, and the waitress dressed in pink and white turns to greet us and freezes in her tracks. My eyes take in the customers and décor.

Pink rabbits line the middle of the walls in a row, that look like they're marching off to their deaths. Most of them are missing parts or have grease stains making the already doomed bunnies look worse. Checkered booths, the same shade of pink, fill the floor space with a beat-up table between each one. The smell, which should be good in a food establishment, is smoke and old ham. Then I spot the poster on the wall, a Fairy - a very human interpretation of one - with a slash through it.

This is a human anti-Fae establishment.

"Sit, they will not harm us." Ciar sounds sure so I slide into a booth seat.

"They better not spit in my food," I grumble.

"They won't, that would be considered rude and they wouldn't want the Troll who lives underneath here to think they were rude to Fae," he says loud enough for all of them to hear.

Ducking my head, I hide my smile. I can see a Troll being a problem. Not only could the troll rip this place apart, he or she will eat them too - slowly.

"Will that be take-out?" the human waitress asks, after making us wait a good two minutes for service.

"I'd like a house burger, rare, and a chocolate shake, and ma'am," Ciar leans close to her, "If I find anything wrong with my food, I will follow you home." His threat is left hanging in the air and as much as I disagree with it and hope he won't do it, I say nothing. I'd rather they not mess with our food, either.

Clearing her throat nervously she says, "And you?" To me.

"A burger, as well, rare, and a chocolate shake," I eye the cake dish on the counter, "And can I please get a big piece of chocolate cake?" There's no harm in being polite. Maybe it will help her make her decision not to dump dirt in the shakes?

"Too nice, Monster Girl." Ciar says, watching the waitress with sharp eyes.

"You know, I've never asked, why do you call me monster girl?"

Ciar smiles, that big toothy smile I like and leans his elbows on the table, his hand idly playing with mine.

"You had no fear of me and the Sluagh as a child. The very first time you wandered into the forest they followed you, watching, and somehow you knew they were there. Yet, you were never once afraid. Instead, you called out to them to play," he smiles. "And you tried to get me to play fetch."

Watching our hands together, I smile. Finding the forest is one of the best things to ever happen in my life. My mother went on one of her rampages about my father - the kind where she got violent - so I ran away to hide. Night came, and I found myself lost in the Dark Forgetful Forest.

He's right, I wasn't afraid. Not then and not now. Something pulled me to that place, something told me to not be afraid. When the whispered-about 'monsters' stepped out of the shadows into the weak sunlight streaming through the thick trees, I felt like I found home.

"Well, you were a dog. It's only reasonable that I thought you'd want to play," I tease.

"You tamed the scariest monsters in creation, Keri, you earned your nickname." He pauses as if he's weighing his next words. After a moment of his unblinking gaze, he says, "You know, Mada told me when I first came to stay in the forest that it would lead me to what I sought the most."

"To go back to high school?" Chuckling, he runs his finger across my palm inciting a shiver.

Our plates of food being practically slammed on the table brought us out of our staring contest, breaking the private moment into a thousand pieces. Sighing, I focus on the food, it's smarter that way anyhow. These kinds of conversations with Ciar always get me into trouble. The last time we had one like this, I Awakened.

Ciar grins at me and takes a big bite of his burger, dripping ketchup all over the place including his chin. When his tongue snakes out to lick it off, I find myself fascinated by it and curious what else it can do. I'm Fae after all, how can I resist something that's so blatantly sexy? And why is it moving so slow? And why, when it disappears back into his mouth am I a little disappointed?

"Naughty Keri," he teases and takes another big bite. Determined to focus on my food instead of his tongue, I start eating. Despite my worry about them tampering with it, Zag, who's been sleeping this entire time on my shoulder, wakes up and takes a big bite out of the burger, squirting ketchup and mayo all over my shirt.

With a snort, he attempts to lick it off. Batting at his head I grab a napkin and pat at it ineffectually.

"I leave you alone for five minutes and you're already a mess. Give me the shirt. And Dragon, if you keep getting her dirty, I'll wash you as well." The Brownie's disembodied voice precedes her. She pops into existence above my plate.

Her little hand hovers in front of me, she's seriously wanting the shirt now? Shrugging, I tug it over my head and hand it to her, surprised to have another, clean one, placed in the same hand.

"Can't have you running around sharing the goods with everyone can we, dear?" she asks with a twinkle in her eye.

"What in the world is your name?" I ask, flabbergasted.

Lickity-split she grabs the steak knife off the table and cuts into the meaty part of my hand then does the same to her much smaller one. Slapping it against mine to mingle our blood. The the bond kicks in immediately.

"Gertrude, your name is Gertrude."

She nods and smiles, "My friends can call me Gertie. Now, do try and not make a mess while I'm gone. I have laundry to finish." With a saucy wink she pops out of existence.

"Well, that was interesting." I've been adopted again, ha.

"She'll follow you until either she dies, or you do. I've never seen one give a blood bond before," Ciar muses, finishing his burger in one bite.

Zag burps in my ear and settles down again. I look down to discover that my hand is now empty of burger. That little piglet. I'm tempted to flick his tail to interrupt his nap but then I dig into the cake instead. He's rather cute when he's sleeping.

"Would you like another?" Ciar asks. Of course, he wants to feed me. I'm starting to understand that it's a thing he does to show affection.

"Na, I wasn't really hungry." It's the truth, and this cake is marvelous for a human made cake. I'll freely admit I like Fairy food more, but human food has its own appeal.

Finishing the cake, I suck down the milkshake and only glance at the check the waitress sets on the table. Ciar snatches it up before I can do anything about it. Dropping some paper money on the table he stands, and I follow.

Pleasantly talking about mundane things as we walk out of the diner means I'm not paying attention to what's going on around me, but Ciar is. He always is. When I'm shoved into the wall of the diner, I'm shocked. The car that he moved me out of the path of, doesn't slow and Ciar is still standing in its way. I yell, knowing I can't help because I'm too far away. He leaps into the air and clears the car as it passes harmlessly underneath him.

That's a neat trick, I can't believe I was worried about a car killing Ciar.

The car keeps going and turns the corner with screaming tires. What just happened here?

Ignoring Zag's cursing, I wait for him to climb back onto my shoulders before climbing to my feet and dusting off my pants. I jog to Ciar to double check he's okay, even though I know he is. He's watching the street where the car disappeared.

"That is why you need a guardian."

"I see that, the question is why?" I'm not anyone important. It doesn't make sense to me. The only person who ever tried to kill me is my mother.

Crap.

"Ciar, why do I have the feeling that someone connected to my mother is trying to kill me, again?" Because it's the only thing that makes any sense. Not that her pretending to be human and then trying to kill me made sense.

"People do things for many different reasons, this is something we need to find out the root cause of, then we can kill it at its source," Ciar says, giving one last look to the road before turning to me. "Be cautious about anything you ingest, bathe in, wear and so forth. In my absence, the Dragon can test any food and drink, he's immune to their poisons." With that, he wraps his long fingers around mine and we head back to the laundromat.

"So why a car? Doesn't that seem like a strange thing to try and kill me with?" I muse.

"I'm guessing it was a weapon of convenience. Someone saw an opportunity and took it. It was a mistake." The cold in his voice shows the depth of his anger. Their mistake isn't just trying to kill me, it's allowing themselves to be known by Ciar.

He is the Lord of the Hunt, after all. His Calling is to hunt down those that Faerie deems guilty, finding an assassin shouldn't be that hard, right?

Walking into the laundromat, I find a napping Fluffy and all my clothes are spinning in the dryers beside him. It's a comical picture and I can't help but laugh which wakes up Fluffy who makes that growly chirp of his and dislodges his hat. Someone close by screams. Ignoring it, I tuck the hat back on his head and marvel that his face is already cleaned up. Gertie is responsible for that I imagine.

Speaking of the Brownie, I find her sitting on the edge of the washing machine reading a magazine. It gives me a chance to study her better. She's young for a Brownie, there are only traces of gray hair in her brown locks. Her eyes are a honey amber color and dancing with amusement at whatever she's reading. Her face bears no true wrinkles but only some slight laugh lines. Gertie has a good sense of humor then. A tiny little button nose and cupid's bow lips finish the face of our newest family member.

She doesn't look like a grandma, but she does look like someone's good natured aunt. I'll take it, especially since she'll do laundry and dishes and it's considered an honor to be chosen. Brownies don't work for free, they take little bits of things here and there for payment. Like food, clothing and jewelry but only things that are given with permission. You're supposed to set them out as gifts.

More importantly, they like sweets and that's something I can provide in abundance. I have candy stashed all over the place and I have no problems sharing it.

Human lore painted the Fae as solitary creatures that lived alone in dark caves and ate all their children. Ugly hags and six-legged monsters that were hideous. Making a face, I turn to watch the spinning laundry. There are hags, monsters and some of them do eat children, but none of them live alone. Fae are family based and those without family or cast outs sometimes choose clans or packs to live with. Fae don't do well alone, they tend to go rather insane and become violent. Something about magic makes us need to be surrounded by others of our kind. No one really understands why, at least that I know of. It's one of those great mysteries of life. Maybe I'll ask Mada if I get to visit home at Samhain, which is the next major holiday.

As far as I know, we can go anywhere we want to, I'm not sure how the rules apply to us anymore. Honestly, I was hoping that my stay in this town would be over by now, but I have a feeling it won't be for awhile. Just like this Awakened business, the sharks will start circling soon - once they find out whether my ability is worth a shit. Some family will try to indenture me and that's unfortunate for them, I'll not be a slave to anyone.

"And if the King of Lafayette came to you and demanded your service - what would you say, Monster Girl?" Giving Ciar a look of disgust, I toss a quarter that's sitting on the washing machine at him.

"Do you want to be indentured to the king, *dark lord.*"

His green eyes narrow and he advances on me, uh-oh. Caging me against the cold metal of the washer he traps me with his hands, leaning his face down close to mine.

"I bow to no king... ever," he whispers, his breath against my mouth. My heart goes crazy pounding in my chest so fast it feels like it's going to pound right out of it. Smiling, I decide it's time to make him realize that it isn't fear I feel around him anymore.

Languidly, I lick his bottom lip from corner to corner and with a quick peck of a kiss to that same lip, I duck out under his arm and move across the room to hide behind Fluffy's chair. Well, hiding without trying to be too obvious. Ciar remains in the same position, leaning on the washer, his posture relaxed. No chase?

Chills roll up my spine and I turn, my senses telling me danger but not for me. There is just a sense of danger surrounding us, thickening the air with the suffocating feeling of impending doom. Frowning, I look outside in the dim sunlight and see nothing. There aren't any passers-by or traffic, vehicle or otherwise.

A sudden snap breaks the silence as cracks begin to form on the large picture window. Racing super-fast in all directions only to be stopped by the frame. In a few seconds, they completely cover the window. Mouth hanging open I step back, pushing Fluffy behind me. Ciar's warm presence beside mine reassures me, but also intensifies the feeling of danger.

"You have nothing to fear." His hand finds mine as the window shatters, the glass raining down on the floor and sidewalk.

Sucking on my tongue, I try to get some saliva in my dry mouth so I can swallow. Clearing my throat, I say, "Ciar, was that you?" I might not be afraid of him but this... this is my fault.

His hand tightens on mine, but not painfully so. "Control cannot always be held, when presented with a distraction like you - even for one such as I." His words are more formal than normal and swallowing again I look up at him.

No, I'm not afraid of Ciar, not anymore, but I respect what he's capable of.

"I'm sorry Ciar -" My hand is jerked, and I'm spun into his arms, his hot mouth finds mine and I realize what it is to be devoured by pure lust.

That quickly, his hot mouth is gone and I'm left standing there feeling like a piece of myself is missing. From across the room, he's watching me with that predatory gaze that makes me want to rip off my clothes and tackle him. I want him more than I have ever wanted anything else in my life.

"Mistress, I realize now might not be the best time to say this, but you should perhaps wait until we are home," Zag speaks loudly in my ear. I pace side to side, my eyes only for the green-eyed Fae across from me. The one mirroring my steps.

Physically shaking myself like a wet dog, I turn away. If I keep staring at him I'll act on my impulse and no matter how mind-blowing sex between us will be, I'm not ready for that yet. If it were casual, sure - but there's nothing casual about this.

Shakily, I turn around to look at Ciar and find him

nonchalantly leaning against the wall. Oh, yeah, he's back in control. Smiling, I take a deep breath and sit on one of the cheap plastic chairs against the wall. Resting my head in my hands, I fight for the control I need to be able to take this at a slower pace. A fight against my very nature.

I don't want him to ever regret his choice.

"Don't be daft, Keri." He tilts his head to the side. "Make sure you're always armed. I expect to find at least two knives strapped somewhere on your body." Against my will I smile, he sounds so irritable.

"Uh, do we have to pay for the window?" It's a fair question to ask, we did break the window. His laugh echoes in the room, and I realize that I'll gladly spend the rest of my life making him laugh with such freedom. Call me crazy but I'm pretty sure that before I came along, laughter wasn't a common factor in his life. Resolving myself, I add it to my mental list of life choices. It only has one other thing on it.

Find the people who gave my mother the dagger she used to try and kill me.

CHAPTER 15

MEAN GIRLS AND MEANER DRAGONS...

The next week passed by in a bit of a blur, today is the first day I care enough to pay attention to anything. Disappointingly, the day is rather uneventful - until we get to music class. We've only danced together once since the assignment was given, but we click together so well that I have no doubt about our performance.

However, when the teacher tells us to pair off and practice, I feel like I've won a prize. For the last week Ciar has avoided touching me. He feeds me still and we've had a few shallow conversations, but there's been zero physical contact since the laundromat. I'm rethinking the taking it slow strategy. It's starting to not make sense anymore. Up until this point, I had no idea how much we touched until it stopped.

It sucks.

"Keri, are you ready?" Ciar asks softly, his mouth close to my ear. Snapping out of my thoughts, I place one hand in his and the other on his shoulder. The contact is electrifying like a light punch to my gut. And my lady-parts.

Ciar's jaw clenches as his nostrils flare, he smells my reaction. I smile up at him innocently and wait for the music to start. A slow smile spreads over his face and my confidence wavers, fudge.

As the music starts he begins to hum, then he begins to move us. As his voice strengthens, it tugs at that new part of me, the magical part, and despite my best effort to stop it my mouth opens, and my hummed notes join his.

Gods bless it Ciar.

As our song blossoms into words and our movements speed up, the world fades away. Magic is thick between us but there's something that's always been there. So solid that no matter how big of a dick he is, I care for him. Exhaling the last bits of reluctance that - really, I shouldn't be feeling anyway, I free myself and our song changes. Smiling down at me he pulls me closer and I feel his magic touch my skin. Oh, the dark lord is coming out to play.

The teacher's throat clearing loudly breaks the beautiful bubble of magic. Glitter from the broken spell, showers down around us and I can't help but give her a dirty look. I'm at least subtle, Ciar looks at her like he wants to rip her head off.

"Yes?" He's using that tone I hate but love to hear him use on other people.

"You two were getting a bit carried away. This is a practice not a performance." Ciar tugs me to his side and refuses to let go of my hand, no matter how I wiggle it. Giving up, I stand there and stare at the teacher staring at him.

"So?" That one word carries a warning in it.

"You don't dance like that with your sister," she hisses out.

"Why does everyone make the incorrect assumption that you're my sister?" he asks, turning to look at me. I shrug.

"You share the same last name," the teacher answers.

"So? Lots of clans all have the same last name." I explain.

"He's a pureblood." Ciar laughs at her response. Yes, he's a pureblood but way purer than the Selkie he's pretending to be.

"Idiot."

"What did you call me young man?" She steps forward, her finger poking him in the chest. Uh-oh. "I can have you expelled and you will be forced to work a mundane job the rest of your life." His eyes narrow.

Double, uh-oh. It occurs to me that I should try to help her save herself, but she's also foolish enough to think she has control over anything in his life. In any of our lives. With her threat she's saying that if you do something to piss her off she can control where you go after this stupid place.

That's not very nice.

Leaning down close to her face he repeats, "Idiot." Then he steps back from her and pulls me to the seats placed around the room in a half-moon shape setting. I sit next to him, my gaze flitting back and forth.

She's standing there sputtering as the rest of the class is staring at her too. Some in anger. The Fae aren't happy about her proclamation. The moment she realizes this she clears her throat and turns away from Ciar, but not before giving him the stink eye.

"All right, let's change things around, I have decided that we will switch partners around. It will—"

Ciar focuses his gaze on her and his magic leaves him in a small targeted wave. "You will not."

For two seconds her face goes slack and then she smiles, all the previous anger gone, "You know what, that will make things too hard for you. Instead, let's plan to share your projects at the Mixer next month." Her smile isn't quite right as she continues, "Now, make sure you're dressed appropriately, ladies and gentlemen. Rumor says there will be several Aristocrats there." She says it with such glee, like we should all be excited or something.

I'm not.

Basically, their little Mixer is a way for the rich and royal to come and take a gander at the livestock. Do they get paid for the 'students'? Maybe they auction us off like property? Considering the expensive tastes of the things in the Headmaster's office, they're getting money from somewhere.

Things like this give my assumptions more substance.

'No comment about my manipulation of her to keep us partners?'

'Uh, no. I don't want to dance with anyone else.' Raising my eyebrow at him I wait for a further explanation. Is he asking me why I didn't react to his high-handed behavior? A smile twitches my lips as I fight to keep it hidden.

'Ah, there it is. You allowed me to get away with it, unscathed, simply because it's something you wanted?' I shrug In a nutshell, yes.

"Miss Nightshade, you and Mister Nightshade will go last. This way the brighter lights shall shine first." Wow, she's a bit bitter about things. And overdramatic. And if one goes by the dirty looks some of the other Fae are throwing at her occasionally, potentially not much longer in this job. The thing about human arrogance is that Fae typically have way more.

Knowing these things - and the whole not caring thing - makes me ignore the slight she's trying to give us. This Menagerie is not an important place to me, and although I can respect others feeling that way about it, I won't let my life be impacted by something petty or someone trying to hold over me their perceived control in my life.

I realize now I'm here for three reasons and one of them is sitting next to me. Once the other two find their way here, I won't need to stay here anymore.

'Does this mean you're ready?'

Looking over at him, the smile I fought earlier slips free. Tempered with a bit of apology. *'Maybe.'*

"Miss Nightshade, if you are unable to acquire an appropriate dress by then, I'm sure the school might have some used ones from previous students." Mrs. Cobbleson's snide comment knocks the smile right off my face.

"We're from the Dark Forgetful Forest, do you think to insult the Elder who rules there by insinuating that she would send us here without adequate provisions?" Ciar's words are so cold I'm surprised icicles didn't form on the woman's nose.

This is the point where a lot of independent women like myself would bite his head off for treating her like a damsel in distress. Nope, it's pretty darn hot of him to stick up for me. It's his nature, he can't help himself. It doesn't mean he thinks I'm incapable, he taught me to be strong after all. He's just protective of those he cares about and it's something I admire in him. It's okay to let a man be a man sometimes and still hold onto your feminine power.

Ciar breaks out in a laugh and Mrs. Cobbleson jumps like a startled cat.

'Mada taught you well.'

'Yeah, but don't always think it'll be this way.'

'Oh, I look forward to seeing those moments too.' There's a promise in those purred words. So, like the intelligent, independent woman I am - most of the time, I throw down the gauntlet.

'Some of those moments require nudity.' I say blithely. The muscles in his legs tense, as if he is fighting himself to stay seated. Smiling, I bat my lashes in an overly dramatic flirt. My teasing, because I am being a tease, has his sex drive on full throttle. The fact that he has managed to not cave-man style toss me over his shoulder and carry me off to ravage me, shows the strength of his self-control.

Fae are sexual by nature but not ruled by it, we're simply accepting of it. Ciar is darker than some, so his desires run deeper. The fact that I bonded with him and that there's a potent attraction between us that's not related to magic at all, is pushing him into Rut.

In our world it's not just the females who go into heat. It's Faerie's way of keeping the various species breeding as much as possible because it's so hard to conceive. Rut for males last twenty-four hours, thankfully. I can't imagine it lasting longer, that would be painful for all involved. Heat for females last two to three days.

We don't menstruate monthly like humans, we ovulate only when we Heat - something I'm thankful for. I can't imagine the bother of bleeding every month and having the hormones and moods fluctuate with such frequency. Heat is bad enough and dangerous, especially for the female's lover. Violence is a common, sometimes uncontrollable side-effect.

The thought of going through that once a month is awful.

In my case, I don't want children anytime soon, if ever, and because of this I take precautions for my Heat. Magical ones that Mada gave me. She's of the same belief as me, Fae children are a blessing but should only be had by those who want them or are ready for them.

I'm in the 'neither' boat right now.

'Strange thoughts to have,' Ciar muses, lightly pushing his shoulder against mine.

'While I was zoned out did I miss anything?' I realize Mrs. Cobbleson is still talking, but I have no idea what it's about.

'You know they have Fairy dressmakers in town.' He says it very flippantly while looking at me out the corner of his eye. Fairy dressmakers? The butt head is taking advantage of my fascination with Fairies and dresses.

'Oh, uh...' There is no way for me not to sound excited about this. *'How long do you think the wait time is?'* My foot starts to bounce in excitement.

'I imagine since you're a favorite of Fairies that the wait won't be

long at all.' I roll my eyes at him. I'm not a favorite of Fairies, I'm just good at making friends with them.

Ciar snorts and bumps me with his knee, pointing towards the teacher.

"Today I want to evaluate your musical abilities. Several elite houses employ musicians on a full-time basis. Miss Nightshade you can go first, pick your instrument."

I clearly remember putting on the application for this class that I don't play any instruments... unless - I stretch out my right arm, the one with the Conduit bracelet on it. Trails of blue climb down my arm to materialize into the form of the violin in my hand. Looking at the shock on her face, I keep the smile of triumph off mine and place the violin under my chin. As my hand hovers over the string the bow appears, and I gently stroke it across them.

Looking past the teacher to the far corner, I take a deep breath. Yes, the Conduit helps me play but I think music is now a part of me too. As the first notes fill the air the large potted plant in the corner shivers. Frowning, I keep playing but walk closer. An odd feeling fills me and then the plant is gone.

'Keep playing, all is well.' Ciar reassures me and this time I listen. I trust him with my life, why not the weirdness of a plant?

Turning my back on the now empty corner I smile at Mrs. Cobbleson all sharp teeth and determination. I think it's time to remind her I'm Fae and by the gods I'm Awakened. Playing until sweat rolled down my back and my arm feels like it might fall off, I'm cocky enough to bow before the gaping mouths of the class.

Eat that, Mrs. Cobbleson.

Taking my seat, the bow disappears and the blue climbs up my arm again to become the bracelet. I swear the thing sighs in contentment.

'*Sentient, remember?*' I choose to ignore the sarcasm in his voice.

Instead, I want to know about the plant. '*Okay, so, the plant.*' He sighs.

'*Whoever it is, can mask themselves from me. I do not sense any ill intent, they're curious versus dangerous. To you anyhow.*'

'*This has happened before?*' Instead of answering, he shrugs.

Kicking his foot, I sit back a bit perturbed. These are things he needs to share with me. Communication is one of the most important parts of any relationship. How can he expect me to always tell him things when he doesn't give me the same courtesy?

'*Relationship, huh?*' he asks.

'*That's all you take from that?*'

'*Oh, no. I heard everything else, but that part is the most important to me right now.*'

Rolling my eyes, I try to pay attention to the rest of class and the dirty looks occasionally thrown my way from the teacher. Freely I'll admit, I probably shouldn't have tossed anything in her face, but she treated me like garbage and I've had enough of that.

"Class is cancelled the rest of the week to give you all time to prepare for the Mixer. I expect you to make me proud. Here are copies," she starts handing out pieces of paper, skipping me in the process, "Of the schedules for your performance. In order to attend, you need to receive an invitation from one of the families who either sponsor or will be attending the gathering."

The look of satisfaction she sends my way makes me want to stand up and smack her. And to push me that far takes a lot, I'm not big on violence if there is another method.

Ciar isn't as nice as I am. "We have a standing invitation to all events related to the Menagerie. Would you like me to have our sponsor contact you to clarify this?"

Mada doesn't clarify, she terrifies.

"Uh, well - that won't be necessary, class dismissed."

As soon as we head out into the hallway, I split off to go to the restroom. My schedule is open for the rest of the day, but I have a feeling - yay - that Ciar is going to take me to the Fairy dress shop.

Jeans and t-shirts are my go-to clothes when I'm outside of the forest, but I love clothes. Dresses and flowing blouses. Hair ornaments and jewelry. Basically, anything shiny and gauzy and I'm all over it. But I never get the chance to wear them. The forest isn't a fabric friendly environment. Speaking of fabric, what color dress do I want? My hair is purple now, so I need to make sure it doesn't clash.

Fairy clothing is made from all sorts of materials. Dragon scale and spider silk to name a couple. Spider silk is soft and beautiful but sticky. Not something I need to wear in such a crowded place, that's more of a wedding dress type of material. Dragon scales shimmer and keep you warm but can be stiff and unyielding, that's something you want to wear for some sort of publicity function.

Maybe like a red or white... na, white washes me out. What about a black with sparkly -

"Oh, look, it's the nerds knight in shining armor." The snotty voice makes me groan. Way to ruin a nice dress day dream.

It's the three girls that were being mean to Lucinda. My eyes narrow, now they think they can pick on me? I'm genuinely not a supporter of violence, but there are moments in time when there's no other choice. The problem is, I always feel bad after the fact.

The first fireball hits me in the chest, flinging me into the mirror which shatters on impact.

Ouch.

For Faerie's sake, why in the world did I tell Ciar I didn't want to learn to use the magic I have? What possible reason is good enough to counter the predicament I'm currently in?

"She's rather weak for a Fae, don't you think Kim?" The Water Sprite questions the other two women.

The Elf with the red hair is too busy lobbing fireballs at me with a malicious grin on her face to answer her. Another fireball singes my hair and I'm pretty sure one eyebrow and all my eyelashes are gone on the right side of my face. Okay, so I don't have their kind of magic but I'm far from helpless.

The knife sliding out of the sheath at the base of my spine is silent. In this situation most Fae I know would kill them. Luckily for them, I'm not most Fae. Water seeps through my sneakers, I like these sneakers.

Water creeps up my body and burns as it forces its way into my nose and mouth. Before I lose vision, I toss the knife at the Water Sprite who is trying to slowly drown me, it clips her arm and just as I expected, makes her cry out and lose concentration. The water falls away and I draw in huge breaths to make up for the lack of oxygen.

"You stupid bitch!" she shrieks at me and I can feel her magic building up again. She's not very powerful and it takes her a bit to have enough juice to control the water. Her I can deal with, no problem.

The vines wrapping around my legs and pulling me down to the wet tile floor however, put me in a bit of a bind.

"Now, Kim she's ready to be a toasty critter." The Wood Nymph who has me trapped encourages the strongest of the trip - Kim - to roast my bum.

Physically I can take them, but magically I'm sunk and unless I can get to them I can't do squat and they'll hand my ass to me or kill me. Great, just great.

'You ready to learn about your magic now?' Ciar teases.

Rolling my eyes, I stop fighting the vines and go limp in their embrace. Of course, Ciar's close by. He would sense my predicament. He's not the only one. A massive reptilian head slams through the door, knocking if off the hinges and coating me in plaster dust.

"Hello, Zag."

"Why is it that every time I allow you out of my sight you land yourself in trouble?" Ignoring his comment, I start cutting myself out of the vines.

The screaming women - because of well, DRAGON - are all huddled together pointing and yelling at the top of their lungs. Not that I want them to, but it seems strange that when presented with a threat like Zag, none of them had the sense to call their Familiars. See, this is why you don't lock them up in your Blank Space. Zag chuckles in my direction and it sounds like a train in the small room, which makes the women scream louder.

"Gods, shut them up, will you?"

Turning his glowing eyes onto the three women in the room with us, he exhales shadows that tangle them up like birds on a spit. The screams and shrieks are still happening, but they're muffled because he essentially gagged them. I can also see their magic being absorbed into the shadows. They'll have a heck of a hangover tomorrow. Being sucked dry isn't any fun, at least not in this case.

"I'm a magnet for fun times," I finally answer his earlier question.

"This is fun to you?"

Giving him a dirty look, I cut the last of the vines away and dust my clothes off as I stand.

"Now ladies, I assume this is the only time we'll have this kind of encounter?" Zag questions as he releases them from the shadows into an ungainly heap on the ground.

None of them say a word, but then the Aura of Kim, the fire bug, flickers with the only spell she has the magic to cast. She's trying to summon her Familiar, finally.

Zag turns his head to her and says, "Let me make myself clear, your Familiar isn't strong enough... and it will die when it dutifully tries to come to your rescue. Now, seeing as I'm hers, I dutifully came to help. Not that she needed it. Had she reached any of you, I'd be feeding your corpse to Fluffy right now."

Zag has a form of flowery speech that you rarely see anymore. All old school, my Dragon. Amused, I lean against the sink and let him work his word magic. Plus, he's stroking my ego a little by insinuating that I would win. We both know that I wouldn't, not this time. Yes, if I can reach them it's guaranteed for me to win. But against magic, I'm toast.

I hate when Ciar is right.

CHAPTER 16

NEW FRIENDS, MORE SHOPPING...

W hen I turn the corner after leaving the shambles of a bathroom - with a grouchy Dragon perching on my shoulder, I catch myself before I run right into Lucinda. Catching her when she stumbles, I pat her shoulder and release her. She smiles at me shyly and looks at the floor before raising her eyes to mine.

"The rumor mill is saying that you and the three witches had a situation in the west bathroom."

I blink several times and look over my shoulder before turning back to her. That happened like two-seconds ago, how did they find out about it already?

Apparently, she saw the question on my face. "Magical place and all, news spreads fast." Oh, duh.

Laughing, I don't think anything of it when she falls into step beside me. She's a nice girl and I'm guessing she doesn't have many friends, either. Looking at her out of the corner of my eye I wonder why they pick on her. It's obvious she's stronger than all of them, so why let them push her around.

I ask her just that. "Why do you let them push you around when you can kick all their butts?" She laughs and even I admit the sound is a bit musical and pretty and contagious. I laugh with her.

"My family is about finding other ways of vanquishing our enemies rather than outright violence." That's right, they're pacifists.

"I saw you leaving music class, are you part of the performing group at the Mixer?" she asks.

"Yeah, are you going to it?" It'll be nice to have a familiar face there that isn't a grouchy Puca or bossy Dragon. Female friends aren't something I've had a lot of. Women can be catty and awful to each other sometimes, but we also like each other's company whether we admit it or not. I haven't had a friend that wasn't Sluagh, ever.

"Have you bought a dress yet? Ciar told me that there's a Fairy dress shop in town and I love Fairy clothing." To my own ears, my voice sounds shaky, but I know it's from being nervous. Who isn't nervous when getting to know a new potential friend? Especially someone like me who doesn't do so well with people in general.

"You want me to go with you?" Why does she sound so surprised? Who better to shop with than another woman?

"Yeah, we can get some dinner too, my treat. I'm not sure what they have there, but I'm sure it's something good." I offer.

"That'd," her voice starts out loud but lowers as she speaks. "Be great." She smiles again, holding out her cell phone.

I always forget I have one. Fumbling mine around, I manage to hand it to her and take hers. Staring at it for a full ten seconds like a dork, I reluctantly admit I have no idea what I'm doing. Laughing, she takes it from me and with a few swipes of her finger adds me to her contact list

"See you in an hour." Handing back my phone and snag-ging hers, she waves and heads down another hallway, singing to herself.

Shaking my head, I walk towards the room. I need a shower before trying on dresses, I'm covered in bathroom water.

CHAPTER 17

HE'S JUST NOT THAT INTO YOU, EVER...

When I walk into the room the vision of Ciar with only a towel wrapped around his waist, leaning back on his bed greets me. He has his phone out and is probably playing a game. I don't think he posed himself that appealingly on purpose but man, it works.

"Your bathroom problem is resolved?" he asks, without looking up from the phone screen. Rolling my eyes, I dig through the dresser and the clean clothes that someone - Gertie for sure - put away neatly. While I'm thinking about it, I put an entire box of Berry Drops on the dresser, it's the last of the ones I brought with me but she deserves them.

"My gift to you, Gertie." I say out loud, knowing she'll hear me, they're never far away.

Turning I meet green eyes, "What?"

"When do we start training you to use your magic?"

"Tomorrow?" I refuse to admit to his face, that he was right. "Lucinda is going dress shopping with us," I call over my shoulder, right before I turn the hot water on.

As soon as the steam starts rolling out I strip, tossing the clothes towards the new laundry basket in the corner of the room, I almost hit it.

"Don't be lazy now, hit the damn basket." Gertie's disembodied voice startles the crap out of me. Laughing at my chicken reaction, I walk over and pick up the clothes making sure they go into the basket this time.

"Yes ma'am," I mumble, climbing into the gloriously hot shower.

Humming to myself, I go through the normal routine, face, hair then body. The new body wash smells like cherry blossoms. The lack of chemical smell and extra kick proves that it's Fairy-made. Rinsing off, I turn to open the shower door and pause. A handprint outline is on the outside of the door, even with my chest. I stand there staring at it and find myself pressing my hand to it. I know that hand and soon I'll know it even better.

Swiping my hand through the steam on the glass door, I see him a few feet away, still in his towel. I know it's his other nature looking at me right now, so I need to be cautious. He won't hurt me, but if he touches me right now I won't be saying no. I realize that my reluctance doesn't make sense but commitment and forever and gods... he looks good in a towel.

No, no. It has to be when I'm ready to go into it with no doubts, no insecurities. For forever because sex between Ciar and I will never be, 'just sex.'

"Tell me about you. You know, the things I don't know," I say, instead of - *Take off the towel.*

"That's a long list."

"I've got a lot of time." Taking a deep breath, I see the minute he relaxes. Smiling, he turns and leaves the room, I'm assuming to get dressed. I'm hoping he's going to get dressed. For all my bluster, my will is weak. Him in a towel makes it damn near nonexistent. I want... no, *need* to make sure that I won't let him down. That I can give him everything that this commitment deserves.

Bracing myself, I grab a towel and dry my hair and body in record time. Walking out into the bedroom, I regret the choice of not bringing my clothes. I'm not shy about nudity but right now might not be the best time, for either of us.

Amazingly, he's completely dressed and once again on his phone, his mood completely relaxed. I wish I had that ability. Hurriedly dressing, I sit on the bed to comb out my hair. I swear the its longer today than yesterday.

"I had no parents, not in the traditional way." When his voice breaks the silence, I pause in my task. Sensing the importance of this moment I force myself to keep going. "I remember the second I was made. Wrapped in this cocoon of warmth and complete safety. A voice steadily whispering in my head telling me who I am, what I need to do in life."

Peeking through my hair, I watch him watching me, but he's seeing another time and another place.

"The world I was born into was different, when Faerie was its own place, and new. Gods Keri, it was beautiful and wild and completely untouched by corruption. When I opened my eyes, the Sluagh were there waiting for me and I knew - as the only one of my kind - even before clawed hands picked me up and cradled me against their furry chest, that I would lead them one day."

The phone disappears into his pocket and he scoots to the edge of the bed.

"There always has to be a balance to everything. For every true evil born there is true good. For every cruelty there is a goodness. That is why the Hunt came into existence to maintain the balance. For the most heinous of sins, there must be a punishment." Moving in that creepy, fast way he does, he's standing in front of me before I can take a breath.

"I like what I do, Keri. I was created for this task. To

bring justice to the creatures of Faerie. I hope that one day you like what you were created to do."

"This Fate Caller stuff?" I ask.

"No, the other thing you were created for, Keri." He parts the hair in front of my face, twirling a bit around his finger in the process. "Loving the Lord of the Hunt." With those words he straightens and gives me that sarcastic smirk. "Hurry up, your friend is here." Crossing to the door he opens it. She's standing on the other side with her fist in the air, her mouth open in surprise.

Laughing, I slip on some flip flops that I'm guessing are an extra pair of Ciar's, since he's wearing some and push them both out the door. A protesting Dragon lands on my shoulder and Fluffy calls forlornly from under the bed.

"Sorry buddy, maybe next time." Him in a dress shop is a big no.

Shutting and locking the door, I feel the ward lock into place as well. Ciar put it on there and If I had to guess, I'd say it's a 'do not disturb'. One that alerts him if someone tries to breach our room. I turn and practically drag Lucinda along. She laughs breathlessly.

"You're very excited to get to the shop."

"Keri is obsessed with anything Fairy. Hang around her long enough you'll see." Ciar comments, walking like he's taking a stroll through the park but somehow keeping up with our hurried pace easily.

"It's not an obsession." Okay, it is, but she doesn't need to know that.

'Don't scare her off.' I practically yell at him in my head.

'Look at how she looks at you, there is no scaring that woman off.' Disbelieving, I look over at her and she's looking over at me with a silly smile on her face. Oh. At least, it's not the other kind of smile. I love women, I think they're beautiful but not in *that* way.

A female won't be part of my Triad and since I'm alone in my head now, I only have room for my Triad in my life at the moment. Ultimately, if I have sex with someone who isn't in my Triad, there's a good chance that Ciar will kill them. Our bond is too deeply embedded now for him to respond otherwise and only requires one more component to be forever.

It's the way of such a bond. He might share me with the Triad without qualm but anyone outside of that and the hunt is on, pun intended. I accept it and have no issues with it. Now, all we are waiting for is for me to stop being a chicken.

I've heard of bonds like ours, they're unique and rare. Plus, I understand a reaction such as that, for the truth of the matter is, if he touches another intimately, I'll gut them. Just the thought makes a flicker of rage churn in my stomach. Very unlike me, but considering what I am, not so strange overall. As the saying goes, I am Fae hear me roar - or at least our version of it.

'Monster Girl, this way.' Realizing that I'm not paying a lick of attention to where we're going, I make a face and drag Lucinda with me as I fall in behind him.

"Why are you starting the Menagerie so late? I've been here since I was 13." Lucinda's shyness is wearing off to ask a question like that.

"How old are you now?"

"Twenty-four, my parents are freaking out because I haven't Awakened. I'd give anything to do it." She casts an envious look at my purple hair.

"What's it been like here for you?" I ask her, and just like that I don't have to answer her questions. It's not like I have good answers for her anyway.

"All of my siblings have either Awakened or became part of a Triad. I'm the last one left, the middle child, so I don't have the excuse of being the youngest, you know? My parents told me if I don't Awaken this year, I'm going to end up being something normal the rest of my life. Can you imagine that?"

I like the idea of being normal, but I don't have that choice anymore.

"You still have five more years, Lucinda." They don't kick anyone out until they turn thirty, if kicking them out is what they do. I'm not really sure about the process. They say they put them into a *productive environment*. When you think about it, that can mean a lot of things.

"You've been here a few weeks and already Awakened. I've been here for eleven years."

There's bitterness in her tone but also sadness.

"I'm twenty-five, Lucinda."

She frowns at my words and then her face breaks out into a brilliant smile. "I thought you were younger."

Shaking my head, I focus on the stores we're passing, she's awful happy about my age. I guess if my family really pushed the Awakening thing and I found out there's still a chance for me, I'd be happy too.

'They do not think the way we do, Keri. Awakening is everything to them. They base their value as living beings on whether or not they Awaken. Not even on how powerful they are,' Ciar explains. This is why I don't understand the way the world works the way it does. A person should be judged on their actions and by who they are, not the likelihood of their children Awakening because they did.

"Did you have a rough Awakening? I've heard that it's incredibly painful. What did your Calling turn out to be?" Her questions are asked all in a rush and I think carefully about which one to answer.

"Yes, it's painful." That's all I say. She doesn't need to know my Calling. I'm not about to tell her that Ciar held me in a bathtub of ice cold water to ease the pain, either. That's too personal.

"My siblings are Awakened but none of them have their full Triads yet. My mother does but she works with plants..." She chatters away, and I nod in the appropriate places.

My gut cautions me about answering too many questions. Maybe it's because I'm a little paranoid because of my childhood or maybe it's instinct, but either way, I'm not going to tell her anymore than I'm comfortable with.

"And here we are, ladies," Ciar says, with a flourish of his hand towards the rather nondescript storefront. Unlike the others around it, there aren't flashing Ley-lights or neon colored paints. It's a simple brick front building.

My inner Fairy lover has a feeling that walking in this door is going to be like opening a Christmas present. It's so right! Pinks and purples of gauzy fluffy heaven greet my wide-open gaze. Hands over my mouth I look around me in absolute covetous wonder.

"Greetings, I'm Adelle, how may we be of—oh, tinkletots you're a marked one. How fabulous that you've come to our establishment." The petite Fairy with translucent pink - oh, my Faerie yes - wings greets me with a smile of pure welcome.

She barely comes up to my waist, her hair is long and wavy and as pink as her wings. Her eyes are huge in her delicate face, a brilliant green haloed with long dark lashes.

My mouth snaps shut as her words hit home. Marked one? This is not the first time a Fairy has used this term with me and I have no idea what the it means.

"What do you mean marked one?" I ask, as she grabs my hand and leads me towards the back of the store.

"A Fairy put a mark on your Aura that says you are to be protected by Fairy kind. It's nothing to worry about, sugar, only Fairies can see it - and that handsome Puca who is watching me like the sexy monster he is." Before I can stop myself, I bare my teeth at her. Smiling, she pats my arm,

"There, there. I have no want of your Puca. I'm too delicate for the likes of him."

True facts, if mating with him didn't kill her, I would. Gods, what's wrong with me? I see the self-satisfied smile split Ciar's face, he's happy with whatever it is.

'Out of my head, dog-breath.' His chuckle gives me goose-bumps as he takes a seat in a chair, facing me.

"Now, what type of function do you need to be dressed for, sweets? We can provide any type of clothing you desire." She steers me towards the pedestal they measure you on and disappears in a cloud of glitter only to reappear seconds later.

"A Mixer at the Menagerie," I tell her, staring openly as tape measures start twirling around me like snakes.

"You're a tall one, but it suits you. Now we need a dress that shows off those long legs of yours." Muttering numbers and measurements she starts fluttering around me, adjusting my arms and legs as she sees fit.

Fairies wings look tissue-paper delicate and, in some ways, like a butterfly's wings. They even have dust on them, just like butterflies. Also like them, Fairies come in all different sizes and colors. Giggling, I wink at Lucinda who's still wearing a bright smile and a look of awe on her face as she looks around the store.

I'm sure I look the same way, probably worse when we first walked in.

"Do you have a particular color you wish to request?" Adelle asks, watching the steady marching line of fabric as a sheath of it stretches out beside of my head.

"Not really. I figure you're the one who knows the most about that. You know, the purple hair and all?" She pauses in her task and smiles up at me.

"Now then, is your friend also seeking a gown?" I look over at Lucinda who nods while clapping her hands in excitement. I climb off the pedestal and go to sit beside Ciar.

"Keri, does your family live in town?" Lucinda asks, and instantly I shift in discomfort.

Clearing my throat, I say, "They used to."

"Oh, does that mean they still own property here?" That's a good question and something I wouldn't ask someone, but I guess this is part of the getting to know each other phase of friendship.

"Yes, but it's been a long time since I was there."

"We should totally go there one day. You can live off campus and have of the freedom you'd have in your own home." Blinking slowly, I shift in the chair my shoulder resting against Ciar's.

"I'm not sure that's a good idea." I know it's not a good idea, the mild curiosity I might have over the old house isn't enough to drive me into going there. "Too many bad memories."

"Bad memories?" Her eyes hold a soft emotion as she says it. She continues, "I can understand that, but you're letting bad memories keep you from moving forward. I figured you for a stronger person than that."

Straightening in my chair, I fight the urge to stand up and walk out, but she smiles at me in such an understanding way that I relax. Apparently, she doesn't mean it to be as insulting as it sounds.

'Maybe this is someone you shouldn't befriend.'

Ignoring Ciar's warning, I lean my elbows on my knees and study Lucinda. She looks apologetic, which proves true as she says, "I'm sorry, Keri. I didn't mean that to sound like that. I guess I see you as this super-hero, and to find out that you have emotional baggage like everyone else surprises me."

"No one is without baggage."

"That's the truth. I still think we should go. Maybe you can get a good look at it and see whether it's worth selling or not."

'*She might actually be onto something there, Keri. Property here can be valuable.*'

I'm not sure if its Ciar agreeing with her or my own morbid curiosity, but I find myself agreeing. "Yeah, you're right. We'll go this weekend."

"Yes! My family will be out of town on holiday." Well, I'm glad she's so excited about it.

"Right then, you're all done Mage. You can both come and pick up your dresses Monday afternoon." Adelle turns to me and smiles, then disappears behind some curtains.

That's our cue to leave.

"So, Lucinda, tell me about you. Any hot boyfriends or girlfriends hiding somewhere?" She blushes and ducks her head as we walk out of the dress shop. This is a sure sign she either has a crush or a significant other. Now I'm curious who the shy Lucinda has the hots for.

"Spill the beans," I tease her, wrapping my arm through hers. She giggles and steers us towards one of the restaurants nearby.

"Well, he's in my history class," Oh, it's a crush. "I'm thinking about asking him to be my plus one for the Mixer, but I haven't gotten the courage yet."

"What's he like?"

"He's human, obviously." What's this? "He has red hair, but I think it looks perfect on him. Our dads work together for the Senate, so I've known him my entire life. We even used to hang out when we were younger..." As she talks about this mystery redhead, her eyes sparkle and a smile stays on her face.

That's not why I'm watching her, I'm doing it because of the human comment. Did she forget what I am? When she leans on my shoulder companionably, I let the weird worry go and just enjoy myself. This is something I haven't had a lot of and it's fun.

Ciar walks behind us like a shadow. He hasn't said anything since the shop, but I can feel him thinking hard. Zag is awake and watching Lucinda, his thoughts are closed to me, but I don't feel any hostility coming off him.

Lucinda is still chattering about 'Mark' the redhead – who's name she finally mentioned. She chooses the restaurant with a point of her finger and since I see no reason not to, we go in. We're greeted by a cheerful teenager who looks like every wholesome teenager you see on the TV programs. I smile at her while she steers us towards a table near the kitchen. It's a bit warm outside so the cool air-conditioning feels nice on my skin. While I cool off, I look around for any type of anti-Fae jargon, seeing none I relax.

I look over at Ciar who isn't sweating at all, lucky dog. Lucinda's face is slightly red and glistening from our brief walk. Which shows that she's a bit out of shape, I'm hot but not winded like she appears to be. She doesn't look it, but her body is telling on her. I don't want to see my new friend get ill, maybe we could exercise together – wait, is that offensive to ask?

'Let her be the one to offer, humans are odd about those things.' Okay, I think he's right this time and he's also eavesdropping a lot. A quick check shows me my shields are nonexistent again. Is that his doing or mine?

We order our food and chat about the school and Lucinda's family, who are not nice people, while we wait for it. It comes faster than I expected. Lucinda ordered bird food. All that is on her plate is a piece of fish smaller than a domino and a floret of broccoli, that's it. Seriously? I have to figure out how to get her to eat real food.

Seeing me staring, she takes a small bit out of the fish and blushes. "My mom makes me take measurements of my waist. She says that no man will have a fat woman who hasn't Awakened."

Wow, just wow.

"She sounds like a great person." Sarcasm is thick in my voice, but Lucinda doesn't pick up on it.

"Oh, yes. She Awakened in her teens, so she's held in high esteem in our social circles." I blink at her and nibble at the burger I ordered, feeling guilty about what I have to eat compared to her speck of food. "And my dad is sought out often for his opinion on government matters."

"Is he part of her Triad?" I ask, raising my drink to my lips.

"My mother doesn't have a Triad." Lucinda frowns at me while I choke on a mouthful of tea. Holding my hand up in apology, I wave for her to continue. "She had a Triad, but the other two members weren't equal to my dad's caliber. They were cast out."

Now, I don't know everything there is to know about Triads, but I do know that you can't cast out a member. You can have a normal relationship with them, you can even live separately, but you can't get rid of them. There's only one thing that can do that, premature death. Typically, all members die at the same time or near the same time. It's the connection between them. How did her mother survive the deaths of two of her Triad?

Unless... "Where did they get sent off to?"

"They were locked up by the Senate for crimes against the crown." So not dead, imprisoned. From the description she gave of her father, it's not hard to imagine that he did it on purpose. That also crippled their Triad.

I don't understand humans.

Lucinda keeps talking and I give up the guilt and eat my food. Mark comes up again and by the end of it, I'm ready to strangle the guy. I know she's not subtle in her attraction to him. She says flat out that she stares at him and giggles around him. Unless he's an idiot, he knows. Either he is shy like her or he's not interested.

"When are you going to ask him to the Mixer?"

"This weekend. He's staying in from visiting family too. Maybe after we get back from exploring your old house, I'll go see if I can build up the courage to ask him."

"I'm sure he'll say yes." Smiling at her, I take another drink to wash the lie out of my mouth. I'm not sure at all.

CHAPTER 18

FIRST LOVE ON THE MENU...

We spent several hours wandering around town checking out various shops and laughing a lot. It's been a long time since I had that kind of fun and I'm sad to see it end. Lucinda is yawning behind her hand, obviously tired. We walk her back to her dorm and she hugs me at the door.

"Thank you for the great day. I've never had that much fun," she says, giving a little wave she shuts the door and we head to our own room.

Changing into my pajamas, a tank top and shorts, I climb onto my bed and watch Ciar strip off his shirt and pants - disappointingly he's wearing boxers - and put on a pair of shorts.

Zag gives me a kiss on the cheek with a flick of his tongue and disappears out the window to go fly. Fluffy is snoring under the bed and that leaves Ciar and I basically alone.

"Are you sure you're comfortable going to the house?" he asks into the quiet.

I figured this question was coming. "She's not wrong, it really is time I deal with it. Like you said, maybe I can sell the property, if nothing else." Mada gave me money but I won't mind having my own.

"Have you considered living there? It was a long time ago." Having our own place, especially considering the addition of more of us wouldn't be horrible.

"I hadn't, but it gives me something to think about. True privacy might be nice. Living here makes me feel like I'm always being watched."

"You mostly are."

"Way to encourage my paranoia." He chuckles and rolls on his side to face me.

"Do you still want to know about me?"

"Of course I do." There's no way I'm missing this chance to get to know who he is as a man and not just the Lord of the Hunt. "Spill."

"As you well know, growing up with the Sluagh is an adventure. My childhood was a happy one. I even fancied myself in love once."

Oh, just, oh.

Clearing my suddenly choked throat I ask, "What happened to her?"

"I ate her."

"I'm sorry, what?"

"She broke the laws of Faerie and was hunted." Blinking several times, I try to wrap my head around what he's telling me.

"Didn't that upset you?"

"Gods, no. She tried to kill me. As it turned out, it was all some big set up by the king to usurp my position in the Hunt."

Licking my dry lips, I ask the question that's burning on my tongue. "Did you still love her when you ate her?"

"No, like I said - I fancied myself in love. I discovered her treachery rather early on and spent several weeks manipulating her into giving me all of her conspirators."

"Wow, Ciar - just, wow." Another question pops into my head and right out of my mouth. "What if I break the law of Faerie?" Those green eyes of his flash in the darkness of our room.

"Then we die together, because there is no force in existence that can make me or the Sluagh hunt you."

"How would we die then, if the Hunt doesn't hunt me?"

"There would be consequences for my refusal." Well, then. "I'm the only Puca in existence and sometimes that makes me feel lonely - made me feel lonely. I haven't felt that way since I met you." I suspected he was the only one but didn't know for sure, now I do. I have no idea what to think about the second half, I feel the same way.

"Were you and Mada ever intimate?" It's a question I've wanted to ask for a long time and well, now's a good of time as any. His guffaw of laughter is not the answer I expect.

"I'd rather eat glass then sleep with that woman. Mada isn't what I'd call easy to get along with." he says, laughing. Then His laughter dies down. "Why would you ask something like that?"

"Well, you know, both of you in the woods for a million years together..."I feel relieved when he starts laughing again. I'm incredibly glad they didn't have sex because I'm not sure how I'd process that. Mada is a lot like a mother to me and that'd be weird.

"My turn. Why are you so obsessed with Fairies?" That's a hard change of subject and it's only right that I answer.

"Peter, my nanny was a Fairy. He was a huge part of my early life." I smile picturing him in my mind. "He had bright green hair that always reminded me of spring grass and I loved to play in it. It's how I learned to braid. He's the first memory I have, his bright green hair and green eyes are forever cemented into my memory. He always had a smile for me." My smile fades but I continue, "My mother hated him but for some reason let him stay. I didn't ask why."

Throat tight with the fading memory of his laughter, I take a breath, and continue, "He taught me to hunt, to be patient and he taught me to laugh. Despite the circumstances. Back then, Peter was my whole world. When she went super nutso and came after me, he got in between us, but whatever Fae she was... way out-classed a Fairy - no matter how strong he was." Swiping at the hot tear rolling down my cheek, I keep going while I can.

"He died, and it distracted her enough to stop stabbing me. The Sluagh... you and the Sluagh who found me might have saved my life then, but he saved it first. I still miss him to this day."

"I'm sorry, monster girl. I'd kill her again if I could." A snotty snort escapes me, and I use the distraction to wipe the rest of the tears off my face. His proclamation is one of the sweetest things ever said to me.

"So, what was the name of this chick you loved and then ate? Should I be jealous?" His chuckle floats through the darkness and the warmth that fills my chest makes the sadness fade.

"Na, she was boney and a bit tough. You'll be juicy and tender." If only my aim were better, the pillow I threw at him might have smacked him in that smug face of his.

"Ha, so funny. Now, about that plant in music class."

"Some creatures have hidden from others for a long time. I suggest patience and the answers you seek will be found."

Cryptic much?

"You're not done with share time already are you?"

He chuckles again, and his soothing voice once again fills the room. "The first time I had sex, I was so nervous and excited I tried to put it in her belly button..."

CIAR USED MAGIC ON ME, HE HAD TO HAVE. WHY ELSE DID I fall asleep mid-sex story? There's no way I'd miss that otherwise. The sneaky butt-head. Rubbing the sleep out of my eyes I sit up and blink at the empty bed across from me. He didn't go far, I can hear the shower running. My bladder is not happy about it, either. With a smile of pure evil, I go into the bathroom and quickly do my business.

"Keri, are you peeing?" As if this is something new?

"Yep." Standing, I flush the toilet and laugh when he yells at me. The dorm has a shared water tank, when you flush a toilet the showers let you know. Just to be a dick, I flush it again while I'm washing my hands with hot water.

A wet washcloth makes a splat sound when it connects with the back of my head. In retaliation, I flush again, looking over my shoulder to vaguely see a soapy Ciar pressed as far away from the spray of water as possible.

Ha.

"Payback is a bitch, Keri." he warns me as I turn the cold water on to brush my teeth. Laughing, I at least hurry it along and leave him cursing at me in the shower that's trying to boil him alive.

What an awesome way to start the day.

CHAPTER 19

CUPCAKES AND CARDIAC ARREST...

F amiliar class leaves me feeling a bit sick to my stomach. Mr. Sputen gave out cupcakes and I couldn't resist them, so I ate two. Which shouldn't make my stomach feel this way. Since they've tried to poison me before, I should have been more cautious and checked them. Instead, I was stupid and trusted the source because it was from a teacher.

Gods, that was a dumb thing to do.

Ciar is strangely absent, he's probably on a Hunt. Something he'll always have to do, Ciar IS the Hunt. Those can call him away without warning, he literally disappears - he's done it mid-sentence before. Zag is snoozing and Fluffy is back in the room.

Something doesn't feel right.

"Zag, wake up, I think the cupcakes were poisoned." The room starts to spin as he raises his head in alarm and immediately hops onto the floor and starts to grow to his natural size. "Zag, not in the room!" He'll bust the walls out at his full size. He's already decimated a bathroom and an entire hallway.

Cold sweat breaks out all over my body, this isn't good.

Zag roars and I feel the room tipping sideways. My vision starts to get wonky, well, there's pretty colors everywhere at least. Putting my head down on the desk, I hope it's enough to keep me from falling out of my chair.

"She needs medical attention, NOW!" The last word is another roar and several people scream. I keep my head on the desk and pray for the room to stop moving like I'm being shaken in a bottle. A warm snout sniffs near my face. "Who dares?" he growls out, his big head hovering over me protectively.

"The healer is on her way, back to her Blank Space, Dragon!" Mr. Sputen orders. I laugh, or try to laugh, it might be coughing. I want to laugh, does that count?

"Make me, Mage." Oh, there's a lot of threat in that sentence. This time I do giggle, I hear it. Actually, I hear it more than once, it's echoing. Uh-oh, everything is echoing.

"Mistressssssss." I giggle again, I wonder how he'd feel if I told him he sounds like a snake right now. An echoing snake in a long tunnel.

"What the fuck is wrong with her?" Ciar's familiar voice demands as he wraps me in the warmth of his arms. I promptly throw up all over him.

"So-sorry... cu-cupcakes." I stutter out, it's cold, like blizzard cold, teeth chattering and all.

If only I can open my eyes, so I can tell him about the echoes and cupcakes. I try to no avail, I'm not even sure when they closed. My body heaves and I feel horrible about throwing up on him again, I can smell it, but nothing I try to do works.

I'm flopping around like a rag doll.

A loud crash is followed by a snarling growl that's so flipping awesome I smile, or I try to smile. My lips are rather numb, like the rest of my face and - hey, my arms are numb too. Be a super great time for a nap right now. A sharp slap to my cheek floods my mouth with the taste of blood. Which is better than the taste of puke, but I can't even swallow it. I want to tell Ciar things, but words are hard.

"Monster Girl, you wake your ass up right fucking now!" I want to listen, opening my eyes seems important somehow. But the colors...

"Ciar, she is fading fast, they hid it with Fairy magic." Oh no, Fairies won't hurt me, Peter promised 'never hurt by a Fairy.' But Peter died and left me. Bad Peter.

Oh, moving again. The colors are going down in the dark tunnel, I want to touch them.

"Don't you dare, Keri. I'll kill every single person in this fucking school, I swear it." A heartbeat is loud in my ear. "Wake up so you can stop me. Wake up Keri, because if you die I can't go. Your fucking Triad isn't complete. I'm going to kill that idiot, hiding like he is." Ciar's words start to run together and some sensible part of my brain should try and remember them, but the colorful tunnel is calling me.

CHAPTER 20
MIND BLOWN, LEGS SMOOTH...

The white magic is pretty, not as pretty as the colors but - hey, why is it grabbing me? Hey! That hurts! Pain fills me like a hive of angry bees. Yelling as my eyes jerk open, I fight to keep in another one as agony flashes hot through me. Taking gasping breaths, I fight to relax, hoping that'll ease it.

For the first few seconds the room is blurry but then it comes into focus. The healer is shoved to the side as Ciar's worried face pops into view and an almost full-sized Dragon blocks out the rest of the room.

"Keri?"

"Hi," my voice is hoarse. "Fancy meeting you here." A glass of water appears as he lifts my shoulders for me to sit up enough to drink. I notice he's not wearing a shirt. Drinking it greedily, I wait for him to refill it and I chug it too. Feeling a bit better, I sigh when he lays me down again.

"Why do you smell like puke?" Why do I smell like puke?

"Because you puked on both of us." He says it as an afterthought while he uses a claw, I'm sure the gaping healer sees, to cut off my smelly shirt. My bra is next and then a warm cloth replaces them.

"I'm sorry," I say, as bits and pieces of what happened before I passed out start to coalesce in my head. The healer yanked me out of near-death-land, because I don't doubt I was dying.

Actually, I'm pretty sure that I puked more than once. That's some love right there, him cleaning puke off me. Wait, love? The warm cloth pauses, and I meet his gaze.

Yes, he loves me. There's not a single shred of doubt about it.

The cloth begins to move again, and I decide to not comment about the love thing, not yet. I'll do that when I don't smell like vomit-y cupcakes and have more clothes on. Or am at least naked in better circumstances.

"Who's hiding?" I ask. He shakes his head, a smile on his face. Is that relief I see? It looks like relief. I wonder if I take him out for a steak dinner if it will make up for the puke?

"The other two idiots of your Triad. You - unfortunately - called ones who don't know how to act civilized. No matter how strong they are."

"You're a Puca who eats people." I say deadpan. He full on laughs and then gently wipes off my face and neck.

"I can pretend to be civilized, Keri. We'll talk about this later, soon enough they'll show themselves." He turns to the healer, "I need a blanket to wrap her in... you're dismissed."

"You should be nice to her, she saved my life," I chastise.

"She barely saved your life, I had to give her a bit of encouragement. She informed me you were too close to death to save." Well, that explains his short temper with her.

Still, "Thank you for saving my life." After a fearful glance at Ciar she nods and practically runs from the room.

"Why didn't you check your food, Keri?" I shrug, or at least I try to. My shoulders are stiff and tender and don't want to move.

"Cupcakes, who blasphemes them in such a way?"

"Apparently, whoever is trying to kill you." Yeah, we both know I was dumb not to. "I think we need to go to the house early, it might be safer for you there."

"I promised Lucinda she could go." He gives me a dirty look but still wraps me in the blanket like I'm a fragile piece of glass. It's sweet, annoying, but sweet.

"Fine, but Saturday morning instead of later," he insists.

"Okay, okay. Can we go to the room now? I need a shower and to sleep awhile I think." Healing requires rest, the healers can only do so much before your own body needs to kick in and do the rest of the work.

Lifting me into his arms like I'm a feather, he carries me in a brisk walk to our dorm room. I'm pretty sure I nap most of the way considering I don't remember the trip.

Staring at the shower from his arms, I sigh in defeat. There's no way I can stand right now, and a bath is a drowning waiting to happen. I feel his eyes roll. Stripping me down, he sets me on the lip of the tub and strips his clothes off. It's nothing I haven't seen before, but I stare anyhow. Wow.

Reaching past me he turns on the taps and waits for steam to come rolling out of the door. Lifting me up, he steps into the shower and I sigh in absolute bliss. Setting me on my unsteady feet, he keeps me in between him and the wall as he thoroughly washes my body and then helps me wash my hair.

No dilly dally time today, he washes himself just as fast and before I know it I'm dry and wrapped in my warm robe. Ciar is my hero, especially when he crawls into the bed with me pulling me into his strong, safe embrace.

Zag appears out of nowhere and curls up around my head, his throat vibrating against me with little warbles of worry as he strokes my neck with his tail. It's adorable. Love you too, bud.

Sleep isn't gentle as she pulls me under in seconds.

AT SOME POINT, THE WARMTH SURROUNDING ME IN A cocoon of tranquility disappears. Of course, I roll over and go back to sleep only to be woke up later by him climbing back in bed with me smelling like copper and fear. Snuggling back into the comfort of his arms, I sigh. Yeah, I'm pretty sure he went out and hurt someone. But right now? I don't care.

There are two things that can pull me abruptly from a good dream, only two. Imminent danger and Brownie Baked Bacon. The smell is so close to my face I wonder if I can just open my mouth and it'll fall in?

"You're not a baby bird. Get up, we've got stuff to do." The pillow disappears out from under my head and the wonderful, mouth-watering smell of bacon vanishes.

"Nooo." My eyes pop open as I sit up, seeking out the source of the heavenly smell. A brown bag, smelling so good I literally start to drool, appears under my nose. I snag it before Ciar changes his mind. Inside it are bacon stuffed biscuits that are so fresh they crumble when I bite into one.

Pausing mid-mouthful, I eye him, and ask, "Why are you buttering me up?"

"It's Saturday." The food in my mouth loses all its flavor, when I swallow it feels like a bunch of rocks going down.

Since the 'PI', 'puke incident', sleeping and occasionally eating have been my only activities. The cupcakes were stuffed with Faebane in an incredibly high dose, masked with magic, so Zag says. This time it wasn't just the poison, there was a spell locked in there too. A small, happy spell to keep me from fighting off the symptoms. All those pretty colors were trying to help kill me.

Today we're going to go to my old house, to all those old memories and I'd rather face those killer colors again than go.

"Can I take a sick day?" His eyes fill with sympathy, but his mouth tells me no.

"It's past time, Keri. You've avoided it for a long time and as much as I hate agreeing with your Mage friend, the time for putting it off has ended." Folding the bag down I set it aside and climb to my feet.

"You don't care for her, do you?" The carpet feels rough on my bare feet as I walk towards the bathroom. It's clean of course. Because Gertie has been here, but the carpet isn't meant for comfort. Why have I never noticed this? We've been here for weeks.

"No," he finally answers.

Digging around, I gather my toothbrush and toothpaste. "Any particular reason?" I stand in the doorway brushing my teeth while watching him and Gertie - who appears from nowhere, I might add - gather our things into bags. All our things.

"Something about her feels off, but you like her so I'll reserve my judgement."

"Why are you packing our stuff?" Bits of toothpaste fly out of my mouth landing on Zag who's hovering in front of me. As he complains and flies past me to the sink, I flick his tail.

He's in on this too.

Stomping back to the sink I spit and rinse, all to the protests of the Dragon perched on the side of the sink and ultimately in the way of some of the spit. "I'm sorry Zag. Here." I clean him off and make sure I stomp louder when I walk out of the bathroom. Ciar needs to hear how unhappy I am about these plans he made without talking to me about them.

The bad dog!

"Keri, I understand you're not thrilled with this idea but," he pulls Fluffy out from under the bed. No wonder he hasn't been his normal blubby self. The sneak cocooned! "We can put wards on the house and we can defend from there. Keri, we need a home because we aren't going back to the forest."

Wait, what?

"Why aren't we going home?" I demand, breaking down and helping him wrap Fluffy's cocoon in a sleeping bag.

I suspected this but hearing the reality of it makes my heart hurt.

"Mada is moving the forest. There's a threat looming on the horizon and for the forest's safety they have to be hidden." After zipping the bag, I sit on the edge of the bed. Why didn't anyone tell me?

"There's a power struggle among the Elders - the king is making some choices that are making quite a few of them angry."

"But you're a -"

"No, I'm your Pinnacle." He sits down beside of me. "They all send their love and will come and visit. Now about this move - soon there will be two more additions and where exactly will we put them?" Logic? He's using bona-fide logic? How dare he.

So I reach, and I reach hard. "They're slinking around hiding, so why do you care where they sleep? They're too ashamed of me to show themselves." Okay, perhaps I reached a bit deep inside myself and ended up with stuff that's true.

A side effect of this whole Awakening business is I can feel them out there. The threads lead out away from me, one blue, one gold, connecting to some unknown person on the other end. The difference is, the link between Ciar and I pulses with magic and life, while the other two are there but still and dim.

"It has nothing to do with shame," he leans his shoulder against mine. "If I had not known you as I d,, I would've have kept a distance and watched. Waited until I knew my reception would be received. It is not you they're ashamed of, it is your reaction to them."

"How do you know this?"

"Only someone like me can survive someone... like me." I can't refute his explanation and I see no reason for him to lie to me.

"Are you saying they're both Pucas?" I can't help it, I have to tease him.

"No, they're different but the same too." This makes me look at him. He's watching me closely.

"Are you telling me that the other two are rare and potentially the only ones of their kind in existence?" Smiling, he bops my nose with his fingertip and climbs again to his feet. That doesn't tell me if I'm right or wrong, the enigmatic pain in my butt.

Watching him pack the bathroom things in plastic bags and then into a box I realize something. If I'm completely against it, I'll fight tooth and nail. Concerning the house, my protests are weak at best and the dread I'm feeling isn't nearly as bad as it would've been even five years ago.

Maybe I'm ready to face my demons because he's right. It's past time. And having more than one bathroom is a perk too.

"Gertie, are you okay with us having a house?" She pops out of the closet, a big smile brightening her face.

"Oh yes, my dear. I can bring my family now." Gods, I didn't think of her family, Brownies typically travel in family groups - I'm an idiot.

"Of course, all of them if you please. There's a guest house that you can live in - make it your own." Her eyes grow rounder and then fill with tears.

Gods, what did I do wrong? Little arms squeeze my neck in a hug and after a moment of confusion, I hug her back. Releasing me she pats my cheek and disappears, along with all our packed things - including Fluffy.

"Did I do something wrong?" I ask the empty air.

"You gave her a house, that's a big deal to a Brownie. It means they never have to leave it," Zag explains, twining around my shoulders. The minty smell of toothpaste emanates from him. I know it's bad of me to laugh at something that I caused but I can't help it. My Dragon smells like a piece of gum.

He blows smoke at me, but I can feel his humor. At least, my Familiars have senses of humor because they're going to need it to be around me.

Okay, I can do this. Standing, I slip on my shoes and head towards the door before I change my mind. Ciar is close behind me, his presence like a blast of heat against my body. The heavy cloud that lingers at the Menagerie lifts as soon as we walk through the gate. Taking a deep breath, I choose to enjoy the walk while I can.

Summer is starting to wind down, so the air is a pinch cooler than it has been. The leaves are starting to turn into those golden browns and vivid oranges that paint the landscape like a dream. Fall is one of my favorite seasons. In the forest the trees sing as they shed their leaf skins. Their songs filling the night sky, lulling me to sleep, is one of the best memories I have.

Smiling, I link my arm through Ciar's and slow my pace, there's no need to hurry. The house isn't going anywhere and although I accept - easier than I thought I would, that I need to deal with things. It doesn't mean I'm in a hurry. Ciar, sensing my need to go slow, stops for ice cream and to watch a street play put on by Gnomes while we enjoy our treat. Arms still linked, we sit companionably until the end and when I start to stand as the small crowd clears, he keeps me seated.

"My favorite color is purple - I think it's because of the heather that bloomed near my home as a child. My favorite food is butterscotch pudding. I can eat an entire package of it in one sitting. The belly button victim is the one I ultimately lost my virginity to, she was a Fairy. I was thirteen years old and I imagine she was much older than that. She also tried to enrapture me with magic and was incredibly disappointed when one of the Sluagh caught her in the process and I dealt with her accordingly."

Which roughly translates to the part where he ate her.

"I, like you, love music and am gifted with the ability to sing." Gods, is he good. Still, I remain silent and let him continue. "I think it has something to do with your Calling." He continues on, sharing stories of his adventures and how he always watched and waited, sensing there was something greater coming for him.

"Everything else you know." Now he stands and pulls me to my feet, tucking my arm in his again.

"How can being a Pinnacle be greater than the Hunt?" He gets to do something incredible and adventurous.

"The Hunt is rather boring. Someone commits a crime - they run and we always find them and then... they die. It's unchanging and tedious and there's no challenge to it anymore. But," he smiles his toothy smile and pats my hand. "Being with you is always a challenge."

I can't refute it.

When he stops, I find out that we've already arrived at my childhood home. I look up at it in trepidation. Stark white with blue trim, it looks so alone and sad underneath it's dressing of brush. The weeds are overgrown and obstruct the front yard and windows from view, while vines are crawling up the walls and digging in the spaces between the siding. Other than that, the house looks the same. Even the house number above the mailbox is still leaning slightly to the right. The formerly red letters faded and barely legible.

Gertie pops into existence.

"We'll have this right as rain in no time, don't you worry," she says and disappears again.

My feet are like concrete blocks as Ciar leads me slowly but determinedly towards the front door. On the mailbox is a blue handprint. Peter and I were painting, and he told me to mark this place as my own. The door opens and the creak sound echoes in my head. Taking a deep bracing breath, I push myself to take the final steps, entering the house for the first time since I was dragged out.

Against my will, my eyes seek out the bloodstains that should be on the floor, in the very spot where I stand. Something inside of me relaxes when I see nothing. Releasing my death grip on Ciar's arm, I run a finger over the bannister to the stairway. A thick layer of dust coats the tip of it. The pictures that used to hang on the walls of my mother are gone. Leaving squares of discoloration in their wake.

The knickknacks and statues that I detested no longer line the shelves along the entranceway. Someone knew these things would impact me, so someone took them away. I bet that someone is standing beside me. Their removal looks recent. Walking through the hallway into the formal living room, I stare at the cloth covered furniture. She loved the velvet junk. Our food money was spent on things like this. Luxurious things that didn't fill our bellies but instead gave her some false sense of worth.

Her worth was all that mattered to her.

"Zag, can you go scout around the perimeter of the property?" Ciar requests, and with a nuzzle of his scaly head, Zag shoots out the doorway. "We can get rid of it all, start over."

Nodding, I turn away and head towards the kitchen. Crossing it quickly, I avoid the dent in the counter and wall. That is where it started. But it is not my destination, that is a small room off the kitchen that isn't much bigger than our bathroom at the dorm. This was my room. The maid's quarters. I'm only half surprised to discover that everything is smashed beyond repair, even the bed and bedding are shredded. My mother vented her rage here. The claw marks down the wall are testimony to her inhuman nature that she hid so well from me.

These things need going through, but I can't do it yet.

Turning away, I wander through the other rooms in the house, it's not a large house so it doesn't take me long. Peter's room is strangely untouched and I merely stand in the doorway, staring into it. Shutting the door, I let the tears roll down my face unchecked. This grief needs to be let out, it's time.

When I've bawled myself out, I scrub my hand over my face and continue on. The last room left is the one I dread the most, my mother's. The door is locked, but a swift kick from Ciar takes care of that issue. The door flings open, banging against the wall, sending something made of glass tumbling to the ground to break in the silence in the room.

Good, I hope it all breaks.

Her bed is perfectly made with silk sheets and the most expensive down pillows. A comforter hand-made by some royal seamstress is folded neatly across the end of the bed. The red silken dressing gown she'd pet like a dog is tossed artfully over the center of the bed.

The closet is open showing rows of expensive dresses and shelves of shoes and jewelry. Those I can sell and will. Nothing of hers will remain here and I need the money to remodel.

I know exactly who I can call for help with that. Calsis, a Leprechaun. He's shrewd and greedy but incredibly honest. He'll squeeze every penny of value out of these items if for no other reason than to get a bigger share.

"Keri, you need to see this." Frowning, I turn to Ciar who is looking at something on the vanity which is lined with expensive perfumes and cosmetics. Closing the distance between us, I look down to find a manila envelope with one sentence on it in an aching familiar scrawl, Peter's.

When the bitch is dead you must watch this Keri.

How did Peter leave this? Hand shaking, I run a finger across the writing. There's dust on the envelope so it's been here awhile.

"Fairies are a tight knit community, this was left by someone who knew him," Ciar explains, rubbing my shoulders with warm hands.

Picking it up I open it. Inside is a round DVD. They haven't used these for decades. Good thing for us, my mother was against the more modern times and kept all types of old technology. Marching to her closet, I dig through her useless dresses until I find the box in the back.

Dusting it off, I leave the room and go in search of the TV in the family room. Ha, family. Finding it, I pull the cover sheet off and sigh in relief when the lights kick on and the TV blares to life. Ciar, reading my mind again. He joins me right as I plug the player in and push the disc into it.

Laughter fills the room around us as the first image pops onto the screen. A young, smiling version of my mother - a very Fae version of my mother. Her hair is blue, a bright ocean blue and her eyes match. And the man she wraps her arms around - his hair is down the middle of his back, a dark purple that makes mine look even lighter. The camera is stationary, and his back is to it but slowly, so slowly, he turns and vivid mismatched eyes crinkle at the corners as he smiles into the camera.

Pain lances my chest and I sit back on the floor, shocked. It doesn't take a genius to figure out he's my father, I look just like the man. The same slope of my forehead, the same small nose, I even have the same mouth. And the eyes are identical. Even those fade as I take in the entire face. Now I know exactly why they're trying to kill me. There's a symbol on his forehead, a hated one that can put fear in even the bravest creatures. It's a Mark of the Moon, not just a mark, it's the mark of a priest. My father is a high-priest of the Moon Clan.

Faerie is only one part of the spectrum, she is the goddess of creation, but she is not the only god of Fae. No, there is another. Checks and balances. The opposite of creation, of life. Donn, the god of the World of the Dead.

Fudge. Fudge. *Fuck*.

My father investigates the camera and it feels like he's looking right at me. Black washes over his eyes before they return to normal - and I can see it there in his eyes - he's old, so old. My father is a First Generation, I can tell by looking at him.

He turns away from the camera back to my mother and the feast laid out on the checkered tablecloth. "Hilda, what's the happy occasion?" he asks her in a voice that can melt ice. My mother smiles, showing the beauty that I saw the ghost of in her face, looking uncommonly happy and full of life. She pulls his hand down to her stomach.

He searches her face for a moment and then kneels to rest his cheek against it. "My child shall be glorious," he whispers. Standing, he kisses my mother once on the cheek and continues, "You have served me well, Hilda. This child shall be stronger than all my other children. You must be protected and moved."

The smile disappears off her face, to be replaced with a

frown that I know from experience means something bad is coming. He continues to rub her still flat stomach, entranced.

Apparently, that's not what she was expecting to hear. Her eyes alight and focus on him like she's going to shoot lightning bolts out of them any second. The love in them is fading to be replaced by hate.

"What do you mean other children, Daya?" she demands.

"You didn't think you were the only one, did you?" He laughs, and when she tries to pull away, he grabs her wrists tugging her against him. "I've searched for centuries for the right woman to bear my fated child. You are that woman and as long as you carry the child, I will protect you and cherish you above all others."

"What happens after the child is born?" Right here is where my life became destined to suck. This is the defining moment of her hatred of me.

"She is all that matters. You are merely the womb." I see the second my mother realizes that he doesn't love her, right as I see the moment her eyes go dead and empty. The eyes I remember.

"You dare cast me aside for progeny?" Things start to fly as my mother's true form emerges. Her blue hair darkens, her skin fades until it is a washed-out gray, her height increases, and long black claws grow out of her fingernail beds. Teeth as vicious as any piranha, push out of her gums, bright white and razor sharp. Wow, my mother is a Graywalker.

"I do not fear you forsaken child of Faerie, but I will not let you destroy the child." Daya's voice booms and I can nearly feel the magic of the spell I hear unleashed as he uses his power word. *Exist*. So close to mine that it's scary and there's no way it's a coincidence.

Somehow, I know what the spell is, she can't abort me from her womb. She can't kill me. I don't understand... I rewind the movie and listen to the seconds while he casts the spell. No mortal weapons, that's what he mutters. The dagger wasn't from a mortal, that's why she needed it - and why she tried to kill me with it.

The camera falls over and other than Daya's laughter and my mother's screeches of anger, there are no other sounds. The camera goes black and the movie stops playing.

My mother is a Graywalker. They're all evil, every single one of them. My father is a Moon Clan high priest, an elder to boot. I'm still not sure of his true heritage, but weakness doesn't survive in the Moon Clan. I'm so screwed.

"Keri, I must -" With a growl of fury Ciar disappears, the Hunt calls.

A knock makes me about jump out of my skin. Climbing wearily to my feet, I go to the front door and peek out. Lucinda stands there smiling. Oh fudge, I forgot. Opening the door, I put as much of a smile as I can muster on my face and greet her. She breezes by me and immediately starts talking about the house. I try to be courteous and pay attention, but my emotions are all over the place and I fail. Instead, I walk back into the family room and take the disc out of the player. There's no reason for anyone else to see its contents.

"That's ancient tech. What's on it?"

"Some old television program my mother liked to watch." Lucinda, boldly annoying, tries to tug it out my hands. "Thank you, but I'd rather keep it to myself." She shrugs and smiles again. I might think she's sweet but she's also pushy and that makes me rethink the friend situation.

In fact, because of that pushiness I send the disc to my Blank Space, something I never use, but my gut is screaming at me to do it. Her smile broadens and she opens her mouth to speak and then something smashes into the back of my head with the force of a hammer.

Black spots swim before my eyes as I stagger to the side

and turn to the intruder. A flipping Elf smirks at me and raises the club in his hand to strike me again. Grabbing a candlestick off the mantle, I block him on the downswing. Lucinda runs between us and the Elf knocks her out with one hit. I hope she's okay! The fight is on. The Elf is good, better than I am, and he has something I don't have know how to use correctly - yet, flipping magic.

Diving behind the couch, I barely miss getting toasted by a fireball. Why is it that everyone but me gets those? Zag roars outside and I feel him trying to get in, but there's a barrier muting the feel of him. The Elf was able to throw up a barrier to keep everyone out of this room. I hear Gertie out there cussing him for all she's worth. Wow, she's creative with some of those names.

Reaching for Lucinda's prone body, I drag her behind the couch and then roll to another piece of furniture. She did try to help me, silly Mage. Why didn't she use her magic?

"Why are you here?" I shout to the would-be assassin.

"Someone paid a lot of money for me to be here," he answers, a laugh in his voice.

"But why?" Unless it's related to what I very recently discovered.

"Dunno, but I don't get paid to ask questions. Shut the fuck up and die already." He's not very nice.

A knife whizzes by my head, embedding itself into the wall a foot in front of me, where it vibrates from the force of the throw. I grab it and, aiming for the last place I saw him, toss it back, smiling in satisfaction when he curses. A smile that's yanked right off my face when magic latches onto me and drags me out of my hiding place. The invisible force holds my upper body against the floor. I struggle but nothing frees me. I hate when Ciar is right. Hate it. Hate it.

A solid boot to my stomach takes the breath right out of me. Scrambling for purchase on the old rug, I try to pull myself away from him. Kicking out, I catch something soft with my foot and take advantage of his magic suddenly releasing me.

I can't win against his magic.

Crawling behind the chair, I duck my head to look at him around the edge of it. The bracelet burns my wrist and the violin materializes in my hand. With it there, something else happens, magic. I can see his fate, it plays above him like a movie. Well, this is pretty neat after all. This Elf is destined to die when he trips and lands on his own knife. A fitting end to someone like him.

On instinct, I sing out a few notes while watching his face, and then my Word comes out in a lyrical phrase. The force of it leaves my throat raw from its passing. His brown eyes widen as he is pulled up straight by invisible strings and the knife laying on the floor beside him moves on its own. The handle against the ground and the blade sticking straight up. Eyes wide, he falls forward, the knife sinking into his flesh with a squishing sound. I see the minute the magic releases him and his life is no more.

The tears are hot and scalding as they slide down my face. Staring at his body I start to hyperventilate. I've hunted food, I've defended myself against others, but I've never taken a life. His dead eyes stare at me accusingly.

"I'm so sorry. I'm so sorry." I repeat over and over and when Zag finally breaks the barrier and curls around me, I let it all out. The whole flipping day I cry out right there on his back, while his wings hide me from the rest of the world.

When the last of the sobs leave me with hiccups, I climb to my feet to see Lucinda sitting on the chair, having a cup of tea. She smiles at me, completely ignoring the Elf's body in the middle of the room.

"Glad to see you're all cried out. Are you okay?"

I shrug.

"So, when do we start cleaning?"

"Go home, Lucinda." My voice is hoarse and hard. I don't want her here, especially as calm as she is under the circumstances. It strikes an odd chord in me and I can't deal with anything else weird right now. She doesn't move, just continues to sip her tea.

Ciar runs into the room, his face thunderous, immediately he takes in the broken furniture and the dead Elf.

"Go home, Mage." His tone leaves no room for argument. This time she puts the teacup down on the coffee table and with a dirty look at Ciar pats my arm and leaves.

"I fucking killed someone." Saying it out loud makes it even worse. My guts are being ripped out of me by the emotional hurricane inside me.

Ciar wraps his arms around me and although I thought I was all cried out, it starts all over again. "I'm so sorry I wasn't here. The Hunt was a false one, a spell summoned us."

Several minutes later I'm quiet again, resting my face against his wet shirt.

"A set up, all of it. As soon as I can get you a little settled, I'm going to start setting wards. When the other two fuckers join us, they can add their own and when you learn how to wield your magic, a fourth ward."

"We'll get this mess out of here and into storage for selling." Gertie says out of nowhere and as she speaks the furniture starts popping out of existence, the body is already gone. I knew Brownies moved fast but this is amazing.

Within twenty minutes the room is empty, even the rug is gone.

"The bedrooms will be done, as well. Which room will you be choosing for your own?" she asks hovering level with my face.

"My mother's." Serves her right, she never let me in there and now I'll make sure every single piece of her is out of it.

Dealing with it all is a little easier. Graywalker, gods - it explains so much. At least I know why she hated me. All because of a man - knowing is much better than not, at least in this case. Looking around the house, I decide right there that I'm going to obliterate every single piece of her from this place. I earned this house simply because she was my mother.

"We're going to get rid of this ugly wallpaper too. All of it, I want none of her left here." Gertie kisses my cheek and is gone. "Let's get some tea. I need tea or alcohol - but tea works for now." Saying this, I head into the kitchen.

Ciar follows quietly behind me, supportive without being suffocating, although once in the kitchen, he steers me to a stool at the kitchen island and starts opening and closing cabinets looking for the stuff he needs. He's being incredibly calm about things considering... wait, his knuckles are white on the cabinet handle. My eyes move up to his face, his jaw is flexing rhythmically which means he's clenching his teeth off and on. The calm is a sham and it's all for me.

"Right of the sink, third shelf." He pulls the tea bags from exactly where I said. "Left cabinet, top shelf." Cups join the tea bags on the counter. "The kettle is bottom left."

Singing under his breath, he washes out the cups and kettle and gets it filled and on the stove. "Who's been paying for the utilities?"

"You have from the small stipend Mada provides specifically for it," he answers, then goes back to singing.

I know what he's doing but I'm not going to complain. My nerves are shot, my emotions are raw and bleeding, and my stomach is killing me. Pulling up my shirt, I look at the mottled bruising of where he kicked me. That'll take a while to go away, but there's another mark towards my hip. It's an old rune and a fresh wound but I know what it is.

It's the brand Faerie spoke of, it's throbbing in a dull achy way. Reminding me solidly of its presence, but the pain isn't intolerable. If I go by what Faerie said in my crazy almost-death dream then this guys fate wasn't too far off from the real deal happening. It's the only explanation I can come up with. Faerie doesn't strike me as someone who exaggerates or understates something.

Ciar is at my side in a heartbeat looking intently at the brand.

"You called his fate?" Meeting his eyes, I nod. "Good." He bends and kisses the brand. The pain eases, not going away completely but not the ache it was. Then he goes back to making the tea like nothing was out the norm.

A tear runs down my cheek and I try to swipe it away before he sees. This is one of those moments in life when you realize just how much someone means to you and it hits me like a truck.

I love Ciar.

CHAPTER 22

FAIRY FOOD FREAKOUT...

Sleeping on the floor isn't as comfortable as I hoped it'd be. Wakefulness brings attention to the crick in my neck, a stiff back and a reminder that my butt was whipped hard by an Elf the day before.

Then I smell it.

Bacon is a smell that grabs you with invisible hands and drags you unerringly towards the source. After a quick bathroom trip, I go in search of that glorious food. Gertie is at the stove, singing a little while she flips scrambled eggs around in a pan bigger than her.

On the counter is a plate stacked high with Brownie Baked Bacon. Without an invitation, I seat myself at the island where a paper plate is waiting with clean, shiny silverware beside it.

"Hope you're hungry, I made enough for an army," she says, smiling over her shoulder.

"Where is your family? I'd like to meet them." She pauses at her task and then picks it up again.

"You really want to meet them?" Why does she sound so doubtful?

"Well, you're family now, so they're family too."

A male Brownie, her husband, I assume, and four kids pop right onto the counter. The kids are in their teens if not older, but Brownie families tend to stay together forever.

"Hello there," I say in greeting. A chorus of hello's spoken at the same time make me smile.

"I'm Ralphie, the oldest and this is Mary, Will and Benjamin. And of course, our Dad, Henry." He leans towards me conspiratorially. "He doesn't talk much, cos Ma does all the talking." I like them all instantly and laugh out loud when a piece of scrambled egg smacks him right upside the head.

Benjamin, the baby of the family, holds out a perfect orchid blossom. I take it and thank him with a kiss to his cheek. He turns a lovely shade of red and ducks his head. Oh, he's adorable. Brownies tend to all favor each other in looks and coloring and these ones are no exception. They all have varying shades of brown hair and eyes, but their faces are distinct. I'm pretty sure I love them already.

"We're going to be helping you redecorate, but I was wondering if it'd be okay to bring in some Fairy friends of mine. They've had a rough go lately," Ralphie asks, wringing his hands.

"That's fine, just let me know what we have to pay them."

He frowns at me.

"Pay them? They'll be happy to just have a safe place to rest. Territory has gotten slim with all of the new laws regarding Unseelie -" his words cut off.

"They can stay here with us, we have several acres of land that we won't be doing anything with," I offer without regret. With a finger I push his chin up and mouth closed.

Next thing I know, I'm swamped in hugs from all four of them. What in the world? Not sure what else to do I hug them back. When they move away, chattering happily together, I look at their dad in confusion.

"I'm Unseelie too, you know." The chatter stops. "Now, let's have some breakfast and talk about decorating. I have ideas, but I don't really know what I'm doing." When they stand there staring at me, I worry I've done something wrong. "What?"

"We can eat with you?"

"Well, yeah. Who's good with colors because if it's left up to me everything will be pink." They laugh, and a small table appears, and we chat all through breakfast. By the end of the meal we have a solid plan.

No pinks except my room and then only minimal. Gertie put her foot down and made a valid point. You can have too much of a good thing. The kids are going to rip all the awful wallpaper down all over the house while I'm at the Menagerie, something that Ciar and I need to speak on.

Wait. "Where is Ciar?"

"He had some errands to run, but said he won't be gone long." Gertie answers, cleaning up our breakfast mess. I stand up with the intention to help but a stern look from her sits me right back down.

"What is today?" I scrub a hand down my face. That's how messed up I am right now, I don't know what day of the week it is.

"Sunday, my dear. Why don't you go get cleaned up? There are clean clothes and towels waiting for you in the bathroom upstairs." With that said she shoos me out of the kitchen.

The upstairs bathroom is huge, the size of our dorm room at least - former dorm room. Gods, did I really agree to move back in here? Yes, yes, I did. Sighing, I cross to the old cast iron bathtub dominating the room. A bath sounds like a good way to relax. Maybe all my problems will wash down the drain? When I twist the taps, I don't know what I'm expecting but it's not the crystal clear, instantly hot water I receive. A nice surprise and probably arranged by my new Brownie family.

I need to get them some nice stuff for payment. I wonder if they like donuts?

Stripping, I walk over and put my dirty clothes in the hamper just in case Gertie is nearby and slip into the blissfully hot water of the tub. The brand twinges in protest but only for a minute. The minute I get comfortable the hot water does its job. Hot water with a perk. The healing magics in it - though small - still feels incredible and tickles my skin as it goes to work. I'm going to love having Brownies around.

Sighing, I cover my eyes with a hot washcloth and let myself enjoy the heat sinking into my bones and the relief of being able to simply veg out for a little while. To float and not worry, not think about all the shit that's happened.

"Do you want me to wash your back?" Smiling, I keep my eyes closed. Ciar is sneaky, I'll give him that - I didn't feel him coming, either.

"Sure. Can you start with my feet first? I hurt all over." I'm only half joking. Several seconds of the sound of the water dripping being the only sound makes me think he left as quietly as he entered.

The shifting of the water around me as another body slides into the bathtub shocks me enough that I freeze. I know that body and the feel of that skin and - those wonderful magical hands as they take one of my feet into their calloused heaven and begin to knead.

Gods, that feels so good. Something the moan that slips out tells him loud and clear if his chuckle is any indication.

"What do you think about dropping out of the Menagerie?" His question almost makes me sit up, but I fight it and keep laying back. I don't want him to stop rubbing.

"What will Mada say?"

"Mada doesn't have anything to say anymore. You did

what she asked and no longer need to remain there. Unless you wish to?"

"Not really, I don't belong with those people."

"I have one request." He moves to my other foot and I moan again. Gods, his hands are absolute heaven.

"What's that?"

"We complete our dance at the Mixer." My lips twitch, but I manage to hide the smile.

"Sure. It means I get to wear whatever wonderful concoction they make for a dress." Something I'm looking forward to seeing. It also means I get to dance with Ciar again.

"You can dance with me anytime you want, Monster Girl."

"Was this the entire point of her sending me... us here?" His hands move up past my ankle to knead the bottom of my calf. It sends an instant jolt of pleasure through me.

"She knew about us, I told her the minute I knew." That's news to me, but the entire thing was news to me.

"What if I hadn't Awakened?" I tense, waiting on the answer that has the power to change my future.

"I'd still be sitting in this tub with you, rubbing your hairy calves." I laugh, a full belly laugh that makes the water splash around us. He isn't wrong, the forest isn't some place you worry about things like leg hair.

He reaches down under the water and pulls the plug. As the last dregs of the water gurgle down the drain he turns the water on again, letting it run but not filling up the tub.

He puts my foot on the rim of the tub and moves around a bit. Trusting him explicitly, I stay relaxed and wait for him to settle back down. His long fingers slide something cool and smooth up my leg all the way past the knee. All the way around and down the back of the leg that's hanging out of the tub. The cool metal of a razor blade makes me tense for half a second before I relax again under his ministrations. Ciar is shaving my legs.

"You're going to paint my toenails, too?" I tease.

"If you wish it." I laugh again and laugh harder when he firmly moves my other foot to his lap, where I encounter other things. Well, that's - it's... holy .... I don't move my foot. In fact, I smile and let him know I know what's under my foot. It's his turn to freeze in place but only for a second.

"Why do you still want to do the Mixer? I know you don't like people." My curiosity drives me to ask.

"I want one magical dance with you before our lives change. One memory where it's just you and I." I can feel his honesty through the bond that's wide open on his end. He's letting me in to see.

Ciar isn't jealous of them - or insecure in any way - but he wants something special that's his alone. I can understand that. After all, he's been with me most of my life. Wiped my snotty nose, kicked my stubborn ass. Picked me up off the ground when I fell on my face.

The other two might be part of our Triad, but this time here is ours. Pulling the cloth off my face, I stare at him. Whether he realizes it or not, he's integral to my life, to my happiness. I can't exist without him, I won't.

Carefully, he slides the razor across my skin, dips it in the running water and then repeats it again. Slow and steady. Rinsing my now clean-shaven leg, he picks up the other one and does the same thing. Watching him slather the shave cream on is borderline erotic.

When the other leg is finished, he reaches down and plugs the water again. As the water rises I follow it up his body. Gods, he's beautiful, all lean muscle and pale skin. There are even a few scars, which shouldn't exist but do and I'm assuming it's like with his calluses. He chose to leave them. The thin pale scar across his right pectoral, I gave him that. Angry that he was pushing me I pushed back as hard as I could and caught him with the tip of a blade. We both know he let me do it.

He kept the scar.

When the water is lapping around his chest he calmly reaches over and turns it off. We sit there, silent, staring at each other. Green eyes burning as they continuously watch me. I plant a foot on each side of his hips and he stretches his legs out towards me.

His feet are even attractive.

Slowly, I pull myself up and then using my arms to hold my weight slide myself onto his lap. My heat solid against his. The water laps around us as one of his hands spans my waist, his fingers moving against my skin. The other hand grasps the back of my neck. Seconds tick by while we stare at each other and I'm aching for him. My hands start their journey at his shoulders and I trace a finger over the scar I gave him, over the ridges of his stomach, and then back up again.

"Are you sure, Monster Girl?" His voice sounds breathy and hoarse. The smile I give him is all woman because now I know how much I get to him.

Staring at his face, I study his expression. His eyelids are half closed, his mouth slightly open, and I closely watch as his tongue flicks out to lick his bottom lip. My mouth on his is my answer.

Our first physical union isn't going to be about love and emotion and all that soft business. We're Fae. The thought is proven true when he unfreezes and reacts. Ciar is not gentle and I love every second of it. His mouth tears away from mine to follow his hand on my body. A hand that's a vice on my flesh as it squeezes my breasts and rolls my nipples against his calloused palm. Sharp teeth and a hot mouth quickly follow. The other hand dips below the water and two magical fingers slip against my aching flesh.

Throwing my head back, I dig my hands into his hair and roll my hips with his movements.

Ciar touching me is a heaven I've denied myself long enough. Growling possessively with a nipple in his mouth and his fingers buried inside of me, I cry out when he yanks them out and I feel him pulsing against the core of me, hard and burning hot. Feeling empowered by his focused desire, I lower myself down enough to take the head of his cock inside of me.

His claws lightly pierce my skin, mark me as his. The bond opens wide between us and I feel what he feels, he feels what I feel. The sensations are enough to make my muscles quiver around him.

When he grabs my hips and slams me down on him, burying himself completely inside of me, the last bit of our bond completes itself. Part of my psyche unravels and travels down the bond to wind around him in a tight, unbreakable knot that can never be undone.

And part of him locks into me. In more ways than one.

Instantly, I orgasm and my cries echo off the walls. I don't care and when he says my name like a prayer, I get louder. When I smother his mouth with my own and our tongues tease and taste and our teeth nip and bite, I feel complete for the first time in my life.

He feels what I feel and fucks me harder for it.

Gods, I'm an idiot for waiting this long.

TO SAY WE MADE A MESS OF THE BATHROOM IS AN understatement. We forgot the tub full of water and managed to flood the entire room, but magic held the water back from the hallway. Gertie at work.

Ciar stands me up and proceeds to dry me off like I'm

delicate and breakable and gods do I love it. Slipping a robe on me, he dries himself off with a wolfish smile, and then picks me up and wraps my legs around his waist.

Feeling my surprise, he laughs and says, "You didn't think that was it, did you?"

"At least you two can't flood the bedroom. Off with you, there's a bed made up on the floor." Gertie appears and pushes us out of the wreck of a bathroom.

Laughing, he carries me to the bedroom and there is indeed a bed made on the floor. Candles are lit, and soft music is playing, bless Gertie's romantic heart. He kneels with me still in his arms and kisses me, keeping our lips together all the way down to the floor. This time when our flesh melds together, it's soft and sweet and I swear I hear the humans' mythical angels singing.

I also hear him whisper he loves me.

Snuggling against his chest I sigh in contentment. For a little while I can forget the mess of things, the world. For a little while.

"I'm a Puca who's waited a long time for his girl. I'm good for at least five more." I scream with laughter as he pounces.

CHAPTER 23
THE AFTERGLOW IS JUST PREP FOR
ROUND TWO...

Laying together exhausted and a bit sore, I rub my hand back and forth over the smooth, soft skin of that magical place right above his hip bone. Occasionally the skin twitches but no other reactions so I keep doing it.

"You're calling Calsis today?" he asks. I nod against his chest.

"He'll buy most of this junk and sell the rest for me."

"Greedy little fucker," Ciar mutters. He lifts my hand to his mouth and kisses my palm. It instantly turns me on and I groan, there's no more energy for that right now.

Ciar is a demanding lover.

Laughing, he does it again and slips from under me, heading to the bathroom. Giving him long enough to do his business, I follow him into a completely spotless bathroom. He's in the shower - of the completely spotless bathroom - and the door is half open. That's an invitation if I've ever seen one. Of course, I take it. With the bare minimum of horsing around, we manage to wash off and get out and dressed without making a mess.

Gertie just achieved godhood in my book because waiting

on the kitchen counter for us are two sandwiches with two pieces of chocolate cake. Still warm chocolate cake. Maybe I should marry Gertie?

"You want to get married?" Ciar asks, a sly tone to his voice.

Choking on the mouthful of sandwich I crammed in my mouth, I wait until I can breathe again before answering. "Isn't that what this already is? A marriage of sorts?"

"Oh, my gods you're a big chicken," he teases, eating half his sandwich in one bite. Instead of saying anything else that will make the hole I'm in any deeper, I cram more food in my mouth. Reaching over to wipe something off my face, he keeps smiling as he eats. I have a feeling I'll be hearing about this a lot now because he doesn't look like he's one bit afraid of the M word.

I'm terrified of it, don't ask me why, because I don't know. I'm now permanently bonded to a Puca and I panicked when he said the word marry. There's something wrong with my head, seriously wrong. Ciar keeps laughing and teasing me about it while we eat our lunch. The doorbell ringing makes me jump. All this jumping is getting ridiculous. I grew up in the forest with flipping Sluagh for crying out loud.

Grow your balls back, Keri.

Voices reach me from the direction of the front door. I frown. Who answered it.

"Gertie. While you were panicking, she got the door." Ciar says matter-of- fact. Throwing my cake at him is a hard no, but I do throw the dish towel hanging on the cabinet at him and miss, per usual.

"Keri, this is Bis, one of the Fairies that Ralphie spoke to you about at breakfast." Turning around, I have to catch my breath when I see him. He looks so much like Peter that it takes my brain a few seconds to realize it isn't him.

Cheeks flaring with embarrassment, I cross the room to

shake his hand. Like Peter, he's of the more delicate type, small in stature but stronger than they look. Smiling up at me shyly, he exposes the cutest dimples in his cheeks.

The ghost of Peter's face vanishes and I'm able to relax.

"Miss Gertie said you might have room for some of us..." He's waiting for me to say no, I can sense it.

"Yes, we do, lots of room. I figure we can take your entire clan as long as they don't mind that there's only a few hundred acres."

His eyes raise to mine. "There's only eight of us left."

This causes me to look at him in shock. Fairy folk have no issues breeding, at all. In fact, they breed twice as fast as humans do. Their clans normally number in the hundreds. Not willing to ask him what happened to his clan, I look over my shoulder at Ciar then back to Bis.

"Are you criminals?"

He shakes his head and then looks incredibly sad, I feel bad for asking.

"We refused to give up an Awakened to an Elf clan, marked one." That rocks me backwards.

"They killed people because you wouldn't give them your Awakened?" He nods his head.

"Can you really be punished for that? I thought it was a scare tactic or some such?" I turn to Ciar.

"His situation is extreme - but they are enforcing the old laws now. Not enough Awakened anymore. Don't you read the news?" Ciar chastises. No, I don't, my heart hurts with all the sad stuff in it and the media makes it worse by sensationalizing every small detail of it. That it's my people causing most of it.

'I think that the worries you have in the back of your mind about who your parents are can be let go. You're a big old softie, monster girl.' For a moment I find myself staring at him with total adoration before I turn back to Bis.

"Go grab your people and bring them here, we'll figure out how to get housing."

"We can take care of the housing and will make the groundskeeping our tasks. We're also helping the Brownies work on the inside of the house. If you need anything - *anything* - you let us know, we'll be in hearing distance." With a bow he turns and in a poof of green dust zooms off.

I slide down the wall and rest my forehead on my knee. I'm setting up a household like a real Triad. This brings it home hard and when the laugh escapes me I'm only a little surprised.

I'm not alone.

Ciar sits beside of me and pats my leg. "Strange stuff to happen to a girl who can't shoot fireballs, eh?" Instead of swatting at him like I normally do, I kiss him. A kiss that shows him exactly how I feel. Breaking apart is necessary, I'm tempted to go further but know we can't right now, his eyes do that eerie luminescent thing and I do swat at him then.

"I gotta call Calsis." Ciar hands me his phone because gods know where mine is. I always forget I have the darn thing.

Not all spells require a lot of magic, some are simple and technically already exist so all you do is tap into them. Like right now. "Existence." I whisper and the phone auto dials Calsis.

"Who the hell is this?" A scratchy voiced old man demands from the other end of the line. I press speakerphone and let Ciar do the talking. Calsis gets mad at me rather quickly because I tell him he's a cheap old fart.

"Calsis, your services are needed." Ciar interrupts, rattling off the address.

"Yes, dark lord." The line disconnects.

"He hustles for you. If I were asking he'd still come but like next week."

"He loves you, but he doesn't want you to know that because then he feels obligated to get you gifts. It's part of their culture, them pretending to dislike each other so they don't have to buy each other things."

"And we call humans strange." He chuckles and climbs to his feet. I take his outstretched hand and look around us. Well, there's work to be done. "Let's get to ripping down ugly wallpaper."

Smacking me on the ass, Ciar runs by me up the stairs. Long legged butt- head, knowing I can't catch him with that big of a head start.

An hour later I do catch him unaware while he's standing on a ladder, a light smack that just makes him throw pieces of old wallpaper at me. Then when he relaxes his guard once again, I smack him hard enough that he falls off the ladder. I feel bad for it, mostly - sort of. Because he heals fast, probably not as bad as I should feel.

Smiling at my one-upmanship I keep ripping at wallpaper. I feel his intent before the burning smack of his hand on my bottom, but not quick enough to stop it. Screeching as his hand connects solidly with my butt with a loud smack, I turn around and jump off the ladder onto him taking him down to the floor laughing.

"I thought the two of you were brother and sister." Ciar is on his feet over me, growling at Lucinda's shocked and kind of snide comment.

We were so engrossed in each other even his senses were dull. Something that might present a problem one day in the future, but right this minute it makes me feel special that I can distract him that way. Ciar's annoyance fills the bond between us. He isn't seeing the situation in the same amused way.

"Huh, I thought I explained we weren't?" Didn't I?

"Are you sure you're not?" Lucinda steps further into the

room, a look of doubt on her face. In the Fae world it's not uncommon for cousins and rarely - but it has happened - siblings to couple or marry. That's gross, but it happens, and I think the stories are a bit exaggerated in among the humans. They have a lot of stories about Fae, most of which existed before the worlds collided. Ninety percent of it is wrong but most Fae continue to let them believe the nonsense. I'm pretty sure it's a law somewhere.

"Yeah, pretty sure, but since we both hatched from eggs it's hard telling." The look of horror on her face makes me laugh so hard I double over.

She stomps her foot. "Totally not funny, Keri."

"What brings you around here?" I ask, pushing on Ciar so I can get up. Ciar moves to let me up but doesn't go far. The speculative look he's giving Lucinda bothers me a little.

'Ciar, I know you don't like humans but cut her some slack. She tried to help.' She got knocked out instead, but at least she made the effort.

He makes a noise low in his throat and then goes back to ripping wallpaper, but not before giving her a hard look. Other voices echo in the house, the Fairies are here.

"Who is that?" she asks looking over her shoulder towards the stairs. We're still on the second level of the house because we messed about mostly. The Fairies and Brownies will be moving much more quickly, but from the sounds of laughter they're messing about a bit, as well.

"My friends." I can't help but smile as I say it.

"But I thought I was your only friend?" That wipes the smile off my face.

She looks hurt and anger keeps peeking out through it. What happened to that shy sweet girl I met a few weeks ago? Catching me staring at her she smiles, bright and happy. I'm starting to think that there's more to Lucinda than meets the eyes and not in a good way.

"I don't want to lose you. You're my only friend, you know?" Oh, it's an insecurity thing where they say one thing but do another.

"Don't be silly, just because I have other friends doesn't mean you are worth any less to me, dummy." Which makes me think of something else. "You weren't hurt earlier, were you?"

"A little bump on my head is all, which is no big deal since I saved your life." Wait, what? "Just kidding, I'm glad you're okay and I'm sorry that I wasn't more help. I panicked." Her face crumples into guilt.

Aw, there's the Lucinda I don't want to strangle.

"What's the adventure today? Dinner or a movie or both?"

"Too much work to do, which you're welcome to help with if you want."

"Manual labor isn't really my thing." Yeah, I'm starting to understand this about her.

"Maybe later in the week?" I ask, going back to the wallpaper.

"Don't forget the Mixer is this week," she reminds me, coming to stand beside me and stare at the wall with a look of disgust. Yeah, I agree with her on that, the wallpaper is a garish orange-red with gold symbols and green leaves all over it.

Speaking of red, "Did you ask the redhead?" Her face sobers, and she drops her eyes to the floor.

"He said not this time." Aw she looks so sad about it, unfortunately I'm not that surprised he said no. I'm glad she got up the courage to try, though.

"He give you any reasons?" I ask, and the cold anger on her face surprises me, but it's only there a moment and the sadness quickly replaces it.

"I guess his parents set him up with some visiting Aristocrat." Her smile returns. "He did say that we can always go out another time."

"See?" Oh, well maybe he really is interested. "He's probably got super controlling parents. Look at yours for example." I smile at her. "You're a beautiful person, if he doesn't see it, someone else will."

"Thanks, Keri." She laughs and starts helping me rip wallpaper off the wall. Little tiny pieces but it's progress for her. A little work doesn't hurt anyone, especially someone who's idea of work is painting their nails.

The afternoon goes by pretty quickly and before dinner, Lucinda hugs me goodbye and heads home for the night. Gertie and Bis introduce me to the new Fairies and we all decide to have a cookout. Zag has been mostly absent, because of the work I'm sure, he's such a diva. And poor Fluffy is still in his cocoon, sleeping and changing.

A loud knock at the door heralds Calsis, little but loud. He makes those harrumphing noises at me as he follows me through the house and to the storage room to sort the stuff I'm selling.

"Some of this is old and valuable, girl. Are you sure you want to sell it?" he asks me, after cataloging the storage room.

"Yes, every bit of it."

"What price are you looking to get?"

"The most you can get out of them." For a moment his face remains in that perpetual frown he wears but amazingly a small smile lifts it away, but only for a few seconds. Long enough for me to see that one of his front teeth are made of gold. Basically getting the highest price is a challenge to him and Leprechauns love a good monetary challenge.

"Only the paper money?"

"No, I'll take gems and other rare goods in trade but only ones I can use to barter." He nods and writes this down on his notepad.

"My normal fee is ten percent."

"Take fifteen if you can get rid of it quickly." Another small smile flashes. This stuff will be sold in a day, ha. He holds his hand out and I shake it sealing our deal. Calsis, gods bless his grouchy soul is shrewd, greedy and hard as heck to get a bargain out of, but he's honest to a fault.

Back at the front door he tips his hat to me and bows - yes bows! - to Ciar before he leaves, notes in hand, with all the stuff I want to get rid of already loaded into Troll baskets. Which are the large baskets that Trolls lift onto their backs to transport goods from one place to another.

Trucks exist but they're super expensive to maintain and are outlawed in most places for pollution. Trolls are used for the heavy lifting and transportation, now. Partnered with them are Fae who can make portals to shorten distances. It works out well and nothing gets broken.

Standing in the doorway I catch myself staring at the place where the Elf died. I'm fully aware that it was either him or me and that it isn't murder when you're defending yourself, but I feel *awful*.

"Sometimes I worry for you, Keri." As he speaks, his arms encircle my waist from behind. Resting his chin on my shoulder he looks at the spot I can't move my eyes from.

"Was it hard for you the first time you killed someone?" I ask.

"No." Well, he's honest at least. "I'm a killer, you're not." He sighs. "Is it because you think his family misses him? Or maybe that he left a kid without a father?"

Nodding, I let myself rest against him and tear my eyes away from the floor. "Keri, his name was Jafe, he was tossed from his clan for raping and murdering several women. When he realized the Hunt was summoned, he murdered his wife for her money and then fled to wherever he'd been hiding.

Someone was using magic to protect him from the Hunt.
Someone strong."

"How did you find these things out?"

"I tasted his blood."

"Ew."

"Are you really grossed out because I licked some blood?"

Laughing I say, "No, the ew factor is because the blood
was cold. Isn't that gross?" Tickling me, he spins me around
to kiss me breathless and then drags me outside to sit with
the Brownies, who forbid me from doing more than pouring
myself a bit of Fairy Wine.

The laughter and camaraderie are a nice change from the
way things always were in this house. It also reminds me a bit
of home and I look at Ciar beside me and he nods, knowing
exactly what I'm thinking.

"They'll come visit soon, the time isn't right yet," he reassures me.

"You know, this 'happy' would totally piss my mother off. I
like it."

Looking towards the lit-up house I see something I can't
recall ever seeing while I lived here, a home. Bis walks over to
me and, with cheeks as red as a tomato, asks me to dance.
Who am I to say no to a dance from such a handsome Fairy?
Ciar rolls his eyes at me and then joins us on the floor with
Gertie as his dancing companion. Well, aren't her cheeks as
rosy as Bis's?

Laughing, I spin around with Bis and start to sing and
when the many voices join me and the sky lights up with the
scales of a Dragon flying over us weaving his own magic,
things feel a lot better.

Yes, I had to kill a man - and that will haunt me forever,
but he was going to take this away from me and I can't have
that. So right there, I accept the consequences of my actions.
I also accept that he won't be the last one and that I'll have to

kill again. Letting the regret fade, if only for tonight, I smile again at my shy dance partner and let my voice fill the night. When a deeper more achingly beautiful voice joins mine, I look across the sea of faces to meet green eyes that are only for me.

Oh, yes. For this, I'll do anything that I need to do.

CHAPTER 24

THE SUPER TALENTED BRASS BAND...

Somehow Ciar arranged for us to only have one class. I'm not complaining though since it means I can sleep in for the last week of my stay in this useless place. I asked him why we still come at all, they know I Awakened. I guess that since my Triad isn't formed I'm not considered fully Awakened.

Gertie, the wonderful person she is, has food ready for us when we make our way downstairs. Ciar is quiet and distracted, but I'm pretty sure he had a Hunt in the middle of the night. I vaguely remember him kissing me goodbye and then hours later, right before dawn, crawling back into bed his hair still damp from a shower.

Messy hunt, I gather.

"You okay?" I finally break down and ask, after thinking about asking it a hundred times. He lifts his lips in a semblance of a smile and pats my hand, then his eyes take on that faraway look he gets when he's thinking hard about something. I want to know what's putting that look in them and I bite my tongue to keep from asking. I need to respect the fact that he'll tell me when he's good and ready.

Ciar stands and kisses me quick and hard on the mouth.

"We need to go." Cramming the last bit of my sandwich in my mouth, I put my shoes on and follow him out the door. At the sidewalk he turns and touches a barrier that I can sense but can't see. His magic makes goosebumps rise on my skin and then he grabs my hand and starts pulling me along with him.

"Didn't realize you liked music class so much." He stops walking and takes a deep breath.

"It bothers me that while I was gone on a fucking Hunt you were attacked and there's nothing I can do about it." That's not what I'm expecting him to say.

"Ciar," I take his hand in mine and stand close enough I can kiss him if I want, but far enough away I can say what I need to say first. "You're always going to have to go away for Hunts and this is something I know and accept. Just as you should, no one can be with me every minute of every day."

I wrinkle my nose at him. "*You* taught me to defend myself, to be independent and not rely on anyone. Stand strong, remember, fleabag? Have faith that you taught me well because I have faith in it."

Both of his hands cup my face and with a smile that makes my toes wiggle in my shoes. He leans forward to give me the slowest, most sensual kiss I've had in my entire life. His mouth is hot and sweet, tasting slightly of the coffee he had with his food. His tongue is rough and long, yet he manages to make it feel like silk stroking mine and the inside of my mouth. When he pulls away from me my body tries to follow and the only thing that keeps my face off the ground is him catching me. Clearing my throat, a bit embarrassed about the whole falling over him thing, I turn and start walking again.

"It fucks with my pride that I can't protect the woman I love." This stops me in my tracks. "There are times you're so confident that I can see the influence I've had in your life, but then you're so innocent about some things."

"Sometime the confidence is a sham sometimes, and sometimes it's not. Like when that Elf was there... it was a bit of both." I don't like admitting it, but it's the truth.

The brand I received from taking his life is even now a throbbing dull reminder that will always be there. Contact with Ciar helps ease it, but it seems to always hurts a little.

"Keri," he says, so softly the wind almost snatches it away.

I continue on, because I need to. "I survived because of you and this gift- curse thing that Faerie gave me. The future is unknown and I hate that. We can guess, sure, but whatever this power is - it's going to cause us a lot of problems. I have to be ready for them, Ciar. I can't always expect you to be the hero. Sometimes I need to be my own hero."

Ciar makes a face at me so I continue, "You made me strong remember? Why change your tune just because you're doing me?" His green eyes flash and then he leans his head back and laughs while pulling me to him in a hug.

"Thank you for reminding me to stop being an idiot." With that said, we start walking again, my hand wrapped securely in his. I swear he's even whistling.

The good mood lasts until the moment we sit down in music class and the 'teacher' walks into the room. Mrs. Cobbleson he's not, it's the flipping Aristocrat from the grocery store.

Now, why is he here?

That slick smile that is 'Fae' attractive turns up when he spots me sitting in the back row of chairs. Ciar tenses beside me but otherwise doesn't react. That beautiful face of his is relaxed, almost bored looking. His ankle is resting on his knee and his arms are crossed. The man is studying his finger-nails like this is just another day while I'm sitting here so tense I can probably crack walnuts with my butt.

Ciar coughs, his mask dropping long enough for him to give me a look of reluctant amusement. That's what he gets for eavesdropping in my brain while I'm nervous, he's lucky I'm not a nervous farter. *I'm* lucky I'm not a nervous farter. That idea is awful, a full brass band would be coming out of my butt right now – bass drum and all. Boom. Boom. Tiss. Bang. Boop. Boop. Ciar coughs again and I stare at the floor, fighting to keep a straight face.

"My predecessor shared the schedule that you're all supposed to adhere to at the Mixer. After some careful thought on the matter, I have decided that only one couple shall perform," he looks right at Ciar and I. "The Nightshades."

The class explodes in protests and cries of favoritism, which are immediately silenced when the Fae – who's name I still don't know – pans his gaze around the room. My nerves aren't acting up because I'm afraid of him. It's because I'm worried about what he can do to me as a whole. I'm not entirely sure I can avoid serving a house since I'm Awakened. Mada can't claim me since I wasn't born there with her. Only blood counts.

'It doesn't work quite that way. But,' I hate buts, at least in this circumstance. *'If they discover who your father is they can. Any house of the king's choosing.'*

'You're kidding?'

'I'm working on it. This one sees something he wants and is accustomed to getting it.' Way to change the subject, Ciar. *'I'm old, Monster Girl, and I'm strong, but there are Fae that can make life very difficult for us.'*

'This guy?'

'Of course not, are you daft?'

'Then who?'

'His father, the king.'

'Well, that can make things difficult.' It explains his arrogance, too.

"Since the Duke of Harleigh is going to be there, I expect you two to give the performance of your life," the subject of our conversation says.

"Aren't you the Duke of Harleigh?" Ciar asks, breaking the sudden silence of the room. For a half a second the look of arrogance fades from the Duke's eyes, and as he stares at Ciar I see a little fear. He might not know what Ciar is, but he knows he's something to be wary of.

The smile he turns on me washes away any wariness and makes me dislike him even more.

"My house is currently seeking an Awakened, you realize the status in society you'd receive being a member of my household will bring you - do you not?"

'Humor him for the moment. I need to look into things before we make him an enemy,' Ciar cautions.

"I have only one member of my Triad, your grace," I say, to make sure it's known if nothing else. This is my only protection.

"That changes nothing. The other two aren't far behind, I imagine," he counters.

"Sounds... interesting." And saying that makes me want to throw up a little.

"Wear something fabulous, Keri Nightshade." With that said, he walks out of the classroom and everyone looks around in confusion. Except Ciar, he pulls me to my feet and we exit the class in a hurry.

'Things will work out,' he says, giving none of his emotions away. Why can't I be one of those people who can do that?

CHAPTER 25

ALL YOUR FAVORS ARE IN BODY BAGS...

"Tonight, we start your magical defense training." That can't be taken as anything other than an order and it makes me laugh. There are times when he doesn't mean to sound bossy but this time it's on purpose and arguing with him won't get me anywhere.

"What got that rock rolling?"

"He tried to use magic on you and you didn't feel the slightest hint of it. If I had not been there to stop it, you would be with him right this moment."

Oh, that's not good. Really, not good. "What was he trying to do?"

"Spell you into looking at him with guppy eyes." He runs a hand through his hair. "Enrapture is a potent spell and if I had been on a hunt..." His voice trails off.

I might not know much about magical defense, not for lack of him trying to teach me, but because as a kid I was a know-it-all who thought that since I didn't have much magic I'd never need to know how to defend myself with it. The only thing I learned how to do back then was mental shields. But I did pay attention to what things are.

"They last days at most, eventually I'd come out of it and cut his balls off."

"Yes, and then be executed by his father for it." He stops walking and faces me, and I swear the world hushes around him. "One-on-one I can take the king, Keri, but I can't stop his entire force. He employs some major powerhouses and combined they're too much - even for me."

Hearing him admit that he's not all powerful makes me a little nervous. Yes, logically I'm fully aware that there is always someone bigger and badder in the world, but Ciar is and always will be the most powerful creature I know. To have him say he can't beat something changes the game.

"Okay, teach this magical defense crap to me. I want to learn everything about it." I instantly regret my words as I go flying backwards, my body connects to the ground with a solid whump sound.

"First lesson. Always be prepared." I take the hand he holds out with a dirty look at the smug smile on his face. He pulls me to my feet and I tense when he moves. Laughing, he starts walking again and I silently mouth insults at his back. As we walk, I dust off the singed threads off my shirt. He did that on purpose knowing I can't shoot fireballs. I can only blow up water bottles.

Wait.

Focusing on the back of his pants and only distracted for a few seconds by the view, I whisper my word and wait for the blow out. Nothing happens. Biting my tongue, I try again this time with more umph. Nothing.

"And this is why you learn magical defense." His words float over his shoulder and I swear he's grinning again.

Anger flares in my stomach and I laugh in shock when the back of his pants disintegrates, leaving his lovely bum hanging out for the entire world to see. Instead of reacting like anyone else in his situation, he keeps walking with confidence and absolute disregard for everyone staring and admiring his bare butt. I'm even staring at it. Pulling my eyes away, I try to zap him again, but this time it feels like I'm hitting a brick wall.

"Not taking any chances this time. Now, it's your turn." Right before I impact with the sidewalk, again, I manage to twist myself mid-air to land with on my knees, okay one knee. At least I didn't hit my face. Pushing myself to my feet, I glare at him.

"You know I don't know how to -" His eyes flash with intent. Ducking to the side, I manage to avoid the fireball that came out of nowhere. "Hey!"

"You're using your eyes too much. Magic isn't always going to be visible. Open your other senses," he eyes me, "The ones I know you have now." He's using that teacher voice that I hate. I also can't deny its effectiveness.

On the way home, I end up on the ground often, but I'm starting to get a sense of when someone is trying to sneak magic at me. It's not going to be easy, Ciar says that it can take months for me to be able to stop a spell like Enrapture. But I'll know it's being cast which gives me a chance to do something. That's more than I have now. I need to find out more on what a Fate Caller is.

"We can go talk to the Old Man Under the Hill." I make a face at Ciar's suggestion. "He is the historian of Faerie and might have the answers we need to truly understand what you are. What I know is very limited and your conditions are different than his were."

There are rumors about the OMUTH, mostly scary ones but those don't concern me, it's the cost of information. He makes you give up something valuable and I'm not talking monetarily.

He stops and looks at me. "He owes me a favor," Ciar says

softly, breaking into the horrible thoughts I'm having about the OMUTH wanting my feet as payment.

"What'd you do? Kill someone for him?" I tease. Ciar looks at me but says nothing, instead he starts walking again.

I jog to catch up with him. "Hey... holy meatballs. You did!"

CHAPTER 26

THE PAST HAS CLAWS...

A fter a brief stop at home for Ciar to change his pants, that I'm still proud I blew the butt out of, we head to the dress store. To say that the dress is perfect is the understatement of the century. I'm looking at a clothing orgasm. The dress is a ballroom style silver and black confection of my dreams. It's so flipping pretty I want to eat it or hide it away and guard it like a Dragon.

Ciar reaches over and wipes my chin with a tissue. "You're drooling."

"But... but look at that dress. It's so beautiful." My eyes eat up the relatively modest heart-shaped neckline and the two thin straps made of the most delicate spider silk braids I've seen, the hour glass bodice and the flouncing puffy skirt - that when worn will spin around me like I'm a princess at her first ball.

The skirt is a rich black with sparkles woven into the material. The bodice is, of course, spider silk. Silver and stunning, it will make the color of my hair a beacon in the myriad of attendees.

"I knew this gown would suit you. As you know, the spells

woven in will make it fit you perfectly, but the spell is only good for one wear. If you need it respelled don't hesitate to bring it back to us." Adelle says, flittering around me while I try to pull my eyes off the dress. She's like a doll sized butterfly and now I'm covered in dust again.

In awe, I step forward to lightly stroke the material of the skirt and find it as soft as it looks. Noticing that my hands and fingernails are dirty I step away and tuck them into my pockets. I'm guessing all the trips to the ground left their mark in more ways than one.

"The dress is... I don't even have a word for it. Spectacular? Mind-bendingly beautiful? All I can say is it's more than I ever hoped to own and wear." I'm fully aware that I sound a bit gob smacked and am possibly even breathing heavy but the dress... drool.

"You will do it justice. Now, will that be cash or credit?" With a wink, Adelle is all business once again.

He looks at me in question, and I nod. I don't mind him paying for it, I can pay him back when Calsis sells all my junk. People get all weird about someone else paying, Ciar and I are partners - partners back each other up.

Ciar steps forward and passes her a gemstone and the light reflects its pale blue color. It's lovely and probably magical, Ciar always seems to have one or two in his pocket. My favorite are the purple ones, I have no idea what type of gem they are, but they tickle your skin when you touch them and make you feel happy.

I have to squeeze every moment of happy I can out of life, doesn't everyone?

Watching on the tips of my toes while the dress is carefully bagged up in a magically protected plastic dress bag, I relax only when Ciar carefully folds it over his arm. Adelle pauses in front of me on her way to the back of the store and whatever they have hidden behind that plain red curtain.

"The Fairy who marked you - loved you. We only mark those they love," she whispers, and then with a quick kiss on my cheek she flits away in a shower of pink dust.

For a solid minute I stand there, staring at the curtain gently moving in her wake. Blinking at the sudden burning in my eyes, I take a shaky breath and swallow the lump that chokes up my throat. Pushing myself to move, I turn away and head out the front door without a backward glance. Ciar follows behind me, quiet but sending comfort through our bond, it laps against me in gentle waves, soothing the rough grief threatening to rise to the surface and take over. Grief owns a slice of my soul and now is not the time to deal with it, so I fight it.

A few deep breaths later I manage to shove it down and lock it away. Tonight, while I lay watching the moon through the window with Ciar's strong arms wrapped around me, I'll let it out and maybe, just maybe, this time for good. A warm hand wraps around mine and tugs me closer as we walk. Looking up at him, grateful for his silent support, I smile and shoulder bump him.

"I wonder what Gertie is making for dinner?" he muses, a soft smile on his face as he looks over at me. "Also, your vacation is over. We're going to start training with weapons, concurrent with your magical defenses." Groaning, I give him a dirty look. That means he's going to start busting my ass again.

"But I'm sleeping with the teacher!" I mock protest.

"That just means you'll get double the workout after training," he teases, wiggling his eyebrows suggestively.

Laughing - because how can I not laugh - I pull my hand from his and break into a run. "See ya at home dog breath!" I yell, over my shoulder. Smiling and out of breath, I fling open the front door only to find him lounging on the stairway. Figures that he beat me here somehow, tricky puppy.

"How the heck did you do that?" Instantly, my eyes seek out the dress and I find it hanging on the bannister with the plastic bag spotless.

"Magic." He waves his hands around like a wizard. Rolling my eyes at him I look around for Zag, he's normally with me but for the last few days he's spent quite a bit of time out and about. I'm snoopy enough that I plan on asking him where he's going. I can feel him loud and clear through the Familiar bond that's tucked in the back of my brain - he's concentrating hard on something, but he's not in any kind of pain or really any negative emotion at all.

Only that stillness that indicates he's doing something that requires his full attention. A fact that makes me even more curious and brings my gaze back around to Ciar.

Sitting on the stair next to him, I snuggle against his side and look up at him, my eyes big and pleading. "Where the hells is Zag?"

His laughter is enough to wipe my attempt at looking innocent off my face. "He's out checking out some things for me."

"Uh-huh. You're snooping on the two that I can feel lurking around, aren't you?"

Shaking his head, he says, "Those two idiots will be around soon enough. Whether they want to or not."

Chewing my lip, I frown at him. "I hate the idea of them having to do things against their will."

Ciar's face turns serious. "You need them, and I'll drag their asses here myself if I have to. They don't have to have what we do, even though it'll make you stronger, but they need to be *here*." He points at the floor, his eyes lighting with irritation.

"You feel really strongly about this?"

"So should you! Not all Triads are about love, or even lust, the attraction to your Center is there - of course - but the follow through isn't required. Just the bonding. I've seen other Triads who weren't romantically or sexually involved at all. But they were a family and right now those two morons are running around fighting the pull, one for stupid reasons that he'll realize soon enough, and the other from fear." Clearly, he's passionate about his beliefs in this system and he knows more than I realized about our two missing mysterious members.

"Yes, Keri, I know that you're feeling the lack of them. It's why you're more tired and why the brand has started to ache." He fills in the blanks for me.

Well, that explains all of that.

"Ciar, if they don't want to be here they shouldn't have to be, though. No one should have to be a slave to magic, it feels wrong." Guilt wraps itself around my heart and gives it a little squeeze.

Turning towards me he cups my face and with a soft kiss on my lips, smiles as he pulls away. "This kindness in you is one of the reasons I love you so much, Monster Girl. But," Yeah, there's always a but. "That's just it, they do want to be here." The guilt eases a little but only a little.

The sudden knock on the door makes me about jump out of my skin. Laughing, he stands and crosses the few feet to open the door. A brief conversation that I can't make out over the sound of crinkling paper follows and then he's turning with something in his hands as the door shuts with a bang behind him.

I'm on my feet jumping around like a schoolgirl. A bouquet of candy flowers, a specialty of Brownies, fill the beautiful crystal vase. Each flower is perfect in its design, identical to its floral counterpart. Except these ones are made from candied fruits and chocolates. The leaves are mint and chewable designed to be used after you nibble on the blossoms. They're flipping awesome and as much as I've talked about them I've never gotten them. Dodging carefully around the vase, I hug Ciar around the waist.

"Keri, I didn't get these, but now that I know how much you like them I'll keep that in mind for the future." Pulling back from him I search the arrangement for a card. If he didn't send them then who did?

Finally, I find one tucked near the center and wrapped around it is a necklace. Untangling it from the card I hold it up to study the delicate silver bird hanging from the black metal chain. I can't quite tell what it is but maybe a raven or a crow?

The card simply reads:

After I take care of things, I'll return. Sorry I've hidden like a coward.

Trick.

Looking at Ciar, who shrugs his shoulders, I hand him the necklace and turn my back to him so he can put it on me.

"Keri, too trusting," he scolds. Turning back around I watch him set the flowers down on the hallway table that Gertie provided. The feel of his magic flaring to life gives me the shivers, good ones, as I watch him carefully check the necklace. With a satisfied look on his face, he turns me back around and moves my hair out of the way and then latches the necklace around my neck.

Feeling the weight of it settle between my breasts, I turn back around and hand Ciar the card. Without missing a beat, I grab a flower and before I can bite into it, I pause. Under his watchful gaze, I first sniff it and then use my magic to check it for poisons. After I'm finished he grabs my hand and does the same. Giving it a final sniff, he releases my hand and I bite into it with absolute glee. Strawberry flavor bursts across my tongue and I can't help but moan a little.

"It seems one of them is going to stop being an idiot," he muses.

"You know exactly who they are, don't you?" Sure, it sounds accusing but I'm not wrong, either.

"Of course I do. You're not the only one connected to them." Leaning forward he kisses me, rather thoroughly, carefully licking the sugar off my lips.

Now, what was I going on about?

A persistent dinging noise pulls me out of the haze that is Ciar and grouchily I pull my phone out of my pocket. It's a text from Lucinda, well actually it's like ten texts from her.

The first one reads - *Mark was found dead this morning in the park.*

Gods that's awful.

The last one - *I can't deal with it, I'm going home to be with my family.*

Skimming through the rest of them, mostly angry rants about how he never gave her the time of day and now it's too late, I text back that I hope she's okay and if she needs me that I'm here for her. After a few minutes of not getting a response, I tuck my phone away in my pocket again.

"I don't know why you like that human. There's something not quite right about her."

"Psh, she's a bit eccentric is all. Her parents put a lot of pressure on her to be perfect. I'd be off too." Despite some of her more annoying traits I really think her heart is true. If I had parents who act like hers I'm pretty sure that my life would be one giant ball of anxiety and self-doubt also. Who am I kidding, because of my mother my life is one giant ball of anxiety and self-doubt. I just cope better than Lucinda does, sometimes anyhow.

Plus, her crush is dead, before any girly fantasy she had about him can come to fruition.

"I wonder how he died?" I muse out loud.

"I can find out." Ciar pulls his phone out of his pocket and makes a call.

My brain goes nuts with thoughts of Trick. Who names their kid Trick? Is it a nickname or something? Maybe a designation? I wonder what things he's got to take care of? At least he admitted he's a chicken, but I don't know about being a coward. All of us have things we want to avoid or hide from altogether.

Oh, Keri, great job not thinking about it. I chastise myself, realizing just how in depth I'm thinking about the one I'm supposed to avoid thinking about. He's this big mystery and I can't help it, I want to know about him.

He sent me candied flowers.

"Are you finished with your inner monologue yet, because I know how he died."

Blushing a little because Ciar is a butt-hole, I look up at him. "Well?"

"He was poisoned and then strangled with a belt or a rope of some kind. The urge to hunt is tingling, but something is keeping us from seeing who to hunt."

"Kind of like with my mother?" After a moment of searching my face with those unfathomable eyes of his, he nods.

"Figures." Chewing my lip, I walk into the living room, the really empty living room. I totally need furniture in here. "How exactly did you break the magic protecting her?"

"Hiding from the Hunt is a temporary measure. Unless the spell is continuously fed, eventually it wears off. We are then called to them. Feeding the spell takes a toll on the caster, so you either need to be really connected or have more than one person maintaining it. Like the would-be Elf assassin."

"Someone was continuously feeding a spell that hid him?" Ciar nods at my question.

"Speaking of the Hunt, I'll return soon." With a hard kiss

on my mouth that left me wanting another he disappears, and I'm left alone with my thoughts.

My brain skips away from the weird death of Mark the 'Lucinda crush' and onto the flowers. I pick off a candy petal and pop it into my mouth. It's a thoughtful present, one from someone who took time to at least learn a little about me. This mysterious Trick person - who is obviously one of my Triad.

The bad thing about my bond with these other two men is that its faint, I can sense them out there in the world, but it's not hard to fool me with magic. Not something I like admitting, it's nothing less than the truth. Either one of them can be right in front of my face and I won't know.

That particular thought makes me look around me suspiciously.

"Why are you looking around like that?" Zag asks, swooping in from the back of the house.

"Where have you been all day?" I immediately ask. He lands on my shoulder and flicks my cheek with his tongue. "Okay, the cuteness doesn't change the question."

"You think I'm cute?"

I prepare myself for the bombardment of reasons he thinks he isn't cute - because he's a big, bad Dragon - but instead he makes his little happy growly sound and settles around my shoulder like a warm, scaly scarf. He's asleep within seconds.

Shaking my head at him, I stroke his tail and debate on harassing Ciar on what Zag is up to, because it's something involving them both. I'm many things but not completely obtuse. Ciar has Gertie checking all the food in the house, just like he checked the candied flowers good and hard before giving them to me.

Deciding that the first thing I need to do is to put the masterful creation of a dress up, I grab the bag and climb the stairs, slowly. I don't want jar the sleeping Dragon. The house is already looking different, the Fairies and Brownies hard at work. They move fast too, as demonstrated when I see my room. I stand there with my mouth open, staring at it. The walls are a beautiful light pink with silver dragons weaving in and out of its textured dimensions. With a cream-colored trim and curtains it looks like a completely different room.

There's a new, bed dominating the room. A four-poster one graces the middle of the room with a soft looking, silver comforter draped over the end of it. There are mounds of pillows eating up most of the space on the mattress, but that's how I like it. Hanging the dress on the back of the door, I carefully slip Zag off my shoulders and lay him on the end of the enormous bed.

Looking around to make sure I'm alone, I leap onto the mattress. This thing is big enough to sleep four or five adults. Which means I can roll around all I want without Ciar griping at me. Giggling, I roll back and forth a few times and find myself facing an awake Zag who is staring hard on the mattress.

"Mistress, lay still." I'm not sure if it's the quiet intensity in his voice or the absolute stillness of him but I freeze in place.

That's when I feel it, a thrumming energy coming from underneath the bed. Gods bless it, I hate when Ciar is right, especially in moments like this. Something is under my bed that's dangerous to me. He told me over and over to always check, always be careful and here I am jumping and rolling around on whatever it is.

Aren't I a genius?

"What is it?"

"Fire bomb, a small but potent one. It's designed to only destroy the bed and its occupants."

"What do I do?"

"Remain calm, Gertie is now under there working on it too."

This entire mess with someone trying to kill me is getting old fast.

"I'm guessing my jumping on the bed like a dunce activated it?"

He shakes his head. "If I'm right, which I am, it is waiting on another presence."

Ciar's.

Someone knows we're together in that way, which means there's a spy somewhere in my life. Automatically my mind goes to Lucinda and although sometimes she can be unpleasant, I'm not sure what she can gain from my death. Still, I'm not stupid enough to take her off the short list. The Fairies and Brownies are clear thought. Gertie would know.

Calsis did have a crew in here yesterday, to take the furniture out and before Ciar put up his barrier ward anyone could have come in and out without my knowing it. But Calsis is super paranoid, I don't see him having an employee playing both sides. At this point, it's frustrating because that mostly leaves one suspect and the burning question of why.

We have a potential who but not a why. Honestly, I need to look at my mother's former friends and their connections to my only suspect. They were the ones who gave her the dagger. My mother who was a Graywalker... wait, I bet they didn't know what she was. That would explain her using magic to hide her true nature under the guise of being human.

Why did she do that? There are too many questions and none of them have answers.

"Okay, it's dealt with, you can move now." Zag says, visibly relaxing. He stretches and yawns, showing rows of sharp teeth that I know are as big around as my arm when he's normal sized.

"Just like that?"

"Yes, whoever planted it was sloppy."

"Can I roll around on the bed again?" Laughing at my question, he curls into a ball and tucks his tail around his face.

"Yes, mistress - roll away."

I do so without needing further encouragement and while doing this I remember something. Daily, my mother would sit at the ugly old desk that used to sit in the corner of the room and write into a leather backed book that resembled a journal.

She always hid it away in the closet.

Hm. Jumping to my feet I go into the mostly empty closet noticing that one of the squares has a deep scratch across it. I push it and discover that it's loose, I open it with only a little effort and dig around inside it. Finding a stack of what feels like books I pull them out and am pleased to discover they are in fact the books she used to write in.

Going back to the bed I climb into it and sit cross-legged with the books spread out before me. I think it's time to get to know the woman who birthed me and hated me for it.

CHAPTER 27
FROSTY THE GUITAR MAN...

Stretching to get rid of the kinks in my back, I sit the open book on the bed and lean back against the headboard, trying to digest what I've read so far. I'm on the third book. The first two were all about her relationship with my father, Daya. She met him at a concert while she was stalking a man for prey.

Graywalkers eat people.

Apparently, my - father seems so intimate, so we'll find another term - donor? Yes, that works. Apparently, my donor helped her catch the guy because he was following her. They hit it off over her dinner and started dating. Daya encouraged her to take on a more human façade and my mother fell head over heels for him. Until I read her words of love scrawled in her elegant - I hate using that word in relation to her but it's true - script, I'd have never believed the woman capable of love.

Gods know, she didn't show it to me. Yet, she practically slobbered over the donor. Every other sentence is about his beauty or his charm. I can also see the little signs of manipulation from him, he's sneaky that's for sure. Little nudges for her to change her hair or her hunting practices. All of this over a year long period.

Which all changed when she got pregnant with me. I saw that video, but her words are awful. While I was in the womb, she tried to kill me several times, but his spell kept her from being successful. By this point, Daya had disappeared and left me at her tender mercy. My creation was deliberate, so why leave me with her? Why never come back for me? Not that growing up in the Moon Clan is something I'd have enjoyed, but it's a valid question and one day I'll need an answer for it.

Rubbing my eyes, I ignore the moisture there.

Even after I was born she tried to kill me, but that spell continued protecting me. That's the reason she got the dagger from her 'friends' in town. Friends who are members of the opposition to the Moon Clan and with their name show their originality, the Sun Clan.

I know a little about the clans dedicated to various deities and this one is young compared to many of them. The Moon Clan is dedicated to Donn while the Sun Clan claim to worship Faerie herself. They both claim to work their god's will.

I highly doubt that they work for anyone but themselves.

I think it's a safe assumption that they encouraged my mother to kill me, wait - that's wrong, she wanted me dead way before that. They gave her the tool to finally make it a reality. That's much better.

The soft strumming of a guitar pulls me out of my dark thoughts. Standing up, I cross to the window. At the fountain in the backyard sits a white-haired man with a guitar on his lap. As he plays, the notes drift on the wind and it feels like, directly into my window. The thread between the two of us lightly pulses. There's no bond but the initial one yet, but I know who he is or at least what role he is supposed to play in my life. This is one of my Triad.

Annoyed with life in general and feeling a bit put out about the entire thing, I stomp downstairs and jog into the backyard before he can run away again. This time he watches me with eyes so blue they're darn near white. As I get closer to him the temperature drops, which is cool and strange. If he were just an elemental of some type, it wouldn't affect the world this easily or drastically. He's not putting any effort into it, at all.

"Who the heck are you?"

Sitting his guitar down on the fountain beside him he crosses his arms and glares at me. Yes, glares. As if he has a right to give me a look like that about anything.

"Who uses the word 'heck' for anything?" he asks with a snide tone that kinda make me want to hit him with his guitar.

"I do. Now, who are you?"

"You went through your Awakening and summoned me here."

I cross my arms in defense. He's angry, I can feel it all around him. Staring at him I take his measure. Spiky white hair, uncommon in the Fae world, vivid colors are the usual. It sticks up in all directions but still looks like he put some effort into making it look that way. His eyes are an unnatural blue, with white stars around his pupils that I swear are shaped like a snowflake. His eyebrows match his hair. The smile his lips curve into is not a welcoming, friendly smile. Nope, it says I hate your guts.

It's a shame too, because he's a really, *really* pretty man.

"Faerie summoned you here. I'm stuck just as much as you are," I counter after staring as awkwardly as I can. He has no right to come into my home and be a dick.

"Release me from my bond," he orders, his voice taking

on a tone like Ciar's but nastier. Makes me realize right then and there that Ciar was never cruel to me or demeaning, Ciar never sounded like this guy.

"Not something I can do, and you know this."

He stands and crosses the distance between us. At his proximity, I get goosebumps, my body naturally attracted to his. It's a Triad thing and I refuse to acknowledge it any more than that.

"I don't want your bond or you. So figure out a way to make the bond go away before I make you." There's menace in the last three words, menace that makes me a little nervous. It's exactly why I punch him in the face as hard as I can. How dare he!

"Holy shit, you punched me!" he accuses, cradling his bleeding nose.

"Duh, don't be so shocked. You threatened me, I reacted. Is this how you treat everyone in your life?"

"Life? You're taking away my life! I have a wife and a child on the way, but I receive a call from a stranger that's so strong I can't refuse it."

My satisfaction from punching him turns sour in my stomach. Wife? Child on the way? I'm not the most educated on all things magical, but if I remember correctly, a Triad member can't knock someone up until after they've bonded with their Center. I'm sure it's a way to make sure that Triads happen. He's definitely a member of my Triad. I can feel the bond demanding to be forged between us.

Something in his life is a lie and this time it has nothing to do with me.

"I don't expect you to ditch your wife and kid, dude. But the Triad has to be completed as much as it sucks for both of us."

"But we have to mate."

I laugh, it's so funny meeting someone who understands less than I do.

"No, we don't. The love you have for your wife should be enough to keep you from having those types of feelings for me."

Triads don't mess with true love. Human fairy tales have that right, real true love is untouchable by magic. But since he's here... that makes me feel sorry for him. He's being duped on two levels.

"Why are you looking at me with pity?" he asks, suspiciously.

Blinking, I try my best to blank my face. I'm not the greatest at it but this time I'm trying. I need to find out more about this wife person and pronto. He might not want to be here, but his mess of a romantic life can impact mine and I won't have it.

'Neither will I, invite them both here to stay. I want to see this woman who claims to be carrying the child of a Triad member.' Ciar's voice in my head only startles me a little.

"You can bring her here to stay with you. I don't have any intentions of forcing a romantic entanglement with a married, soon-to-be-father." Even though I don't think it's his kid any more than Ciar does. The love part I can't judge. I love one man and it's still all new.

'You admit it at least,' Ciar teases.

This new guy - who's name I don't know yet, might be part of the Triad but he's not family. Not yet.

"You're not going to force a connection between us?" Making a face at him I shake my head. Does he know anything about Awakening that's true?

"I didn't ask for this, either, so we'll just take things nice and slow. The bond doesn't have to be a love bond. You know that, right?" I can tell by the dumb look on his face he didn't know. "Where did you grow up?"

"Everywhere until I met Penelope." I watch his face for the dreamy look people in love tend to get and there's nothing but a slight softening of his gaze. "She pulled me in off the street and we've been together ever since."

"Long time then?"

"Three years this October." He answered that fast.

"Can't wait to meet her." I do mean that just not for the reasons it sounds like. "Now, first things first, what the heck is your name?"

"Rime," he answers automatically, his beautiful - yeah, they are totally beautiful, eyes narrow at me. "You're really not going to force anything?"

"I'm not sure where you're getting your information about Triads from but someone is feeding you a line of crap." The mask of anger slips back into his eyes replacing the doubt that was there.

That's great, I made him mad again.

"Penelope is a Mage who knows her magic. For you to even insinuate that she is being dishonest about anything makes me want to throttle you."

"I wouldn't recommend it, Frosty," Ciar says, stepping out of whatever shadow he was lurking in. I'm actually quite thankful he's here.

Rime might seem a bit air-headed, but he's strong, incredibly so, I can feel it coming off him in waves. He'll hand me my butt in a hot minute. Ciar on the other hand, is his match or more. He's the Pinnacle after all.

"This is Keri and she is your Center and deserves a lot more respect than you're showing her." Ciar says, stepping in between Rime and me.

Leaning around Ciar's broad shoulders to look back and forth between the two men. I realize that although they are both alpha males, Ciar just burns a little brighter or darker, depending on how you look at it. Rime can see it too. It's why he backs down and adopts a more relaxed stance.

"I don't care what her name is. I'm not giving up my life for some mystical shit I don't agree with or understand." His eyes land on me. "I will take your generous offer to allow us to stay here and bring Penelope for a temporary move. This pull won't allow me to do anything else, yet." In a swirl of snow, he vanishes.

Why does everyone but me get cool powers?

"You can call someone's fate to them by whistling and you don't think that's cool?" Ciar asks, one black brow arched.

"I want to blow things up or portal out or throw a fireball once in awhile." There's no shame in wanting something... normal.

"Normal is boring."

The backyard, or courtyard as my mother called it, boasts a variance of Faerie fauna, some of which are trees. One such tree has a branch that hangs low over the walkway. Grabbing my attention is a blue raven perched precariously on the very tip of the branch.

Blue raven? That's not normal, either. Just like with Rime, a thread goes from me to this bird.

"I thought you had some things to take care of?" I ask the bird, surprising Ciar, who turns on his heel to face the bird. The bird, who chitters in what can only be described as a laugh.

"It's not him really, it's simply a golem for him to be snoopy with," Ciar informs me, and turns and walks into the house.

I look back at the bird. A golem huh? I've heard of them, but never saw one before. They're made from blood or flesh of the caster, typically used to spy.

"Well, snoop all you want. At least you're nice enough to

send me candy." With that said, I head back into the house to catch up with Ciar in the kitchen.

Now I have hopes for Trick, he at least didn't come in full of anger over something I have no control over any more than he does.

"Frosty needs educating. He's young and foolish and more than likely under some type of spell, or in the least stupid over a wet pus- "

"Ciar."

"It's nothing less than the truth. If he doesn't want to pursue romantic ties with you that's fine, more for me but he can and will respect you whether he wants to or not." Ciar has that tone, the not fooling around one. Smiling, I link my arm through his and kiss his cheek.

"What's that for?" he asks with a smile.

"For making me feel like I'm worthy of something."

Turning suddenly, he yanks me up and slams me gently against the wall. Without a word, he fastens his mouth on mine and plunders it. Yes, plunders. His tongue is a hot dominating presence that seeks out every single inch of my mouth and lips.

Wow.

Biting down, not so gently on my lip, he pulls away and stares at me with bright eyes.

"You are worth everything, Monster Girl. Never doubt that for a single second." And I'm pretty sure he mutters something about killing Frosty under his breath, but my heart is beating so loudly in my ears from his kiss I'm not sure.

Releasing me enough to let me slide down his body and to the floor, he steps back and smiles the devastating one that says, run away little girl. With a squeal that, to my shame sounds real, I turn and run for all I'm worth.

I almost made it to the stairs.

CHAPTER 28

AS THE LYING, PREGNANT, JERK TURNS...

Somehow, we end up in the bedroom, on the bed that almost exploded.

"WHAT?!" he yells, sitting up with a jerk. Whoops, I forgot to tell him or think about it.

"What she neglected to tell you is that there was a magical fire bomb planted under her bed that would've gone off if not for myself and Miss Gertie," Zag fills in, flying into the room from wherever he hid while Ciar and I were having our escapades through the house.

Ciar gives me a dirty look and drags me onto his lap. Flipping me over, he solidly slaps my bare butt cheek.

"OW! What was that for?"

"For thinking that wasn't important. For not being vigilant. Keri, this isn't just your life. You're playing with our lives too." His voice grows steadily calmer as he talks but the anger is still a spark in his eyes.

"Okay, okay! I'll be more vigilant. I didn't think to check in my own home."

"Until we catch the people responsible for these attempts, expect it from anywhere. You're smarter than this, act like it."

"Well, in my defense, there's a lot going on right now! I didn't ask for this crap to happen. I wanted a nice quiet life in the dang forest."

"No Fae has a nice quiet life."

"Mada -"

He cuts me off, "Has just as many struggles in a different way. Power is coveted." To dig home his point, he smacks my butt again and I bite his thigh. Laughing, he tosses me off his lap and pauses when one of the journals thumps onto the ground.

"What's this?" he asks, leaning over to pick the leather-bound book off the floor.

"My mother's journals, I figured that maybe I could find some things out reading them."

"Did you?"

"Yes and no. I have an idea who's trying to kill me if that helps?" He makes a face and goes to grab me again, probably to abuse my poor bum some more, so I slither away from him and slide to the floor. "The Sun Clan."

Face palming, he lays back on the bed. "Gods, it's those idiots. They think they stand for Faerie and take fanaticism to a dangerous level. Are you sure?"

"Pretty sure, yeah. I'm guessing you've made their acquaintance before?"

"Several years ago, when we found you. Some of them tried to breach the forest wards. They were like birds beating their heads against a glass door." Rolling onto his side to study me, he pushes the hair off my face. "I didn't connect the two at the time, it wasn't the first time they tried, I should've. They were more persistent than normal, but you were fighting for your life. I was focused on more important things than a clan full of idiots."

Standing, I cross to the bathroom, pausing in the doorway

to look at him over my shoulder when he calls my name, "Keri?"

"Yeah?"

"Do you want to go to the beach this weekend?" Standing there, staring at him lying naked on the bed with only a sheet across his hips, his lean muscled body still bearing the marks of my teeth and on display to my hungry gaze, I do the only thing a woman in my situation can do. I run and jump on him like a cat. Of course, he catches me. Laughing, we roll around on the bed and - no surprise, I end up on bottom. Laying on me, his hips cupped between my thighs he kisses my nose.

"You've never been to the beach, so I thought you might like the trip. I had no idea that you'd like it that much."

"Had nothing to do with the beach," I murmur, letting him see my thoughts. Laughing, he pushes the result of those thoughts against me. Then his eyes turn serious and thoughtful.

"You're not saying much about your wayward Triad."

Oh, there's the question that I was hoping to avoid.

Taking a deep breath, I explain, "Rime has some hoopla going on, that's for sure. With the pregnant wife and all that, something is wrong with that arrangement. Since he is *definitely* part of my Triad, then a child with her is impossible. Which means more drama for us."

"Agreed, him having a child is an impossibility, a mate... I highly doubt she's his mate."

"Why?" I ask him, curious despite myself.

"I've known from the moment I saw you that life with you in it will never be the same. Something that goes for your Triad, as well. I think ultimately, we'll all three end up mated to you. I also know that you won't do what I would in this situation and force the bonding."

"That's wrong and you know it. Plus, I didn't know I could do that."

"Yes, you can and it would solve the problem. The goal is right whether or not the method is."

"There are times when talking to you makes me feel like I'm talking to an old wrinkled man, and other times, someone my age."

"Can't I be both?"

"Wait, does this mean you're going to get old man balls?"

"I'm going to rub them all over your face too, Monster Girl." I end up laughing so hard my bladder gets upset with me. Crawling out from under him, I creep off to the bathroom and while sitting on the toilet notice the blue raven in the window across from me, staring.

"That's rude to stare at someone while they pee, bird." It chitters at me and I toss a roll of toilet paper at the window. Of course, it doesn't hit the bird, but it startles it away. Which means he is watching me through the bird.

Well, Rime is a jerk - maybe because of his circumstances, but it stands regardless. I wonder what Trick is like? Not as big of a jerk because he did send me candied flowers. Gods, I hope he doesn't have a wife hiding somewhere too, because as much as I hate Ciar being right, he often is. And my gut agrees with him this time.

Finishing up my business, I wash my hands and go in search of food. Ciar chuffs when I walk by the bed without a backward glance. Smiling, I keep walking. The key is not to look, which I barely manage to avoid. Looking is a trap.

"Keri."

"Sorry Ciar I'm hungry, the rest will have to wait until I eat."

"Not that I mind another hour of fucking you, but I thought you should know you're still naked and there's a houseful of Fairies downstairs." His laugh follows me as I turn and run into the closet. I'm not ashamed of my nudity, but there is a point where you shouldn't just parade around naked as the day you're born.

Especially in front of a houseful of male Fairies, or Fairies in general for that matter. The majority of them aren't shy like Bis, and all of them have an extremely high sex-drive that's set off with the slightest provocation. Me, strolling by them naked, might be considered that.

Clothed and feeling a bit better than I did when the day started, I run down the stairs and straight for the kitchen. My stomach protests loudly as I swing open the fridge door. Patting it, I sort through the gobs of leftovers. Settling on spaghetti and meatballs, I load up two plates and toss one of them into the microwave. When I lean my hip against the counter and look up Ciar is in the doorway watching me.

"What?" I ask. His eyes darken in that special way that ends up with me naked.

"Nu-uh, I just put the food in." I know that look and I swear a woman in a kitchen turns some men on. Backing away from him, I jump when he rushes me and manage to do laps around the kitchen island to avoid his grabby hands. Both of us laughing - me borderline out of breath - I take the chance to change the plates out when the ding interrupts our game.

"Aw, you made me some too." He wraps his arm around my waist when I set the plate of hot food down.

"Of course I did. I figure since you don't have the leg of some strange guy in the freezer, that spaghetti will do."

"I don't eat people outside of work," he teases, taking a fork and attacking my plate of food.

"Hey!"

"Too slow, Monster Girl." Grabbing the plate, he turns in circles to avoid me. Giving up, I wait for the second plate to be finished.

"You have sauce all over your chin," I taunt. His tongue

snakes out and licks his entire chin clean. That must come in handy when he licks his own butt. I sputter as noodles rain down on my head. Oh yeah, he heard that.

"Well, you were a dog."

"I never licked my own butt," he protests.

"Liar, I saw you licking other parts." Which is true.

"That's a perk of the canine form!" he defends, throwing more noodles at me. Some of them smack me in the eye and makes me laugh, even as it stings.

"You two are worse than little ones, I swear." Gertie comments, popping in above the spaghetti covered island. Whoops.

"Sorry, Gertie." We apologize at the same time.

When she turns to clean part of the counter, I smack him in the ear with a handful of sauce saturated noodles and run. Like the children Gertie accuses us of being, we run through the house leaving bits of noodles all over the walls and floors.

I vow to clean it up as I dive away from hands that reach for me and head outside into the backyard. The blue raven joins the game, dive bombing both of us and making that gurgling laugh. At least Trick has a playful nature, I hope. The bird's behavior gives me hints that he does.

Running around the fountain, I head towards the front of the house and look back into the smiling face of Ciar, the predatory smiling face. Laughing out loud, I push myself to run faster. We both know that he's barely moving and can catch me at any point. I think in this case he's conserving his energy and simply wearing out his prey, who happens to be me. Seeing the spaghetti in his hair and all over his clothes, I can only imagine how bad I look, and that makes me laugh harder.

Aren't we a pair?

"Ciar, you know—oof." My rather clever insult is ruined when I collide, full-throttle, with something solid and warm.

Hands grasp my upper arms to try and catch me but it's too late, my momentum is going to take us both down hard.

Coming to a stop, I make a face when I meet the ice-blue eyes of Rime.

Scrambling off him, no matter how much my body decides to like the feel of his, I roll to my feet and step back out of his space. He's returned rather soon, and I don't feel like having my happy moment dimmed by another one of his temper tantrums.

It's then that my eyes decide to work properly and take everything in, including the blonde human standing to the right of him. I'll be, he actually brought her. In a glance, I take in the red spots on her cheeks, the hate filled look she's giving me. The gobs of suitcases at her side and the single duffle at his. And somehow, in all that jumble, I see the swell of her stomach. Looking at her I have to wonder who the father really is, Ciar and I know it isn't Rime. Now, how do we go about telling him that?

"You are covered in spaghetti," Rime says dryly.

Looking at the orange handprints all over his white shirt, I smile and say, "You are now too." For a split second he almost smiles but then Penelope elbows him, and it fades before it ever reaches fruition.

That's a shame.

"There's a bedroom on the third floor you're welcome to use. If Gertie wants to help you she will, but I'm not going to make her." I caution.

"Who's Gertie?" the woman demands. Her tone makes my teeth hurt and I have to force myself not to wince. Yeah, she and I aren't going to get along.

"The house Brownie," Ciar says over my shoulder.

"Are you going to take our things to our room, Rime?" she demands of the man glaring daggers at me like I've committed some grave sin.

"Frosty, I suggest you explain that this isn't a hotel or a luxury resort. This is our home and she is merely a guest here." Sensing an impending disaster, I step directly in between the two men. Rime is now looking at Ciar like he wants to pound his face in and Ciar is looking at Rime like he's a dog turd on his shoe.

"Penelope, this is the woman I was telling you about and her companion." Rime attempts to introduce, a bit late.

"Oh, the whore that summoned you against your will and the dog that follows her around?" The whore? The dog? Gods I'm going to punch him in the nose again. He sees the intent and flinches away while Ciar grabs me before my fist connects.

A mean part of me wants to blurt out that I'm onto her scam and wipe that smug grin off her face. Ciar and I are both aware that Rime is mostly ignorant about Awakenings and how Triads work. Ignorance doesn't forgive his or her behavior. Instead of ruining his day, I grit my teeth and disentangling myself from Ciar, turn away and head into the house. I want to hit something but choose to go shower.

'Why not tell him? It's the truth and he does deserve to know,' Ciar asks, as he joins me on the stairs. See, he could've caught me at any time.

'I don't want to be the one he hates, so I'm going to do something you did to me a long time ago.'

'Monster Girl, that's a long list.'

'I'm going to give him the book.' Ciar pauses, then throws his head back and laughs.

The book is a history of Fae kind specific to Awakenings. It's magic and no one mortal can tamper with it. Ciar made me read it as a child and it's how I have the limited knowledge I do have. It's also how the book may or may not have gotten the scribbles saying that 'Ciar is a buttface' in the margins.

Ciar's laughter increases. He caught that thought, did he?

"There's something off about that human," he states, tugging off his jeans when we reach the bathroom. I eyeball him but choose to say nothing and turn the shower on.

The fact that she's lying about Rime being the father of her baby is more than enough for me to agree with Ciar. The way she looked around her like she's adding up dollar signs didn't set well with me, either. That was only from a couple of minutes in her presence. I can't imagine spending more time than that with her. Keri, you can't strangle a pregnant woman, I remind myself, and wonder how many times I'll have to say it around this Penelope.

"You forgot to eat," Ciar says.

Sonofabiscuit.

CHAPTER 29
THE DOOMED PILLOWS...

To say dinner is an awkward affair is a complete understatement. Gertie somehow produced a large dining table to fit the dozen or so dinner guests.

Rime is staring at the plate in front of him like he wants it to catch on fire. Penelope is chattering about mundane things in a snotty rude way while watching the Fairy men with a bit of envy in her rather dull brown eyes. Fairy and Brownie servants are considered a boon in society. To me they're just family who are nice enough to clean up after my messy bum.

She's pretty, with a cherub face and those pouty lips that men covet so much. Her hair is a thick wavy blonde that some might say resemble feathered velvet, perfectly laying on her head like the cloud of goodness it is. Her makeup is immaculate and in a roundabout way she reminds me of Lucinda, except this time, I hate her. Every time she opens her mouth and speaks I hate her more.

Rime, other than the occasional grunt, has remained silent throughout the entire endeavor while Penelope hasn't shut up. Not that I mind chatty people, I can be incredibly chatty myself, I mind what she's saying.

How she thinks Fairies should lose all their rights. That all wealth owned by 'servants' should be turned over to the 'master.' And the worst thing, this obvious mother to be that's supposedly pregnant by a FAE - all mixed blood children should be placed in servitude.

Does this moron realize who she's talking to?

The Fairy and Brownies are stone-faced, and I don't blame them. Gods, this is my fault. I let him bring this awful woman here all because I didn't want to force him to choose. The pull of a Triad is strong, and since there isn't true love between them, that pull is stronger than his pull to her. Even magically enhanced like she's probably making it because something fishy is going on here and I think Rime knows it deep down inside.

'Is it one of those Enrapture spells you told me about?'

'No, it's worse, whatever it is. I can't see the spell through his wards.'

'If you can't see through his wards, how did a spell get in there?'

'Sex is a very vulnerable time for many Fae. Especially if you trust the person you're having sex with.'

That's good to know, and when I meet Ciar's eyes he rolls his, knowing what I'm thinking. *'You're not putting your finger there, Monster Girl. Unless I can put mine in yours first.'* Coughing to cover a laugh, I pretend to wipe my face with a napkin to hide my smirk.

"Karen, what did the Menagerie pick for you as a job? Since I don't see any clan or house banners I'm assuming you were chosen for manual labor?"

First off, she got my name wrong, second... no, can't think the second, it involves me causing her bodily harm. I open my mouth to reply but Zag saves the day.

"My mistress is an independent, if you must know. As well as Awakened, which is something you aren't familiar with I imagine. Something that will never happen to you since

258

you're breeding. Speaking of breeding - " I wrap my fingers around his nose to quiet him.

"Rime, since you don't seem to know a lot about what's going on, we thought we'd give you the Awakening handbook. It'll give you ALL of the information you need to move forward in this incredibly messy situation," Ciar says, way more diplomatically than I expected him to be.

The book appears on the table in front of Rime, right in his plate of untouched food that he's been pushing around for a half-hour. Penelope attempts to touch it, but it zaps her.

"That's a Fae only kind of book," Ciar states, with quite a bit of amusement in his tone.

My eyes fall on Rime to find him, surprisingly, looking at the book with a bit of awe on his face. Has he never seen a Fae book before?

"This will tell me everything I need to know about what's going on?" he asks quietly.

"Yes, *everything*." Ciar stresses the word but no one gets it. Okay, everyone but Rime and the twit next to him gets it. I swear, even Gertie lets out a little laugh. Rime tucks the book away in his Blank Space and starts picking again at his food. Ignoring the whole lot, I finish my steak and thank Gertie for a wonderful meal.

"It's okay, I guess. Shouldn't she be a better cook since she's a Brownie?" Penelope's whiney voice filters through my happy food coma.

Aw, it's a shame that after three helpings the food isn't what you expect. I figure that's something you notice on the first helping. I manage to catch the thought before it leaves my mouth, barely.

Ciar chokes on his food and I can hear his laughter mixed in with the coughing. I look everywhere but him, because I know I'll laugh and there won't be any disguising it.

Instead I say, "You can buy pizza if you prefer."

"What are you insinuating, Keri?" Rime asks, quietly. His spectacular eyes pin me to my seat. Instead of shifting uncomfortably or feeling guilty, which is what he wants me to do, I smile.

"That maybe she prefers buying her own food?" I put as much innocence into that statement as I'm capable of. It's taking everything else to keep my face straight. His jaw clenches, he senses more, but because we don't have a full on bond he can only guess. Continuing to smile inanely, I put my dishes in the sink and go to leave the room.

"We need to practice the dance," Ciar says, surprising me.

"We're still doing that?" I was hoping he forgot since the last time we talked about it.

"Yes, because of our circumstances we need to establish our power base in the Fae world and rubbing it in their faces is the best way to do it." Why are we having this conversation out loud? Taking our audience into account, slyly I look at Rime and see his interest, even though he's trying to hide it by staring at his untouched plate. His head is turned to the side to hear our conversation.

'He's paying very close attention. Her hold on him isn't only magical like I first believed, it's coupled with something older than that.'

'What's older than magic?'

'Guilt.'

I have no idea about the history of these two, no information from which to make an educated guess. For all I know, Rime is a wife beater. *'How ignorant is he of things to think that the kid is his?'*

'Relatively so. He's angry with you for Awakening and summoning him here, it'll take him awhile to get over that childishness.'

'You don't agree with his stance on things?'

'I find it hard to believe that a mature member of our Triad -

which for all intents and purpose he is - demeans himself into thinking that someone like her deserves the title of 'wife."

Whoa, Ciar sounds angry.

'Keri, I know that you don't expect a physical relationship with your Triad, but you should. This is not a run of the mill type of connection and he knows it. It's why he's so pissed off at the situation.'

'I don't want either one of us to be forced into anything.' And I won't allow it to happen that way, either. Ciar sees this entire situation differently than I do, he's known a lot longer, and had more time to prepare for its eventuality.

'This woman is a big part of his life - whether or not that's his baby. Maybe she's super sweet when no one is around and makes him feel over the moon?' Chancing a glance at Rime, I catch him staring at me with a frown on his face. He suspects something strange is going on but isn't sure what.

'You refuse to use the magic you've got and unless this idiot wises up and acts accordingly, the threat to your life is very real. I can't always be here because of the stupid fucking Hunt and this one can't pull his head out of his ass enough to guard you.'

'I'm perfectly capable of protecting myself.'

'The bomb under the bed. The poison in the food.'

'Okay, I'm mostly capable of protecting myself.'

'You're splitting hairs here. The entire point of a Triad is to protect it's Center.'

'Wouldn't it make more sense to talk to him about it instead of talking about him?'

'Go right ahead.' Well, I didn't mean right this second.

Clearing my throat, I turn back towards Rime, super uncomfortable because I have no idea what to say that isn't going to come out rude. Ciar, of course, saves the day.

"Read the book, you know it isn't tampered with. It's the real information about an Awakening and Triad." Ciar has that no bullcrap tone going on. It's kind of hot.

Grabbing my arm, he pulls me behind him out of the

room and up the stairs. Playfully tossing me on the bed he pins me against the mattress and stares down into my eyes.

"You're too kind at times."

"How am I being too kind this time?"

Kissing me softly, he rests his face in the crook of my neck. His breath is hot on my skin and gives me little tingles every time he exhales. Chuckling, he nips my throat and lifts his head.

"You're fully aware of the fact that an incomplete bond can be highjacked."

Sitting up, I push him off me. "Is someone trying to do that?" I fumble around with it but don't feel anything.

"No. The Duke has noticed."

"Are you fucking serious?" The shock on his face almost brings me out of the near panic state this news has me in.

Blinking a few times, he opens his mouth, then closes it, then repeats it. "Did you just say fucking?"

"Yes. Now, answer my question," I demand.

"His magic tested it the last time we saw him."

"So, you mean to tell me that unless idiot upstairs cements the bond you think the Duke will try to take it?" After a moment of carefully looking at my face, he nods. Every pillow on the bed explodes in a cloud of stuffing that drifts around us like fat snowflakes.

CHAPTER 30
A FAIRY DID IT...

Ciar has disappeared off to wherever he goes to get ready for a Hunt which leaves me alone in the dark, listening to the argument happening above me. I'll freely admit that it's more interesting than I imagined it would be. Her voice is shrill and tear-choked as she rails at him for not making sure she has money for more maternity clothing. While Rime, surprisingly patient, asks her what happened to the other new clothes he bought her.

She informs him that it's not enough. She needs a few outfits a day to feel happy. Wow, just wow.

"Why are you reading that stupid book. I already told you about Awakenings." Her voice is less shrill but snider now. I don't like the woman and I never will. It's obvious she's manipulating him magically and otherwise.

If only I knew how the guilt plays into it.

"I hate to say it Penelope, but I feel like you're not being completely honest with me about all of this. You disappeared for months and then tracked me down saying you're pregnant with my baby."

"It's your fault I left! You said you were sensing an Awakened. I didn't want to be second in your life and now that we're here, I don't want to share you with that fat troll."

Fat troll? For a moment, I want to go punch her right in her whiney mouth, but then I remember that she's pregnant and in her place, I wouldn't be thrilled if my husband went off chasing some strange person. Then again, it's an Awakening and I'd probably be more understanding about it. It's not like I'm all up on his lap or anything. In fact, I'm pretty sure I don't really like him much, either. This situation isn't my fault any more than it is his.

"It says here that a member of a Triad can't have a baby until the Triad is formed." Oh, things are getting interesting now.

"That's a bunch of bullshit and you know it. You're looking at me gross and pregnant with your baby and saying that?" I can feel the spell she is casting lapping around his Aura, which is new. Or maybe it's because I'm sitting here being a creep and listening in on a private conversation, so I'm concentrating harder.

"These books can't be tampered with," Rime defends.

This is something all Fae are taught as children when they first start to show magic, but she won't know that because she *isn't* Fae. This is about to get incredibly interesting now.

"I don't understand how a book can't be rewritten. Your Fae gods make no sense to me. Give me that and I'll throw it away." She squeaks when it zaps her. You'd think she learned the first time. Is there a chance that the wards on this place are interfering with her magic on him?

There's some stomping above me and a slamming door, but no more words are exchanged. Slightly disappointed he didn't straight up call her out for her deception, I roll over and fluff my pillow. Rime isn't demonstrating a lot of intelligence here. I'm kind of magic dumb and even I can see her magic coating him in its oily residue. Looking at him, feeling what I can feel from him - he's too strong for someone like her to be able to pull this off.

The guilt factor must be strong for him to sacrifice his freedom for someone who is lying about something as life-altering as a child. There's no going back from being a parent. At least, a decent parent. And if I had to guess, dumb or not then he'll be a good parent. After all, he's willing to accept that baby without question.

I'd bet money on it.

There's also the chance that the woman has more than her own magic involved. There are such things as enchanted objects and such. It can also explain why I don't feel it. I can't pick up something like that, but I know who can.

"Zag. I know you're awake because you were eavesdropping too." There's a grumble from the covers at the foot of the bed, then he pops his head up, his eyes glowing in the dark room.

"It was a rather engaging episode. I look forward to others that involve less door slamming."

"It's not TV you butt head." I poke at him with my foot.

"Close enough. Now what is it you need?

"I need you to find out if there is a spelled object on Rime or Penelope. I can't sense them, but I know you can."

"As you wish." He settles back down into the blankets, "I don't like that human Mage."

Me neither, but I keep that to myself. "Thank you, Zag."

"The dark lord is right you know." Isn't he always?

"How's that Zag?"

"With this foolish man's reluctance to forge the bond he creates an opportunity for that Duke."

"Isn't it true that in order for him to take it over he has to be compatible?"

"It has to be someone similar to the destined one."

"So, how are they destined if someone can take their place?"

"Normally they aren't reluctant." Well, that answers those questions. Great, just great.

"You know, I've never asked you, but how do you talk so well for someone who supposedly lived alone and far away for an eternity in some dank cave?"His chuckle makes me smile in the dark.

"TV, duh." He cuddles my foot and sighs as he settles in for sleep. That's what is making my eyes heavy and my body sink further into the bed.

"How did you learn the way you did, living in the forest with a bunch of monsters?" he asks into the sudden stillness of the room.

"TV, duh." Clenching my hand to tuck it under the pillow, I freeze. My hand is no longer empty - instead the warm wooden neck of a violin fills it. Is this some kind of weird cosmic hint? Because I'm not hurting a pregnant woman. Nope, nu-uh.

Gods, I almost forgot about the violin. So much has been going on and apparently, it's tired of me forgetting about it. Ciar did say it's sentient. Patting it, I close my eyes to sleep. It's not glowing or making noises, it's simply there, so I take that as a sign that it's safe to go to sleep.

Maybe it wants a cuddle too.

I realize something as sleep claims me hard and fast, having its presence there reminds me a little tiny bit of Ciar.

"Run, Keri!" Why is Peter's face all bloody? Mother runs behind him, black claws swiping at Peter. Mother did it! Mother hurt Peter! Running through the hallway I look behind me, seeing the

shadow of my mother creep around the corner, the dagger held high in her hand.

"Come here pretty girl, mommy has a present for you."

I want to help Peter, but mother is scary. She never calls me a pretty girl. Peter's delicate hands grab me in a strong grip and drag me backwards towards the door, just as mother comes around the corner.

But... but she doesn't look like mother anymore. Her hair is a tangled mess around her head and her face has streaks of something dark down one of her cheeks. But her eyes, her eyes scare me.

"Okay Keri-bell, you have to run as fast as you can, you ─" Peter starts to say, right before I'm jerked out of his arms and find myself dangling from the floor against the wall. My mother's hate filled eyes stare into mine.

"Now he'll pay for everything."

The knife digs into my flesh, burning, burning so bad. A sharp pain that turns into a wave of agony that I can't hold back. I scream each time the knife goes in. Then I see Peter, my Peter, with blood on his pale face.

He grabs my mother from behind and with all his strength, tosses her out the door.

"Remember our game, Keri-bell? Play dead for me. Whoever does it the longest wins," he whispers into my ear, giving me a hard kiss on my cheek.

No Peter! Something bad is going to happen...

"KAREN, WAKE UP." THE UNFAMILIAR BUT FAMILIAR VOICE pulls me out of the nightmare that's ripping through my brain. Memories from so long ago that I hope every day to forget.

"You," I swallow the lump in my throat, I'll be darned if this man sees me cry. "Know that my name isn't Karen."

"You were having a nightmare."

"Thanks for that stunning observation, Rime." I sit up and barely give him a look, cringing at the foot of the bed. I'm amazed he didn't sit on Zag whose head is out of his blanket nest and watching Rime carefully.

"Why are you in my room?" I ask him, turning around to get a drink out of the glass of water on the nightstand. I always keep water close at hand. These nightmares are more familiar than I like admitting.

"I came to ask you a question."

"What?" Not that I'm in the mood for them but at least it'll distract me from those horrific images. Catching myself rubbing a scar on my chest, I tuck my hand under my leg to keep me from doing it again.

"Can someone tamper with that book your friend gave me?"

"You know they can't. You're Fae, Rime - you should know the stories about those books." Fighting the urge to look at him, I stare at the glass of water in my hands, at the film of frost forming on the top of it.

"Unlike you, I didn't grow up in luxury."

I laugh, luxury? "I grew up in the Dark Forgetful Forest with the Sluagh, it's not what I'd call luxury."

"Oh, well... I didn't know that, did I?"

"You know, I didn't ask for this anymore than you did. It's not my fault that your life isn't what you wanted it to be or whatever. As welcome as you are to stay here, you and her - you can't treat people like shit. Especially me. Understand?" I look over at him this time. His eyes are on me, looking at me like I'm something he hates and wants at the same time.

I wonder if I ever looked at Ciar that way? After staring at him staring at me for a few seconds, I'm assuming I did.

"I grew up in an orphanage." Yeah, I don't like him but that hurt my heart a little. To me, that word represents being alone because I was almost there growing up.

"Sorry." And I am, but that doesn't change anything I said.

"I don't want to leave, in case that's what you're going to say." Okay, that's surprising.

"You can leave my room though, so I can go back to sleep." He sits there staring for a bit, before standing up and walking out without a backward glance. Him and I won't be doing any secret best-friend handshakes any time soon but we made it through that entire conversation without saying something rude to one another.

That's a win. Crawling back under the covers I flip around until I find that sweet spot. When sleep finally claims me again, it's to the gentle music of a violin.

CHAPTER 31

RIDE 'EM COWGIRL...

Morning starts out disappointing. Gertie had an appointment so no hot breakfast. Totally spoiled now, I dig around in the fridge for something.

"You need to mind your own business."

The voice jerks my head up and right into the shelf above it. Rubbing it, I straighten and look at the glowering Penelope. Hungry, caffeine-less, I'm not in the right frame of mind to deal with her.

"Good morning to you too, Penelope." I'm pretty sure my teeth are clenching, but I persevere.

"If you don't back off you'll get your ass kicked."

Gritting my teeth even harder, yeah, I'm gritting them now, I try to smile and fail. Fine. "By whom?" I look around the empty kitchen.

"Me." Her hands swings out and I simply duck out of the way.

"That sucked, Penelope. Can this wait until I get my coffee?" The next swing I catch her hand in mine and squeeze just a little teeny tiny bit. This won't hurt the baby, right? "Didn't your parents teach you that it's rude to hit someone

271

who can hit harder than you can?" I release her hand when she tugs on it.

"I'm a Mage and that means that ‑ "

"That I can hit harder than you, in case you weren't understanding that bit." I sigh and step back away from her. "I don't know what you're trying to prove right now, but all its making me do is want to throw you out of my house. Is that your goal?"

Penelope looks towards the stairs. "I think your puppy is calling you," she spits out. With a dirty look to beat all dirty looks directed at me ‑ no shocker there ‑ she turns and struts off.

Ciar pops into existence in front of me, his hair still wet from the shower, his skin glowing. He's looking at me in confusion and I'm so flipping happy to see him. I throw my arms around his waist and bury my face in his shirt. He smells so flipping good. I want to crawl all over him until I smell like him.

Leaning back enough to see the surprise on his face, I stand on my tip toes and grabbing his face with both hands, pull him down to me. Before he can say words, because I can see the movement of his lips, I cover his mouth with mine.

For a full five seconds he's shocked enough for me to be in charge of the kiss, for me to explore his mouth that tastes like mint. Sliding my tongue along the tip of his and then half-way down the side I repeat it on the other half. With caution for his sharp teeth, I lightly graze the points of them with my tongue. As I pull away, I suck his bottom lip into my mouth and release it, satisfied that it's a little plumper and still shiny from being in my mouth.

"I want you to know that I love you and I am thankful that you're such a big part of my life." Hugging him again tightly, I slide my hands across that incredibly toned butt and then release him and step away, and head upstairs without another word.

Smiling as I slowly climb the steps, I count down in my head.

Five, four, three - as my feet leave the ground, I laugh. Turning me and tossing me over his shoulder, he smacks my butt and takes the steps two at a time. He stops abruptly, and I feel the happy drain right out of him. Levering my upper body enough to be able to look around his shoulder, I see Rime standing there his blue eyes glowing white.

"Did you put your hands on Penelope?" he demands.

Oh, heck no. Kicking my feet until Ciar releases his grip, I slide down his body to my feet and turn on Rime. Closing the distance between us I stalk toward him. Poking him in the chest, I let him see the anger on my face.

"First off, you're an idiot. A destined Triad member can't impregnate anyone, ESPECIALLY a human, until AFTER the bonding with his/her Awakened. I suspect you already know because I heard your little argument last night. Second, she's using magic to keep you interested in her - something I'm starting to think you suspect, as well, but haven't fought too hard to prove. Zag told me this morning that its connected to something you keep in your pocket. Quite possibly your idiotic ding-dong." He opens his mouth to speak but I poke him in the chest again, hard. "Being raised in an orphanage is no excuse for ignoring your instincts, Rime."

"You're jealous he doesn't want you," she taunts over his shoulder at me.

"I have yet to find anything about him I even like, let alone enough to be jealous over." My temper rising brings forth the magic that always seems to be churning inside of me now. My eyes burn, and I know that they're doing that weird glowy thing they do when the magic is working.

Turning towards Penelope, I see her fate playing in front of me like a movie. Quick as a snake, I grab the amulet around her neck and pull, ignoring the stinging pain in my hand. I hold it up in the air as Zag appears out of the shadows at my shoulder and blows a small stream of magical fire over it. With satisfaction, I watch it catch fire and burn to nothing.

The dreamy look that was previously on Rime's face when he looked at Penelope is completely gone now. I see the guilt in his eyes, but also his anger and, although I'm a bit curious about what happened to make him feel guilt like that related to her, I don't ask.

"There, now take your rose-colored glasses off and see her for who she is." Dusting my hand off on my pajama clad thigh, I turn back to Ciar. "Where were we?"

Ciar stares at me for so long the smile on my face starts to fade. "What?"

He looks over my shoulder, I'm assuming at Rime, and says, "This is what you could have in your life, Rime." The emotion in his words... the world distorts as tears fill my eyes. I blink them away because I refuse to let them fall in front of them.

Ciar turns those intense eyes back to me and leaning down, so softly that it feels like a brush of wind, kisses each cheek. Then, without warning, he bends and puts me over his shoulder again.

This time I smack his butt. "Yee-haw, horsie."

Snorting, he walks around Rime who is watching me with an intensity I've not see on his face since he came here. So, I do what comes naturally, I wink at him. The corner of his mouth twitches and slowly starts to lift. In a blink, he's smiling and my heart rate increases. Gods bless it, why'd he have to go and smile? The smile that is barely there falls and he turns to Penelope with thunder in his eyes.

Glad I'm not her. Ciar smacks my butt again and this time rubs the sting away. Oh, yeah, I'm totally glad I'm not her right now. Especially when Ciar's hand dips lower to rub along my inner thigh and then to the heart of me, reminding me why I like his hands so much.

CHAPTER 32

DRESS-GASM...

The next morning Ciar wakes me up with those light teasing kisses that tickle but still feel good, all along my stomach. Giggling, I roll over to avoid them, to find that they are just as bad on my back.

"Wake up. We've got things to do today." Frowning, I roll back over and give him a look that I hope transmits the depth of irritation at being woken up to go somewhere.

Unless. "The beach?"

"That's in a few more days. There's somewhere else I think you'll like." What can I possibly like to do when I can be sleeping instead? "There's a Fairy Festival." I'm out of the bed and pushing past him before the last syllable leaves his mouth.

"Excited, are you?" he asks, dryly.

Ignoring him, I head to the bathroom for the got-to-get-ready-to-go-to-the-awesome-Fairy Festival routine. While brushing my teeth I try to squeeze into a pair of jeans and, failing miserably end up propped against the wall next to the sink to finish brushing my teeth, with both legs in one pant leg.

I love festivals and the Fairy one is the one at the top of my list. The food alone is worth going for. There's no time to waste on dumb things.

"You realize that putting your pants on one leg at a time won't make the festival disappear?" He's leaning against the doorway, looking at me with that sexy amused look on his face. You know, the one where their lips twitch a little and even if you don't want to, you think something dirty? Yeah, that.

"And thinking thoughts like that won't help you get there any faster, either."

Smiling through the toothpaste I'm sure covers my mouth, I spit and rinse my face off while balancing on the balls of my feet. Drying my face, I finally turn to the pants situation and remedy it as quickly and gracefully as possible.

Throwing my hair into a loose bun, I clip it and turn to him.

"Not that I mind the view, but you might want to put a shirt on," he suggests, eyeing the goods. Horrified that I almost left the house like that, I run to the closet and grab a random shirt. Tugging it on I slip my feet into my shoes, sans socks, and head out the door with Ciar close behind. Gertie tells us to have a great day and I'm only able to keep walking when I see Rime waiting for us on the sidewalk because Ciar pushes me forward.

"Do you want to come with us to the festival?" I blurt out before I can catch myself. He looks as surprised by the question as I feel about asking it.

"Uh... sure?" His eyes widen, he's doubly surprised he accepted.

"If you two are done being awkward together, can we go?" Ciar teases.

"You weren't complaining about being awkward last night when I was doing that thing with my tongue." Sticking my tongue out at him I wiggle the tip of it to emphasize that thing.

Ciar laughs and drags me along with him, with Rime pulling up the rear.

"What thing?" Rime asks, breaking the silence. Shocked, I look over at him and his beet red face.

"Do you really wanna know, Rime?" Wiggling my eyebrows suggestively, I can't help but pick on him a little.

"Oddly enough, yes?" He sounds so unsure that it gets a reluctant laugh out of me, easing the awkwardness Ciar accused us both of having.

"You see, she has you bend over and touch your ankles..." I smack Ciar's arm. He's not as funny as he thinks he is. The sounds of the festival reach my ears, laughing children, the ohs and ahs of those on the rides, and the general chatter of happy people. I pick up my pace. I don't want to miss anything and these two are walking too slow now while they talk about the principles of magic.

Who does that?

"I hope you like Festivals, Frosty. Because we're going to be here all day." Ciar cautions as we pay to get in.

Grabbing both of their hands I drag them along, eyeing the first booth in a long line of them. This one is a game booth and the prizes are stuffed animals. Lots of stuffed animals. I eye a pink dragon and realize that Zag isn't here.

"Where's Zag?"

"He's running an errand for me," Ciar says, giving money to the Fairy vendor for the bright red balls to throw at the moving cups.

"I'll admit that I really want to know what these "errands" are that you keep sending him on. Are you sure he isn't your familiar?" Taking aim, Ciar throws one of the balls and it's a direct hit. Somehow it remains on its stand.

"Now, this isn't one of those games where there's cheating

involved, right? Because cheaters end up on the wrong end of sharp teeth." He sounds bored, but I know he's anything but, because Ciar hates cheaters.

The red-haired Fairy catches on quickly. The cup mysteriously falls.

"How many cups do I need to knock over to win that pink dragon?"

"For you sir, one," the Fairy stammers fetching the dragon for Ciar who promptly hands it to me. Cuddling it, I smile in happiness thanking Ciar for winning it for me.

With one last dark look at the vendor, we move onto the next game. This one is where you pick a random rubber duck from the small stream of water going in a circle inside of the booth. The number on the duck tells you if you win or not. The prize is a Water Fly and its number is one. Water Flies are a lot like goldfish, minus the fact that they're not fish or gold. In fact, they look more like dragonflies with people's faces.

For the most part they're harmless but can attack in swarms. I want one.

Tossing some money on the counter, I start selecting random ducks. But none of them match the number for the Water Fly. Sighing in disappointment I take the balloon and stuffed snake I won and turn away from the game.

Rime steps around me and hands the vendor some cash. On the first pick he gets the Water Fly number. With a rare smile directed at me and my overactive hormones - because that smile gets to me - he takes the globe containing the Water Fly in it and hands it to me.

Looking at Ciar I feel a bit guilty about my reaction to Rime. He pats my lower back in comfort.

'My place in your life is secure.'

Holding my prizes close to my chest, I race off to the next

booth, but not before pausing long enough to give Ciar a kiss on the mouth and Rime a quick peck on the cheek.

Squealing when I see what's in the next booth, I almost drop my stuff.

Clothes, clothes everywhere. Fairy made clothes. Oh, my gods, I'm in heaven. My precious bundles are gently removed out of my numb arms, and now I'm free to touch things versus contorting myself in weird ways to graze them with my fingertips.

Spider Silk, Fairy Velvet and holy crap they have Dragon Shell Silk.

"She looks like she's going to have a heart attack, is this a concern?" Rime asks from beside me, a pink dragon tucked under his arm.

"This is her on overload. In a few seconds, she'll blow her top like a pressure kettle and start making odd goo noises while rubbing the fabric between her fingers like an old miser does a gold coin," Ciar adds, holding the Water Fly globe.

As predicted, I start making said noises as I rub the edge of the Dragon Shell Silk between my fingers, and as I get to the fur selections I squeal again. No matter how much I yell in my mind to stop or not do it, I still bring his predictions to fruition. How come I didn't realize how well he knows me? Because I'm pretty sure he knows me better than I know me. That thought makes me smile so hard my face hurts.

After buying a couple of sleep sets and some dresses - I love dresses - we head on to the next booth. Looking back and forth between the two men, I hide a smile. Rime's arms are full of packages and Ciar is balancing the globe on top of a box and I'm about to add to it. This is what they get for being gentlemen and carrying things for me.

After a few hours, we've managed to work our way through all the booths and have finally hit the food vendors.

About half way through, Ciar runs out of room and rents a pull wagon to tote our things around. I say our because they end up buying things too.

Fairies cater to their customers exceedingly well and Fae males are a big part of that. Ciar picks up some shirts and a package he tucks away out of sight and Rime gets a leather jacket and some T-shirts, one of which is in a baby size.

"You know, after today you're going back to your training schedule, I mean it this time too. All of these sweets are not good for you."

Pausing I level a glare at Ciar. "Are you saying I'm fat?"

"Uhm."

"You're fucked now," Rime says, laughing as he steps forward to order a sandwich.

"Here, have a roast sandwich. You love those." Ciar practically shoves the thing in my mouth.

After eating most of the sandwich, I feel bad enough to let him off the hook. "And you're right, I do need to go back to training. I'm getting soft." It's nothing but the truth. Being here in this town has ruined the careful alertness I tailored in the forest.

Penelope snuck up on me. Speaking of her...

'Leave it, Monster Girl.' Ciar cautions, and since Rime is smiling and seems to be having fun – he's right, for now I need to leave it. And I'll be darned if I don't like him a little, and other parts of him a little more. My eyes slide down his chest to his stomach of their own accord, admiring the way he fills out his shirt. Mentally shaking myself I turn away.

What in the world?

'It's the true bond calling you. Now that he's here and away from the influence of that creature he's more relatable, it's allowing the bond to be... natural.' He paused when he said 'natural', which means that isn't the first word he was going to use. I raise an eyebrow at him.

'It allows your desire for him to manifest.'

He's still hedging, so I push. *'Still not the word you were going to use.'*

'Sexual. It allows the bond to be sexual.' There it is.

'Are you really okay with it doing that?' I stare at him steadily, gauging the emotions as they cross his face the best I can. Which isn't the greatest, but I can feel them too, which helps decipher the depth of them.

'We're Fae. With Awakenings this is always a possibility and somehow Faerie balances that. The three of us form our own unique bonds that enable us to so freely share and possess you simultaneously.'

'Still not sure how I feel about all of this possession and stuff.' And I'm not. I'm perfectly aware that my attraction to Rime is part of the Triad business but not all of it, some of it is straight attraction. I look at him through my lashes.

He's tall, almost dead even with Ciar's six foot plus. He's a bit bulkier than Ciar but not by much, they're kind of like night and day side by side really. Ciar with his pitch-black hair and green eyes. Rime with his white hair and blue eyes. It's like two sides of a coin, and that means one thing about the third.

He'll be the monkey in the middle of these two.

Just the thought of both of them in my bed at the same time... the temperature of the air heats up suddenly and sweat breaks out on my upper lip and chest.

Whoa.

Ciar's and Rime's gaze turn to me at the exact same moment. Waving at them inanely, I turn my back on them to slurp on my drink and try to think about things that don't involve nudity. What the heck is wrong with me? I barely tolerated Rime yesterday and now I keep picturing him naked.

'The bond is giving you a nudge, but I promise you that your feel-

ings are genuine too. So, don't second guess the shit out of yourself like you're likely to do.'

"Let's ride the mini-coaster," I offer, heading towards it without looking back. I'm not really ready to talk so plainly about it yet. My luck, the seats hold three and I'm squished in between the two hard muscled bodies that I want to – gods, stop it, Keri!

After the uncomfortable ride – that took ten years – on the coaster I plop down at a table and proceed to pout. Yes, pout. I'm woman enough to admit I do it. Rime sits across from me and Ciar beside me. Linking his hands in front of him, Rime leans forward and pins me with those ice blue eyes that my heart, the traitorous thing, uses it as an excuse to beat fast.

"I'm sorry that I brought that mess to your home and I wanted to thank you for still allowing me to come there." Mentioning the mess that is his 'wife' instantly cools my hormones, thank the gods. "Everything is just moving so fast and I thought that you were going to force me to give up my life. It helps that Ciar told me about the bond. I had no idea that –" He's moving before I can blink, and then Ciar pulls me to the side as an ice barrier pops up in the space my head previously occupied. An arrow, vibrating with magic, is stuck in the ice.

"Are you freaking kidding me?" I blurt out from where I'm laying under Ciar. How he managed to get me under him on the ground I have no idea, but he did.

"These assassination attempts are becoming tedious. It's time to do things my way now, Monster Girl."

"Which is different how?" I snap out, not mad at him but the entire situation.

"Instead of making yourself a target because you won't do anything to protect yourself, I'm going to make an offensive move. They aren't magically protected from my gaze this time." Somehow, he's on his feet and I see the monster he keeps contained under the skin shift and push against his hold.

Am I wrong for thinking that's attractive? Because I do. Then he moves, and a shiver skitters down my spine. The Lord of the Hunt is Hunting. Definitely hot - seriously - like, if we were at home right now there'd be nudity and the tongue thing.

"Are you turned on by that?" Rime asks, offering a hand to help me up.

How does he possibly know that? "Uh, maybe?"

He laughs. "I felt it, does that mean the bond is forming now?"

Taking my mind out of the gutter, with effort, I look at the bond between us and the thread is indeed darkening and starting to pulse with life.

"Once we do a blood bonding - " He grabs my hand and then there's a knife in his hand that he uses - without permission I might add, to unceremoniously cut the tip of my finger. To further this violation, he then sticks my finger in his mouth. Before I can rail at him for being rude, I *feel* my blood hit his tongue. Heat flashes through my body, intense and aching, and makes me think about things that I shouldn't be right now. Against my will, I moan from the force of it.

"You could've picked a better time for this." I hear Ciar say. He's so far away in that tunnel, but then his warm arms are around me and the inebriation is starting to dim a bit. "I'm here, with Frosty the Idiot who decided to start your bond at a picnic table in public, right after someone tried to shoot you in the head with a magically charmed arrow."

"Wow that was a mouthful... speaking of mouthful," giggle, "When we get back to the house..." another drunken giggle follows. Gods, is that me talking? "I'm tooooootally doing the tongue thing." Holy meatballs, that's awful. I sound like I swam in a lake of wine and drank half of it. I can't have this.

Gritting my teeth until I taste blood, I force myself out of the haze that's from the bond forming. Without asking first, I might add. The one good thing about it right now is, Rime isn't any better off than I am. He's sitting on the ground across from me, a dumbfounded look on his face as he stares at me.

"That's what a real bond feels like, Frosty. Now compare the two and tell me which one is true," Ciar chastises, lifting me into his arms.

He walks over to Rime and pulls him to his feet. With as much warning as Rime gave me, he grabs Rime's hand and using a claw, cuts open the thumb on his right hand and shoves it in my mouth.

Instinctually I suck and, once I get past the metallic taste I discover that his blood tastes like the snow I used to eat in the winter. All fluffy and cold with fat flakes that are soft enough to make into a ball but not stay that way. My stomach lurches and my head spins and for a moment I'm inside him. His shock at my intrusion and exchange of memories because I can feel him rooting around in my head too, I find the source of his shame and guilt concerning Penelope.

"Gods you idiot." I mutter, resting my head against Ciar's shoulder. Wait a minute, "Ciar, you took advantage to finish the bond."

He kisses my forehead and tucks me closer to his chest. "Of course I did. Come on, I think it's time to go home." I peek at Rime over Ciar's shoulder as we walk towards home, me being carried like a baby because I'm pretty sure that my legs are made from water and won't hold me.

Rime is staggering side to side behind us but still

managing to move forward. The handle to the wagon in his hand doing the zigzags with him on the sidewalk. The blue that's normally in his eyes is gone and those frozen orbs are on me the entire way home.

All my sappy butt can think is, aw that's sweet, he didn't forget my prizes.

CHAPTER 33
KICK THE KING'S ASS...

I woke up with one of the worst hangovers of my life. The sad thing is, I don't remember the fun that usually comes with drinking. No table dancing or bad singing to lift my spirits. What I do remember is...

"Ciar, where the hells are my pants?"

"On the ceiling fan where you threw them while you were doing your awesome strip tease." Oh gods. Oh, my gods. Unable to help myself I look up at my pants spinning lazily on the ceiling fan, the memory coming back to me in pieces.

My strip tease consisted of me slinging off my pants and falling over face first on the bed where I'm pretty sure I proceeded to pass out. I cover my eyes with my hands. I did some other dumb crap, too.

"Did I tell Penelope to -"

"Yep, you told her that her face was permanently stuck into 'I smell farts' position and that she'd smile more if she did in fact, smell farts."

"Did Rime get - "

"No, he snorted when she turned around and got caught

making faces behind her back. That bastard was as drunk on the bond as you were."

Groaning I cover my face with a pillow.

"I didn't take my clothes off in front of *her*, did I?"

"No."

"Thank gods for small mercies." Sighing, I let myself relax and realize that I can feel them both now. Ciar's bond is calm and dark, soothing really. Rime's is cold - big shock there and light. Right now, he's not light. I can feel his anger thrumming along the bond and it's not at me.

This time.

But he does learn fast. He's already blocking me out of the conversation, he just can't hide his emotions from me. Ciar does the same thing. Now, I need to learn how to do it. I thought I had it, but when the bond between Ciar and me opened I lost it.

The only person I know has the answer, is the one I want to hide my thoughts from, so it looks like I need to go to the library. Knowing he overheard everything that went through my mind, I move the pillow and stick my tongue out at him.

"Why did you complete the bond, knowing that he's still hung up on the crap that she's spewing?" I ask.

"I wasn't about to leave something like that up to him to decide. He'll take forever and with what's going on, I can't have that."

"You can't have that? What about what I can or can't have?"

He sits on the bed beside of me, leaning over me to stare into my face. "Monster Girl, losing you - losing you would destroy me. Completely, utterly. And selfishly I don't want that to happen." With a quick kiss he climbs to his feet and continues his task.

Which I realize is packing a bag.

"Are you leaving?" I ask, even as I watch him put a pair of my shorts in the bag.

"Yep, that's exactly why I'm packing your bikini, I figure I can make a stylish get-away." Throwing the pillow at him isn't effective but it makes me feel better.

"So what's the bag for then?"

"The beach." Jumping out of bed I wobble over to help him.

"We're going for the entire day?" He removes the jeans and socks I toss in, refolding them before putting them back. Well, isn't he a peach?

"We're going for the entire weekend," he pauses, then continues. "After the Mixer tonight."

"Ugh. What is the big deal about basically rubbing noses in stuff?"

"Someone like me doesn't become part of a Triad often. We need to clearly establish that I have, and your status because of it."

"You know I feel like I'm missing some big detail here, and for the life of me I don't get it. You're a Puca."

"He's not merely a Puca, mistress. Your dear Ciar is a king," Zag pipes up from the bed.

I turn on him, "Are you serious? A king?" Ciar actually gives Zag a dirty look.

"I was going to talk with you about it."

"You've had most of my life to talk with me about it. Why the hells didn't you tell me?"

"Would it have changed anything?" he asks softly, continuing to pack the bag.

Thinking about it, I sit on the edge of the bed. It's a valid question, even I see that, but it's a big secret and I guess I'm a little hurt he didn't tell me. The weight of him sitting beside me brings me up against him.

"I love you, Keri. I don't care what stupid titles I have. If you don't want to do this, we can go to the beach early and they can fuck right off," he offers, and for a moment I'm tempted, only for a moment. He's right, I hate it but he's right.

It's all about maneuvering on the game board of life with the Fae and this is a good move. Sighing, I lean my head on his shoulder.

"What are you wearing tonight?" The smile that spreads across his face kind of makes me want to climb on his lap.

"It's a surprise. Now go get some breakfast, Gertie said she made choco chip pancakes." At damn near a run I head out the door, I love pancakes. It's one of my favorite foods in the world. And choco chip ones are the elite of pancakes.

Impatient to get down the stairs, I jump over the railing and land easily on my feet. Rime is in the kitchen when the swinging door flies open and Penelope has a bite of pancake halfway to her mouth. My eyes take in the scene in one swoop. The empty plate in front of her has a note beside it that clearly says my name with a little heart next to it. She's eating my flipping pancakes.

This time Rime can feel me, can probably eavesdrop on my thoughts. His apprehension pulls me down from the anger zone. I'm a nice person, mostly, but it's a crime to eat someone's food without permission.

Penelope smiles like the jerk she is and pops the last bite in her mouth. The urge to cross the room and shake her is a hard one to fight, but then her fate flashes above her head. The one I saw before. Inside of me something loosens, and I feel the whistle shape my mouth and come out with the skill of a songbird. The table begins to shake and the plate rattles against it.

"Existence." The word leaves me with effort.

Penelope's fate isn't to die like a lot of them are, hers is... worse really. A roar like a Dragon's echoes outside of the house and then the entire house starts to shake. Still, I continue to whistle.

"Keri, what are you doing?" Rime's voice holds his concern and he goes to step towards me, but the forcefield around me holds him back.

"Giving her the fate she deserves a little early."

Everything stops. The roaring, the shaking and rattling. Everything. Turning on my heel I walk towards the front door and am not surprised by the knock. Swinging it open I look at the frazzled human man in front of me.

"I'm terribly sorry but I was walking in the store and then suddenly I'm here," he says, nervously.

"That's okay, there's someone in the kitchen who has some things to tell you." I step aside and wave for him to walk by me. As the skinny, buck toothed fellow slips past me, the burning of my upper arm begins to throb incredibly painfully.

Hissing through my teeth, I pull up my sleeve and look as the rune for liar appears on my skin. This brand hurts more than the other one because this time it's earlier. But it's her fate. This man, whatever his name is, is her real husband and the real father of her baby. Her fate is to be with him, at first miserable but slowly over the years, happy.

It could be much worse.

"Kirby what the fuck are you doing here?" Penelope demands from the kitchen.

"I can ask the same of you. How the hell did I get here?"

"Who are you?" Rime asks, softly, with menace in his voice. Sounds a bit like Ciar.

"I'm her husband, who the hell are you?" Even out here if a pin dropped in that room I'd hear it. "Is this the reason you've been gone for months?" Kirby demands, I imagine pointing or looking at Rime as he says it.

"Kirby, you were ignoring me." Wow, petulant much?

"Ignoring you? I was working to pay for the house you just had to have and the car that you've yet to learn how to drive. Those things aren't cheap."

"You and your brother weren't in the orphanage, were you?" Rime interrupts, sounding sad and defeated.

"Her idiot brother is in jail for embezzling from the Leprechauns. Orphanage, ha. I doubt she's ever seen one, let alone been in one." Kirby adds.

"Why then, Penelope?"

"You were so damn gullible when I met you, and when you were drunk you told me a few stories and I embellished them a bit when I returned."

"Did you two have relations?" Kirby sounds shocked, but I have a feeling this isn't the first time Penelope has wandered.

"She and I met at a club, had sex - protected sex - and she returned a few months ago claiming that while we were drunk that we got married, and the baby is mine." Rime is nothing but honest with the man.

Kirby laughs and it's one of those laughs that hurts your ears.

"This scam never gets old for you does it, Penelope. The pregnancy is new but how else can she explain the size of her ass? I don't even get mad at the man she dupes anymore, it's not your fault for being a sucker." Penelope sobs in the background. "Rest assured, the two of you aren't married and that child she carries is mine. I had it tested to be sure." There's a beat of silence. "Now, unless you want to be disinherited, Penelope, I suggest you get your things and come along. I have to figure out where I am, so we can go home."

Pushing open the kitchen door I take in the occupants of the room. Rime has his hip against the counter, his face in one hand, shoulders slouched. Hopefully, with relief. Penelope looks like she swallowed something that tastes bad and Kirby is looking around the bare kitchen with distaste.

Good riddance I say.

"What did you do?" Penelope screeches.

Oh, she's talking to me. "I simply made your fate come a little earlier. Which happens to be Kirby here."

There's a noise and at first, I think it's a sob coming from Rime. Concerned I step towards him as he looks up. His emotions bleed into mine, those aren't tears of sadness in his eyes it's something else entirely.

"I've never been happier to say goodbye to someone in my life. Take her and get out of our house," Rime says, going from laughing and smiling to dangerous in two seconds.

Kirby looks a lot less cocky now and grabbing Penelope's hand, drags her towards the door. With a last look at Rime, she puts her head down and follows but that doesn't last long. Almost immediately after the front door slams shut behind them,I hear the shrill tone of her voice again.

"I spent my life savings on baby clothes and furniture." Rime's voice is barely above a whisper, but I hear it.

"That was nice of you." Clapping my hands together I smile at him. "Now, are you going to make me more pancakes since she ate all mine?"

"Is she really gone and this isn't some strange dream?"

"Uh, yeah, pancakes." I point at the stove that isn't on and the frying pan that's still hanging above it. "Your fake wife ate them, so you have to replace them."

"Keri, I don't know how to cook."

"Are you serious?" He nods. Rolling my eyes, I putter around and first make a pot of coffee and then drag out everything to make choco chip pancakes.

"You know how to cook?" he asks, surprised.

"Despite what most people think, we had TV in the forest, lots of them actually. One of my fave things to watch were the cooking shows. I kind of obsessed over them a little." Ruefully I smile, remembering the looks I got during that time in my life.

"Eventually, I became the designated pancake maker. Oh, and cookie baker and cake maker and all around sweet stuff person. I think that's why I love sweets so much because I like cooking them so much." While I stir the batter, I continue to chatter on. Happy to have someone in the kitchen while I do something I actually enjoy doing.

"What's something you like to do?" I check the pan to make sure it's hot enough and then drop my first circle of batter on it.

"I like to play the guitar." Yes, I remember his guitar music calling me to it.

"And?" I prompt.

"You aren't going to say I told you so or anything like that?"

Thinking on it, I shrug. "No, why should I? Looks to me like you're already beating yourself up enough about it and the reasons you were putting up with her kind of top an I told you so."

"You saw."

"Of course, I did. I was in your brain. I will tell you." I flip the pancake when I see bubbles. "You need to let that guilt go sometime. Blaming yourself for something you had no control over isn't a way to live."

There was an accident and the orphanage caught on fire. Penelope convinced him her brother was one of the children killed. To this day, he thinks it's his fault because he didn't properly turn the lights off.

"If I hadn't seen inside you, I'd tell you that you had no idea what you're talking about." So, he did see it. Well, that saves a lot of explanations when we go to the beach and most of the scars will be out for people to see.

I refuse to hide them and be ashamed.

"She had me fooled, I can't believe I fell for a scam like that." Apparently, he needs to talk about things, I can feel the turmoil inside him.

"It happens to everyone, Rime. Now you gotta move forward, not backward. Her life won't be horrible, just not what she wanted to make you have with her."

Which would've been miserable for Rime.

"Who's trying to kill you?" There's that subject I was hoping to avoid. Might as well be upfront and honest. If he didn't see it when the bond was formed then I buried it deep enough. But I believe in being upfront.

"My father is a high priest in the Moon Clan, so someone out there gave my murderous mother a knife and, since that didn't work they are trying to finish the job."

"Are you sure it's them?"

"Oh, yeah. They're protecting most of their group by magic. Speaking of that." I poke my head out of the kitchen door and yell, "Pancakes."

"The day we bonded, who is that man that Ciar's friend took?"

Do what? "What man?"

"Right after the arrow thing, while I was sucking on your finger, he grabbed some guy and a big wolf took him."

"Well, I kind of feel sorry for the guy, but my guess is the Sluagh have him." Ciar hadn't mentioned it but I'm guessing it has to do with the comment about hunting.

Normally, I would pay more attention but the whole drunk bond thing with Rime dominated that particular moment in my life. I feel the heat of him come up behind me and ignore the goosebumps that celebrate his arrival.

"I have to ask, how the hell did you end up married - fake married to a pregnant human Mage."

"I wish I can say it's a funny story." He's so close to me I can feel the vibrations of his voice. "It's incredible how much of you I can feel."

"Back to the story."

"Right. I am a bit of a collector, I do it for money. Most of the time it's stolen items but beggars can't be choosers."

"There are always other choices, just saying. Continue."

"I went out to celebrate and Penelope was there, she's a hot piece of ‑ " he coughs to clear his throat. "She's a hot woman and came on pretty strong. Once I had quite a few drinks in me, she looked even better. Sadly enough, I don't remember the sex at all but I woke up naked next to her and that's a pretty sure indication of what transpired."

"The nudity made you jump to the sex conclusion?" Not that it's a wrong conclusion but it doesn't always mean sex.

"The used condoms in the bathroom trash can made me jump all the way there." That's pretty good proof. At least, he had enough sense to be protected.

"How did you end up thinking you were married?"

"She showed up a few months ago talking about her 'brother' that died in the orphanage fire, I fell for that line of shit, too. And she also convinced me that I was the father of the baby and that while I was drunk we got married. Gods, she had papers and everything."

"That sounds like complete fiction. How much of her hold over you was guilt and how much was magic?"

"Honestly? I'm not sure. When you destroyed the charm, it cleared a lot of the cobwebs out of my head, making me notice lots of shit I'd overlooked but it didn't make me want to leave her."

Pausing long enough to put the cooked pancakes on a plate for him, I wave the spatula at him to continue.

"I mean, what if it had been my kid? I was left alone, I couldn't do that to my child."

"Do you love her?"

"Gods, no. I think I was starting to love that baby because finding out its not mine... hurts a bit more than I expected." Looking over my shoulder at him, I see him literally rubbing his chest above his heart.

I think at that very moment I start to fall a little for this confused but incredibly sweet man.

"Here ya go, breakfast." I slide my own pancakes onto a plate and sit at the island across from him. Slathering them in syrup, I moan when I bite into them. Warm and delicious and... why is he staring at me like that?

"What?" I ask, trying in vain to catch the syrup that dribbles onto my chin.

Rime surprises me when he leans forward and uses his thumb to clean my chin, he surprises me even more when he pops the thumb in his mouth and then keeps eating.

"What's this Mixer that Ciar is talking about?"

"It's in front of the Duke of something. The king's son, I guess? Ciar wants to establish our Triad relationship." Gods, I can cook, these things taste like heaven.

"These are really good, what else can you cook this way?"

"Well, see if its baking or pancakes, I've got it. Regular cooking is beyond me and more than likely I'll burn it or turn it into something totally different than its supposed to be."

"Like transmutation?"

"No, like lump of smoking black coal." Laughing, his entire face changes and gods does it affect me.

"We're going to the beach right after the Mixer tonight. If you'd like to come I suggest you pack, Frosty. Also, you need a suit for tonight, we'll take care of that now," Ciar says, breezing into the kitchen, a secret smile on his face. He can read my thoughts and has heard or seen everything that went on in this kitchen.

With a quick kiss, he with Rime in tow are gone, leaving

only the smell of Ciar's subtle cologne behind. Sighing, I look at the dishes, might as well get them done.

"You've attracted some interesting characters for your Triad, mistress." Zag's presence is welcome, and I smile at him over my shoulder.

"Right? A Puca king and whatever Rime is, ha."

"Jack Frost."

"Beg pardon?"

"Rime is Jack Frost, he simply doesn't know it yet." Why is it that this Dragon likes to deadpan important crap to me?

"*The* Jack Frost?"

"Mm-hm. Only one can exist at a time and he's that one." Leaning my soapy hands on the lip of the sink, I turn and look at the encyclopedic Dragon, sensing there's more. "Ciar is a King that is a Puca, not the other way around. He was born a king unlike that sop that sits on the throne now."

"King of what?" I know I shouldn't ask but I can't help myself.

"Faerie of course. Ciar is the first-born son of Faerie." There isn't a single memory that I can recall of me fainting and as the room spins around me and the world violently tilts and starts to go black. I can't deny that it's happening right now. Unable to stop the chain of events, I watch the floor coming up to meet me.

CHAPTER 34
AND ON THAT NOTE...

The first thing I hear is Zag's voice and the second thing I hear is the buzzing of a million bees. What the heck is that noise?

"That's your senses returning."

"You can read minds?" I blink, and he comes into focus more.

"No, you spoke out loud." That explains why my voice sounds so loud. Slowly, I lever myself up on my elbows.

"I fainted, and that's a fat load of crap." I grumble. Fainted? That's what wussy people do, not me.

"I did find it rather strange, but I found no sign of poisoning or magical interference. You're not pregnant, either, although a little version of you would be adorable. I think you were genuinely that overwhelmed."

"You're telling me that I," of course I point at myself because there are so many other 'i's in the room, "who can run three miles barefoot, uphill, passed out because I was emotionally overwhelmed?"

Sitting like the cat I quite often relate him to, he curls his tail around himself and gets a rather smug look on his face. "That's exactly what I'm saying."

Many things have happened to me in my life, I've almost died - a few times, but I can't recall ever passing out before. One good thing that I can see glaringly clear right now, at least I'm not pregnant. Kids are great and all, but I don't want any at this moment in time, if ever.

Not that it's a concern when I'm not on my heat cycle. Shaking myself out of this odd circle of thoughts, I climb shakily to my feet.

"I really wish they were more upfront about these kinds of things. I'd rather not have another shock that's bad enough to make me face plant on the kitchen floor."

"If it makes you feel any better, the counter tried to catch you on the way down."

"Oh look, the Dragon has jokes." I toss the bowl of left-over pancake batter at him and am completely satisfied when his angry roars fill the kitchen. The little twit is now covered in drippy thick batter. Laughing, I scrub a hand down my face and chug a glass of cold water. Feeling a lot better, I turn to finish up the dishes and find a cross looking Gertie standing on the counter tapping her foot.

"What do you think you're doing?"

"Uh, dishes?"

"Are you trying to take my job away? I go away for a few hours to shop and I come back to you cleaning. I'll not have it."

Feeling adequately chastised I turn and glance at the clock. Oh, gods it's only three hours until that stupid Mixer.

I've got to get ready!

"You will have several of us on hand to help you prepare yourself. The dark lord wants you to shine." Rolling my eyes, I head upstairs.

I'm only half surprised when I find my bedroom full of

Fairies. Mostly male, not that it matters. Fairies aren't cut and dried sexually. It's one of many things I love about their culture.

"Now, in the shower you go." Gertie's daughter ushers me towards it with a swat at my butt. Smiling, I head in there and after one of the longest, hottest showers in my history, dry off and walk back out into the bedroom wearing the underthings that were waiting for me on the bathroom counter.

A pale pink silk that is so soft and delicate I'm almost afraid to walk fast in them, afraid that the friction will damage them.

"Those fit perfect, I must say. Adelle outdid herself." Adelle made them for me? Well, that's flipping awesome. I'm wearing Fairy-made underoos.

"Now, let's get that mop of hair beaten into submission." Mary, Gertie's oldest daughter, looks at my uncombed wet hair with a frown. "Did you at least condition it?"

"I did." Although, sometimes I'm in a hurry and forget.

Two hours later, I'm staring at myself in the mirror and can't believe it's me. My makeup is done in a classic but light way with the silver eyeshadow and black eyeliner accentuating the colors of the dress. The final touch is a dark red lipstick that I can't feel on my lips. My hair is loose and wavy, brushed to a sheen and looking way better than anything I can do to it.

I look a bit regal and part of me wants to cry because of it... in a good way.

"All right now, let's wiggle you into that dress." Mary waves towards the dress that's being held up by two levitating Fairies. A bit excited, I practically skip over to them.

"Arms up." Following their instructions, I smile when the smooth, soft fabric slides down my body. There's no shame in loving clothes. With a few tugs and pulls the dress is fastened around me and I twirl a little to watch the skirt poof out.

Wow, just wow.

"Now, we were going to put you in heels but Ciar said no, so Bis made these especially for you." Mary holds out a pair of delicate flats that still hold the shape of a spiderweb.

"But I'll break them."

"Pish, a Troll stepping on them won't break them. On they go, time's a ticking." Never in my life have I worn a shoe so soft that it embraced my feet. Apprehensively, I look at them.

"Are you sure? I'm good at breaking things." The group as a whole, laughs. Well, then.

"Now, have a look see." A floor length mirror appears and inside of it stands this beautiful woman who I've never seen before. In wonder, I touch the mirror just to be sure it's real.

"Is that really me?"

"Silly girl, of course it is. That beauty is always there, you simply needed a bit of polish to bring it out," Gertie says from the doorway, and when I turn to look at her, her eyes are a bit moist. "You've never done yourself up before?"

"My idea of doing myself up is a shower, ha."

"Good gods, Keri." Rime's shocked voice pulls me out of my happy floating-on-a-cloud moment. Turning to him at the doorway, I raise an eyebrow.

"Yes?"

"She's breathtaking, isn't she?" Ciar asks, strolling by him into the room. Now, it's my turn to be shocked. Ciar is a spectacular looking man. I mean, on a level that he's prettier than all the women too. Dressed in his traditional black court clothes with the cravat and the weird half pants and hose - looking manlier than he should in that getup, he's beyond even that.

It makes me feel good staring at him. It's like drinking a tall glass of water after crossing the desert and almost dying in agony. Like jumping off a cliff to land in a bed of feathers and clouds.

'Bit dramatic now aren't you, Monster Girl?'

Laughing, I wink at him, *'I was wondering when you'd comment.'*

'You look just as beautiful covered in dirt, I want you to know that.'

Lifting the skirt of the dress, I run at him and jump. He catches me easily and kisses me until I'm breathless.

"Why does it feel like you two have conversations no one else can hear?" Rime's question makes us look at him simultaneously.

"Does it?" Ciar asks, gently placing me on my feet and stepping back to allow Mary and Gertie to fuss over the wrinkles in the dress. Blushing a little, I turn to Rime and pause as my already high hormones climb even higher. Good gods he looks almost as good as Ciar. His suit is so black it makes his white hair and blue eyes stand out in stark contrast.

It also makes me notice for the first time how tanned his skin is. This thought helps me shake off the still new sexy thoughts about him. How does Jack Frost get a tan? That's a great question to pose to the know-it-all Dragon. A smile dimples his cheek and my already hot skin burns, especially the brand on my upper arm.

Which I notice is standing out like a beacon and starting to throb.

"Can we cover this or something?" The dress is strapless and sleeveless, so the brand is very noticeable. And now it's red and angry and in general unhappy. Rime steps forward and gently places his cold hand over the burn, the pain subsides immediately. When he removes his hand, I see that, although it's still there, its faded like a scar versus a fresh burn.

"Don't hide it, it's a mark of your power," Rime whispers, stepping back away from me.

Lifting my chin, I smile. "All right fellas, it's time to go."

A Pegasus drawn carriage takes us to the district castle. The line to wait is ridiculously long and the vehicles range from the magic powered cars to a variation of creatures, including one bored looking Troll.

I won't admit it, but I'm nervous. We were so busy with things that we didn't get to practice much, but then again, I'm not sure we needed to. Something magical guides us when we dance together. Something beyond what I know. All that's left for me to do is to hold on and ride out the cadence of Ciar.

"What put a smile like that on your face?" Rime asks. He and Ciar are both sitting on the seat across from me, while I have this seat all to myself. Mary didn't want the dress to get squished. My eyes meet Ciar's and the amusement and small bit of softness in them informs me he's snooping in my head.

"Just thinking about dancing," I answer, realizing that he's waiting on one.

"You must really love dancing," he mutters.

"My lord, please let us direct your carriage to the appropriate line." Turning towards the Elf who is wearing the old timey footman outfit, including the white wig, I look back at Ciar who is wearing a look so cold and haughty. For a moment I almost don't recognize him.

"Took you long enough, servant. I expect apologies to be made to myself and my guests."

"Of course, my lord." The footman bows, and our carriage is moving towards another section of the road. One with armed Goblin guards and a large silver gate blocking the road. As we draw near, the guards bow and the gate opens.

"Ciar?" I question, a bit apprehensive about this change up in things.

"They pushed it to the point of insult but not quite past it. Now we shall be given respect due our monetary station," he says, his eyes lit and swirling. This isn't just Ciar I'm faced with now, this is the king that Zag mentioned. This is the Ciar who taught me to do many things and always pushed me.

"Ciar, when were you going to tell me you were a king?" For the first time he looks a bit uncomfortable as his green eyes flicker to me.

"Eventually. I didn't figure it for something super important."

"You're the flipping Fae king, Ciar. That's super important."

Ciar smiles and rolls his eyes. "Na, I'm uncrowned. Besides, I'm waiting for the wedding."

Wedding? I look around for something to throw at the sarcastic butt head but find nothing, and I refuse to throw one of my beautiful shoes at him.

"My lord," the footman begins to say, then pauses as if listening to something, I imagine he is. "If you'll come this way."

Ciar inclines his head and stands. Climbing out of the carriage, he puts his hand up for me and helps me down. With effort, I keep from rolling my eyes. Now is the time to behave, even the smallest slight towards royalty can end up with my head on a spike somewhere outside of the castle, like a pumpkin on Samhain.

Ciar stops walking and looks over and down at me.

"I'd level this kingdom." Then he continues walking, his face stoic and his posture ramrod straight like he didn't say he'd kill them all. Looking around carefully, I slap him full on the butt and my face, as straight as I've ever been able to keep it, reflects none of it.

To give the man credit, he didn't pause for a second.

'Tonight, when you're naked and exhausted from the dirty things I'm going to do to you, that sweet ass is mine, Monster Girl.'

Biting my lip, I keep my mouth shut, but it's a barely kept thing. Not only did he threaten me with wonderfully lascivious things, he shared images from his mind, as well. Two can play that game. I think of the most pervy things that have ever crossed my thoughts to do to, or with him in vivid delicious detail.

"What are you two doing that has this fucking bond going nuts?" Rime whispers, loudly I might add, from behind me.

I'm so used to it being just Ciar and I that another person will take some getting used to. I might be starting to accept the inevitable bond and future sexual relationship between Rime and me. It'll happen, I can feel it. Rime just hasn't earned his place in my life yet. I don't care about the magical wahoo, he has to earn it.

He doesn't get to just say okay, let's get naked and he's part of the family. Not that he's said that, yet. Unless I'm mistaken in that look he gave me, he's thinking about me along the same lines.

'Oh, you're not mistaken.' Ciar reassures me. That's something he does a lot and now I'm starting to see it and appreciate it for what it is. *'Took you long enough.'*

"Seriously though, I can feel a lot of things, but I'm not getting any telepathic voodoo and shit," Rime insists.

A squawking blue raven dive-bombs Rime's perfectly gelled hair. It's cawing laughter echoes around us as it lands on his shoulder and begins to ruffle his hair. Trick has joined the party. I wonder if the creator is as entertaining as the golem bird?

I don't have time to dwell on it. A set of floor-to-ceiling double doors are at the end of the walk-way, they open of their own accord and inside is bright and loud, and a cloud of perfumes and smells rolls out of the open door.

Is it too late to back out?

Ciar grabs my hand and tucks it into the crook of his arm. Yep, it's too late to back out now.

'You got this, so don't be a chicken.'

A dirty look from me goes unnoticed as we enter the overly bright room. An elegant, open, round ballroom greets me, packed full of a myriad of creatures and colors. Waiters, balancing trays on multiple hands, cruise by dodging and weaving without their tray wobbling at all.

That's some skill right there.

"Why are you admiring the waiters instead of the dancers, Keri?" Rime asks, coming up to touch my elbow.

Shrugging, I turn to look at the dance floor. It is beautiful. The room is made with purple and green glow stone. Marbled and seemingly alive, it pulses with the magic of the spell feeding it. Glow stone is expensive to make, and this right here is a banner saying, 'Hey, I'm richer than you are.'

Considering it's the Duke of Harleigh - aka the King of Lafayette's son, yeah, they're richer than anyone here. Except maybe - I look at Ciar, who smiles at me like the cat that's got the canary. Apparently except Ciar.

"Have you been around much royalty, Rime?" I ask.

"I've stolen from a lot of them." He doesn't crack a smile while he says this. Instead, he looks around with calculation in his frost colored eyes. "No matter where you go, the rich are always the same. I've attended quite a few of their parties, mostly to case a place, and I've yet to see any that aren't egotistical, empty-headed twats."

"Ciar's rich," is all I say.

"Yeah, but he's not these guys." He isn't shocked at all. That's no fun. "I can smell money and he reeks of it, Keri. I've known since the first time I laid eyes on him." He says it in that duh tone that makes me want to smack him. "But he's nothing like this lot. They covet it, seek it out - destroy for it. Ciar IS power."

Okay, he's forgiven, I don't want to smack him anymore.

"As are you." He smiles a devastating smile that leaves me a bit open mouthed as he bows all courtly like and disappears into the crowd with the raven still on his shoulder. Yet, I feel him out there because the bond has grown more.

"You know, I think that Rime is growing on me."

Ciar's answer is a chuckle. We pause at the top of the stairway and wait to be announced. Well, Ciar waits. I have no idea what to do, I'm simply following his lead and paying attention to what's happening around me.

"My Lord Ciar of the Forest and," the announcer leans towards Ciar who whispers something in his ear. "His consort, Lady Keri Nightshade." Ciar inclines his head and I curtsy in the precise, perfect way that Ciar made me practice over and over as a child. It feels like every eye in the place is on us and I understand why he taught me.

'Why didn't you just tell me then?'

'Oh, that you were destined to be Center and would one day be the Consort of the King of Fae? I'm sure you'd have taken that well, celebrated it even.'

'Well, you can shove it up your wazoo, buddy.'

'Which is exactly what you would've said then too.'

I can't stop the laugh that escapes. I cover my mouth, but it still slips free. He's completely right, it's almost word for word what I'd have said to him if he told me this crap then. And probably throw in a dog breath for good measure.

'At least, now I know why you made me learn all that crap about Triads and stuff. Stuff we have to teach our special snowflake.'

'Our?'

'Well, yeah. We're a team, aren't we?'

'Always.' The seriousness of his tone makes me look at him. His eyes, vivid and alive with the magic of the night, are

looking at me with such love it takes my breath away. How in the world did I ever doubt his feelings concerning me?

'Will I love him one day?' I'm not sure how that will work. I know it's possible to love more than one person, some of the Sluagh had multiple mates and Triads have proven it over and over.

Will ours?

'I think that's on him. You've got a lot of love inside of you. More than enough for three fools who don't deserve it.'

Before I can argue with his fool's comment, the voice booms through the room, "His Grace the Duke of Harleigh!" Instantly the room goes silent. I might think he's an arrogant tool, but he's the son of the king. And for some reason he's staring right at me.

"Good evening ladies and gentlemen. Welcome to the annual Mixer of the Bordertown Menagerie. I want to thank you all for coming and for your generous donations to the school. As you all know, we depend heavily on them for our future generations. Now," the smile he gives me is all ego, indicating that this next part is going to twist my tail. "As you know, every year the students from the dance class at the school perform at the Mixer, however, this year I've chosen only one couple to entertain us this evening. Maestro?" With a wave of his hand towards us, the music filters through the room.

Ciar, always on his toes, makes me walk with him to the center of the room. Taking a deep breath, I get into position and look up into his eyes.

'Let's show them what we're made of.' Winking, he parts the lips of the mouth that I suddenly want to kiss, and the first note leaves it, taking part of my soul with it into the air above us to spin around in a magical storm. Following his lead into the first steps of our dance, I begin to hum. Slowly, a step forward and step back. Half-spin...speed up. And as we

dance, his eyes hold mine captive and the hum turns into words to match his, and together we move, and we sing and my stomach burns - in a good way with the magic we create together.

The moment our voices completely harmonize is the moment the magic leaves me to twine with his around us. A colorful tornado made of the magic from our life together, of the pain we've endured, of the love we've shared.

Around us, faster and faster it spins, to finally lift us into the air. Faster we move, faster... so fast now that only inhuman eyes can follow. I find myself laughing with the jubilation of it, the freedom of it. As the last notes of the piano fade into the silent room, we float back to the ground, breathing heavily, smiles on both of our faces. Leaning down, he kisses me softly, soundly and when his mouth parts from mine he leaves a promise behind.

A promise of something so deep and profound there isn't a word for it. It's more than love it's more than life. It's everything that he is, that he will be - and it's mine. I don't try to stop the tear that treks down my cheek or the one that follows. I don't try to look away or step back. I can't.

"And that, ladies and gentlemen, is why I chose this couple to share with you tonight," the Duke says, coming to stand beside us.

This does make me turn away, if only to keep this incredible emotion between Ciar and I. I look over at the Duke to find his speculative gaze on Ciar, who is looking at him with boredom in his emotionally flat eyes. Harleigh suspects but he can't prove anything, Ciar's glamour is good, the best I've seen.

The Duke raises his arms and then claps his hands, slow at first and solo in the quiet room and then the roar of others applauding follows. Its thunderous in the ballroom and my head immediately starts to hurt. Ciar weaves his fingers through mine and pulls us backwards into the crowd. Rime meets us at the entrance to the terrace. The bird is still on his shoulder.

"That was one of the most beautiful things I've ever seen. I had no idea that you sing, Keri." Rime says, his eyes alight with pleasure and a smile on his face.

"Each member of the Triad is musically inclined." Ciar observes, his eyes searching the shadows past the farthest edge of light.

"What?" I ask.

"We are being watched."

"How do you know that?" Rime asks, visibly relaxing, but his eyes subtly look around us.

"I can smell them... but - DOWN KERI!" I don't even hesitate, I drop to my knees and roll, grimacing when I feel the dress tear. There's nothing to be done about it. A spell bomb hits where I was standing two seconds ago.

Rime has an ice barrier around the part of me vulnerable to the direction the bomb came from and Ciar is already gone, chasing someone if the fire I see flare in the darkness and yelp of pain is an indication.

'There are more of them and ... you're not going to like - '

"Why won't you die already?" The familiar voice saying something so damn nasty brings my full attention to the woman now standing in front of me.

"Lucinda?" I'm not really surprised. More annoyed than anything. She's the only one on the list.

"How in the world are you so surprised that I'm trying to kill you?" She apparently thinks she completely deceived me.

"I was hoping you were too stupid to be a bad guy." I kick the hem of the dress out and loosen my stance. There's a knife sheathed on my thigh.

I never leave home without one now.

"Are you serious? I planned this entire fiasco. I tried to

give you a gentle death and poison you but that didn't work. Then I hired that stupid 'world-famous' assassin and look what happened to him? He fell on his own knife... how fucking clumsy do you have to be to do that?"

Lucinda is a total nutball, I can see the light of crazy in her eyes now. Before, I thought she had a tear duct issue or allergies. Isn't that something humans suffer from quite commonly?

'I didn't realize that you had figured it out.' Ciar teases.

'My brain does work sometimes.'

'Pay attention to the threat, assess her. Defeat her.'

"What are you smiling about? I tell you that I want you dead and you smile?" Lucinda demands.

"Fell on his knife, huh?" She doesn't realize I'm the reason that happened.

"Right? Fell on his fucking knife. Then I tried the bomb but somehow you survived that shit too. Then the arrow that supposedly never misses its target missed you. Where did that ice come from? You don't have elemental powers, so it wasn't you. And a Selkie doesn't have those kinds of abilities. Did you hire a bodyguard?" She rambles on and on.

"Do you ever listen to what comes out of your mouth? Because you sound ridiculous." Her sane ship has sailed, that's for sure. I don't even think she realizes she's in a ballroom with the son of the king.

Her face scrunches up and I sidestep, sensing that she's going to do something. In disbelief, I watch as the small, sort of pathetic fireball goes whizzing by. Honestly, I could've stayed where I was and it would've missed. It reminds me of those cheap fireworks you buy at a human store. The ones that never work right and fizzle out before they actually do much of anything.

And here I was complaining about not having fireballs.

"My father told me that if I kill you, I can have the same

status as my Awakened siblings. I'm sorry, I actually am - because I kinda like you but you have to die, Keri."

"Why does your father want me dead?"

She likes to talk, let's see if any of it is actually useful. My eyes pan around the strangely silent room and I find everyone watching us intently. No one is doing anything to stop her or help me. These idiots like the show.

"Because of your father or something. My father is working under the mistaken belief that you have power. I tried telling him that you can't light a match with a lighter, let alone do anything dangerous."

Edging to my right, I move slightly closer to her.

"Kind of like your own abilities, eh?"

"Right? I studied hard! I can speak four languages, I know the history of all things Faerth. The fact that my magic isn't - wait, there's nothing wrong with my magic!"

"Too late you already admitted you suck. Your family is part of the Sun Clan?"

"How'd you know that?"

"How is someone so smart so stupid?" I smile at her. "You answer first."

"I'm... you... oh, my gods, someone kill her!" she shouts. I wait for something to happen, but nothing does. I look past her. Ciar is leaning against a small fruit tree of some kind cleaning his bloody nails and Rime is sitting on the bench twiddling a knife over his knuckles. Which is also bloody.

Lucinda's backup isn't coming.

"Uh, Lucinda..."

"Shut the hell up! Where are those morons? Can no one do anything right?" Then she surprises me when she pulls a gun out of her pocket. She can barely hold the thing up, but it's still pointed right at me. Guns are illegal in Faerth. The penalty for owning one is death. Ciar's face jerks up.

I can do a lot of things but there's no way to stop a bullet, not when they're made of iron and burrow right through any kind of magical shield that we might throw up in time. Instead, I use one of the two magical abilities I know I have.

Pushing as hard as I can, the magic finally cooperates, and the gun blows up in her hand. Squealing in agony, she screams obscenities at me while cradling her hand close to her chest.

"Your whore of a mother should've done the job right and killed you the first time. Instead, my life is hinging on your death. You have to die!"

Something in me snaps, I'm sick of it. The crap my mother did. This stupid mess with Lucinda, who I thought was my friend... all of it. The whistle lights her fate up for me in her aura. Grimacing, I let the notes fade and sigh. Her fate was sealed the minute she raised that gun.

"I'll keep trying, Keri. I'll kill your stupid handsome friend like I did Mark. I'll go after that new loser sniffing around you too. They'll all die." She stomps her foot like she normally does in a tizzy. "Why are you whistling? Will a dog come running out of the bushes to save you?"

The violin materializes in my hand and without looking, I put it under my chin and play with the bow that appears in the other hand. A note leaves the temperamental instrument and then another and soon I'm playing a sad song about lost love. Because really, that's what made her finally lose her marbles, the mess with Mark.

She couldn't bear that he didn't love her.

If only she knew. Ciar meets my gaze, sensing what's happening, he's waiting patiently for me to finish. Owning a gun is outlawed in all Faerth, sworn on by magic and the Hunt. The minute she drew the weapon, she called on a different magic than mine. I'm only hastening it along a few hours.

Ciar smiles a shark's smile and then moves.

"What are you doing? What is that magic coming from

you? Why - oh!" Ciar grabs her none too gently and throws her over his shoulders. Pausing only for a second, he blows me a kiss and then vanishes as the need to hunt calls.

She'll be turned loose in the forest, prey for the Wild Hunt, it's how the Hunt works. Although, her clan protected some of their own, Lucinda isn't afforded such protection. She's a throwaway child to her parents, the one who didn't bloom. It's all kind of sad.

"Are you feeling sorry for the woman who tried to kill you multiple times?" Rime asks.

"Uh... maybe?"

"Gods you really are a big bag of moosh aren't you?" he teases, patting my shoulder. I don't say anything. I'm waiting for the backlash, for the brand that I know is coming.

It'll be similar to the Elf assassin's brand. Her fate was due to happen regardless, tonight in fact, but I still called it and there's still a cost. Then it hits me, the burning of it first appearing on the skin of my calf. Moving the torn skirt aside, I look at the rune for deception that appears on my calf. It's smaller than the other two, about half the size and not as painful as any to date.

Rime kneels and touches it with his cold hand. "This worked last time so let's try it again." It instantly eases to nothing more than a little twinge.

"How did you know it worked before?"

"The bond." Oh duh. I'm tired.

Ciar will be gone for hours and I'm ready to go home. I just have no idea how to get there. "Rime, do you know how we can go home?"

"Actually, yes. Ciar left a phone number for me to call."

Ciar is my hero and will always be. Sitting on the concrete bench, still cool from the night air, I let myself relax a bit. Rime talks briefly on the phone and then joins me on the bench.

"Troll service incoming." He leans back and studies me, I can feel it. "Fate Caller, huh?"

"I guess."

"Even I know that's rare."

"Not as rare as being Jack Frost."

"You're not the first person to call me that. Do you know why?" He's got me there, so I say nothing. I honestly have no idea why, we can ask Zag... tomorrow.

When I sense someone staring at me I look up and, on the balcony, overlooking the courtyard we're in, is the Duke and he has a smile of absolute satisfaction on his face. With a small wave he turns and walks out of sight.

"Shit."

"What?" Rime is tense and ready to defend me, I can see it in his posture.

"Where's the bird?"

"No idea, he flew off when the fun started. Are you okay?"

Yes and no. I'm not sure. Am I? Shivering, I wrap my arms around myself. A warm jacket smelling of fresh snow wraps around me. Odd that it's warm, considering.

Saving me the effort of trying to have a conversation with the suddenly talkative Rime, a large basket is deposited on the concrete in front of us. Our ride is here. Flicking a brief glance at the Troll, I stand up and climb into the passenger basket. The seats are surprisingly soft and cuddling down into one I decide a little nap won't hurt.

The rocking of the basket keeps me in a light doze for most of the trip home. I only wake up because Rime pulls me closer to him to rest my head on his shoulder. When the basket is put down in front of my house, I stand and stretch. Gertie stands in the open doorway, the light casting a long welcoming glow towards us. I'm so glad to be home. Her eyes take in the torn dress and she schools her expression to a neutral warm smile.

"Come on in for hot chocolate and marshmallows. I decided that you needed something warm before bed after such a busy night." Trudging inside I go upstairs first to change and fight tears as I see the condition of the once beautiful dress. Still, I carefully place it in its bag and hang it in the closet. Maybe one day I can have it repaired.

With my feet feeling like blocks, I walk back downstairs and to the kitchen. Inside, there's friendly chatter from Bis and Zag who alights on my shoulder and nuzzles me, and Gertie and her family. The only quiet one is Rime, who's watching me like I'm going to fall apart any second. I'm not, no matter how much I want to.

I feel bad, there's no way around it. I thought, flawed or not, that Lucinda and I were on the way to being friends. And to have to call the Hunt on her... I don't like this part of it. I don't like how I feel afterwards.

And that's why she chose you.' Rime's voice in my head startles me so hard I knock my hot chocolate over. Gertie starts cleaning it up immediately and pushes my hands away when I try to help.

"Did you just talk in my head?" I demand.

"Yes, it took some figuring out but, as you can see, I managed it." He spreads his hands in supplication. Now, this will take a little getting used to but really, I've had someone in my head most of my life, what's another voice? Feels kind of like he belongs there anyhow.

"I don't think I'll be able to do it all the time, but you were thinking so hard without any filters I caught that bit of it." That's good to know. He's not telepathic like Ciar but he can talk to me this way. "You love him, don't you?"

"Who?"

"Ciar."

"Yes, I think I've always loved him," I answer, honestly.

"Do you think," he pauses and runs his finger around the rim of his cup, "that you will ever love anyone else?"

Studying him, I put thought into my answer. I'm aware of what he's asking me, maybe even more so than he is. What I see is a man who's been crapped on a lot. Penelope, the most recent example.

"When I love, it's forever - there's no 'love them for now' in me. And from what Ciar says, I have a lot of love in me to give." He smiles at my answer and takes a deep drink of hot cocoa. I can't help but smile back, especially at his huge chocolate mustache and solitary piece of marshmallow stuck to the tip of it.

CHAPTER 35

COMMITMENT ISSUES AND LOTS OF TISSUES...

No matter how many times I switch positions I can't find sleep. When I feel Ciar's presence wash over me I know why. On silent feet, he slips into the room and after pausing a moment next to the bed where I'm pretending to be asleep he crosses to the bathroom.

The shower turns on.

Realizing how much I worry when he's gone, regardless of the surety he's safe, I climb to my feet and creep to the bathroom stripping as I go. The light is off, he can see in the dark after all, so I don't have to worry about turning on the lights.

As quiet as I can possibly be, I take off the last bit of my clothes and step into the shower behind him. He's got his face in the spray and maybe the pounding of the water on his head blocked out the noise.

"Can you wash my back, monster girl?" Nope, he heard everything. Smiling I grab the loofa and lather it up super thick and start scrubbing. The skin is smooth and unblemished, he heals radically fast, and I can't help but slide my hand down his back. Down his soft skin, carefully over the ridges of his muscles.

I love this man.

Turning towards me he tosses the loofa gods know where and pulls me into his arms. Holding me close he buries his face in my hair and stands there, lending me his warmth, his strength. The sob comes out of me with force. Loud, it catches me off guard and I push my face harder against him. Another sob racks me and he tightens his hold on me.

"I love you, Monster Girl. I've always loved you and I always will love you. Now, let that big heart of yours grieve," he kisses my neck, "and then we'll shave those hairy legs of yours."

The sob turns into a choked laugh and a piece of me relaxes a little. Ciar is here, Ciar will make it all better.

CIAR PASSED OUT AFTER WE SHOWED EACH OTHER EXACTLY how many positions you can do that thing with your tongue in. Unable to sleep, I wandered downstairs. Rime is asleep on the couch, one leg thrown up over the back, the other with his foot flat on the floor. His mouth wide open.

Hopefully, nothing crawls in there.

I cover him with a blanket and move on to check on Fluffy, who's still sleeping the sleep of change. Resting my hand against it, I find it warm to the touch and know he'll soon wake up. Zag is still upstairs, snuggled against Ciar's butt. I'll make sure to tell my proper lizard tomorrow that he slept next to a butthole and see how he likes that.

My wandering takes me to the backyard to the fountain where I first saw the frost from Rime. The water gurgles happily and the Water Flies - including my festival prize - swim around it, happily coming to the surface in the hopes of a treat.

I don't have anything this time, but I promise them I'll

bring something next time. A blue feather floating in the water catches my attention. I pluck it out of the water and stroke it. Another one floats by, then another. Curious, I follow them. Kneeling, I find the blue raven, lifeless on the ground. This can mean a lot of different things, but two things jump immediately to mind. Either the creator is too far away to give it life or they're dead.

"Bit pessimistic, yeah? Jumping straight to dead." The accented voice pulls me to my feet and turning, knife in hand. The man standing before me has the prettiest cyan colored eyes, bright in his gorgeous face. His hair is a soft brown that looks reddish in the moonlight.

But that accent - he's definitely not from this part of the world.

"How'd you know, Trick?" It's a guess, but I'm pretty sure it's a good one. The suitcase at his feet is a good indication he's staying or hoping to stay.

"You're clever, aren't ya?"

"Mm, are you planning on staying?"

He laughs, and I get a shiver. "There isn't a force in the world that can move me from here."

"You can go pick from the two rooms left on the second floor. I'd suggest you not wake the sleeping Puca, he gets grouchy." Trick smiles again and this time I look away so I don't react.

Since you can read my flipping mind, Trick.

"I'm your Anchor, clever girl. I have to be able to read ya." He has a valid point there, but I still start working on the shields I've been lax at keeping up. For now, they need to go up. He might be sure of his place, but I'm not.

He turns to walk into the house. "By the way, there's some official looking gits heading this way - I'd expect them in the morning."

"How official and how do you know they're coming here?"

"Mark of the king identifies them as his men and I may have borrowed an identity or two to have a look about." With that said, he walks into the house without another word.

King's men? I need a fucking vacation.

I want to thank the Savage Squad, you all make me laugh during some hard days.

Jason—hump-muffin, I love you. More than I'll ever be able to show you in this lifetime. You're the main reason I get through well, EVERYTHING, the tears of frustration and the daily crap that constitutes life. Wanna wrestle?

Felicia and Korah, what a wonderful miracle. Love you both!

Vicky...there's no hurry—take the dog back. (inside joke!) I love you !

Thanks for my fantastic Beta Team... I wasn't sure I had a book at all, but you got me there!

Last but not least, thank you reader—for joining me in this journey. I do believe in Fairies, do you?

ABOUT ZOE PARKER

In these worlds, I can fight for the poor dragon, I can cheer for the black knight. I can make the little guy strong enough to toss cars, and if you allow it, I'll drag you right along with me. I do believe in fairies, do you?

Www.zoeparkerbooks.com
https://www.facebook.com/ZoeParkerAuthor
https://www.facebook.com/groups/ZoesSavagesquad

38128829R00195

Made in the USA
Middletown, DE
06 March 2019